D1373378

RUNLOVEKILL
VOLUME ONE

STORY BY **JON TSUEI**
jontsuei

WRITTEN BY **JON TSUEI** AND **ERIC CANETE**

ART BY **ERIC CANETE**
ericcanete

COLOR, LETTERING AND DESIGN BY **LEONARDO OLEA**
oleatv

COVER & 3D BY **MANU FERNANDEZ**
el_big_manu

RUNLOVEKILL·COM
RUNLOVEKILL

RUNLOVEKILL created by Eric Canete and Jon Tsuei.

RUNLOVEKILL, VOLUME ONE
First Printing. August 2015.
ISBN: 978-1-63215-445-3

Published by Image Comics, Inc. Office of publication: 2001 Center Street, 6th Floor, Berkeley, CA 94704.

RUNLOVEKILL

VOLUME ONE

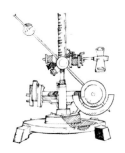

TSUEI · CANETE · OLEA

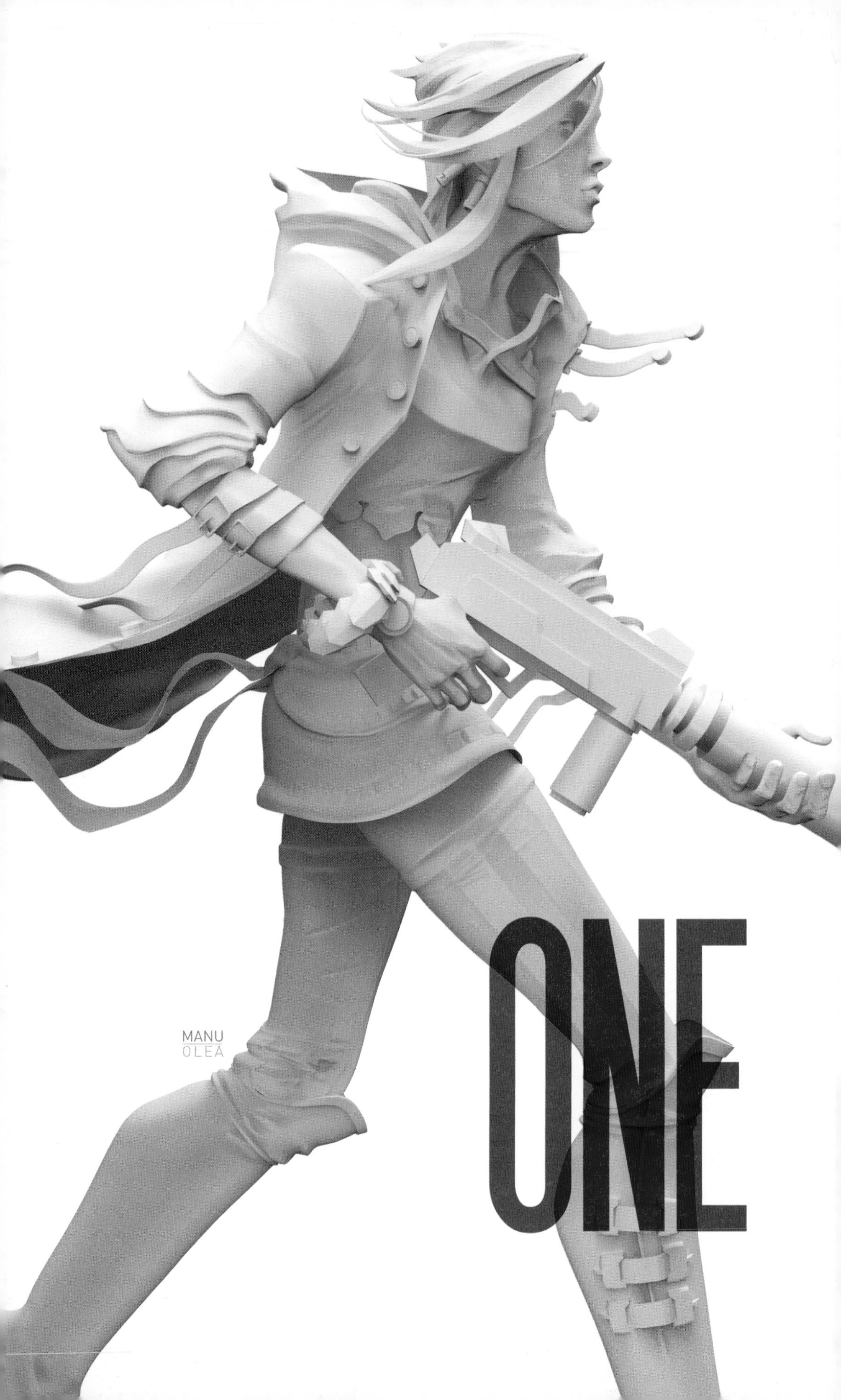
MANU
OLEA
ONE

IMAGE COMICS

P R E S E N T S

A Jon TSUEI, Eric CANETE & Mafufo / OLEA

P R O D U C T I O N

TIC TIC TIC TIC T TIC TIC TIC TI

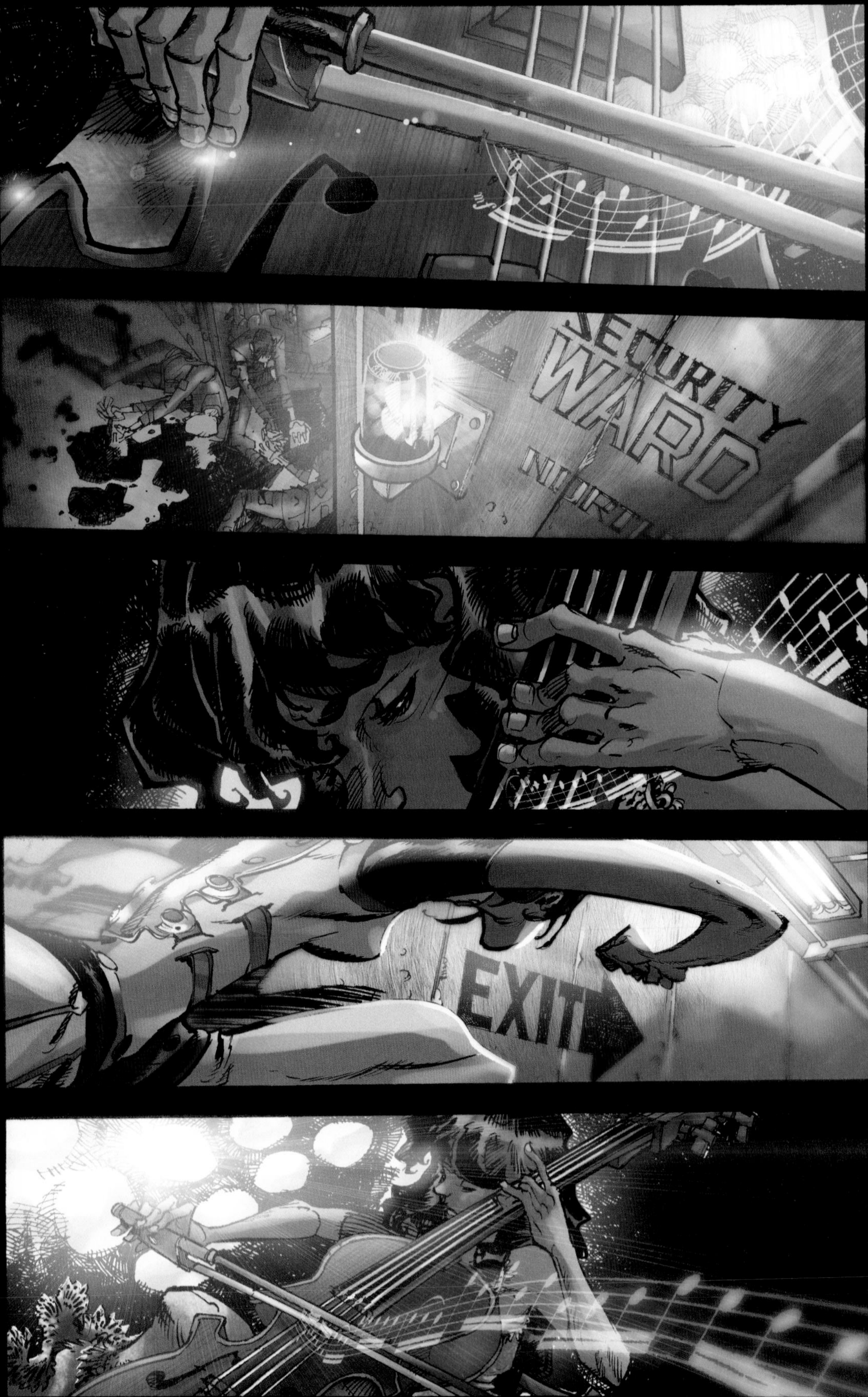
SECURITY
WARD
EXIT

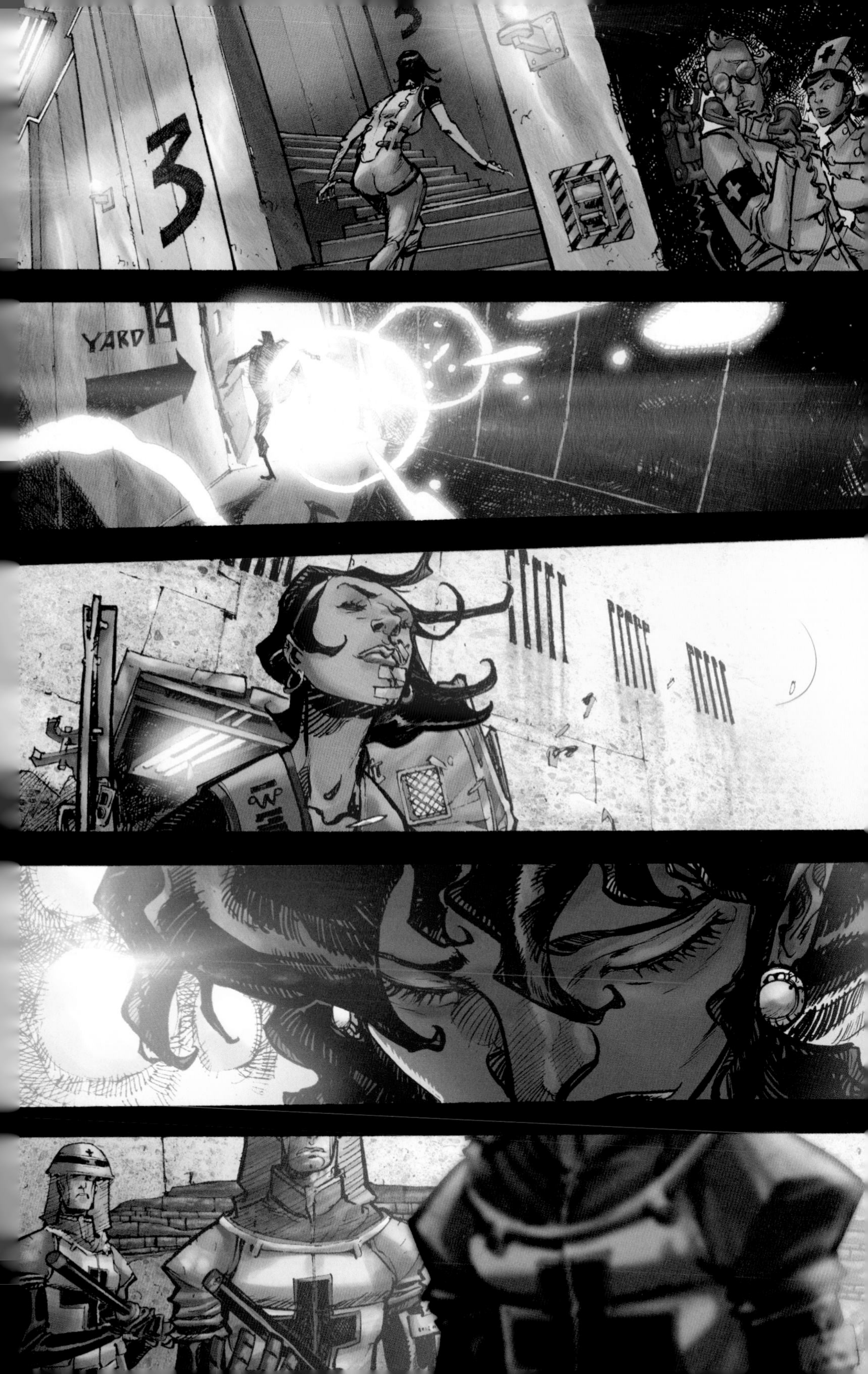
3
YARD 14

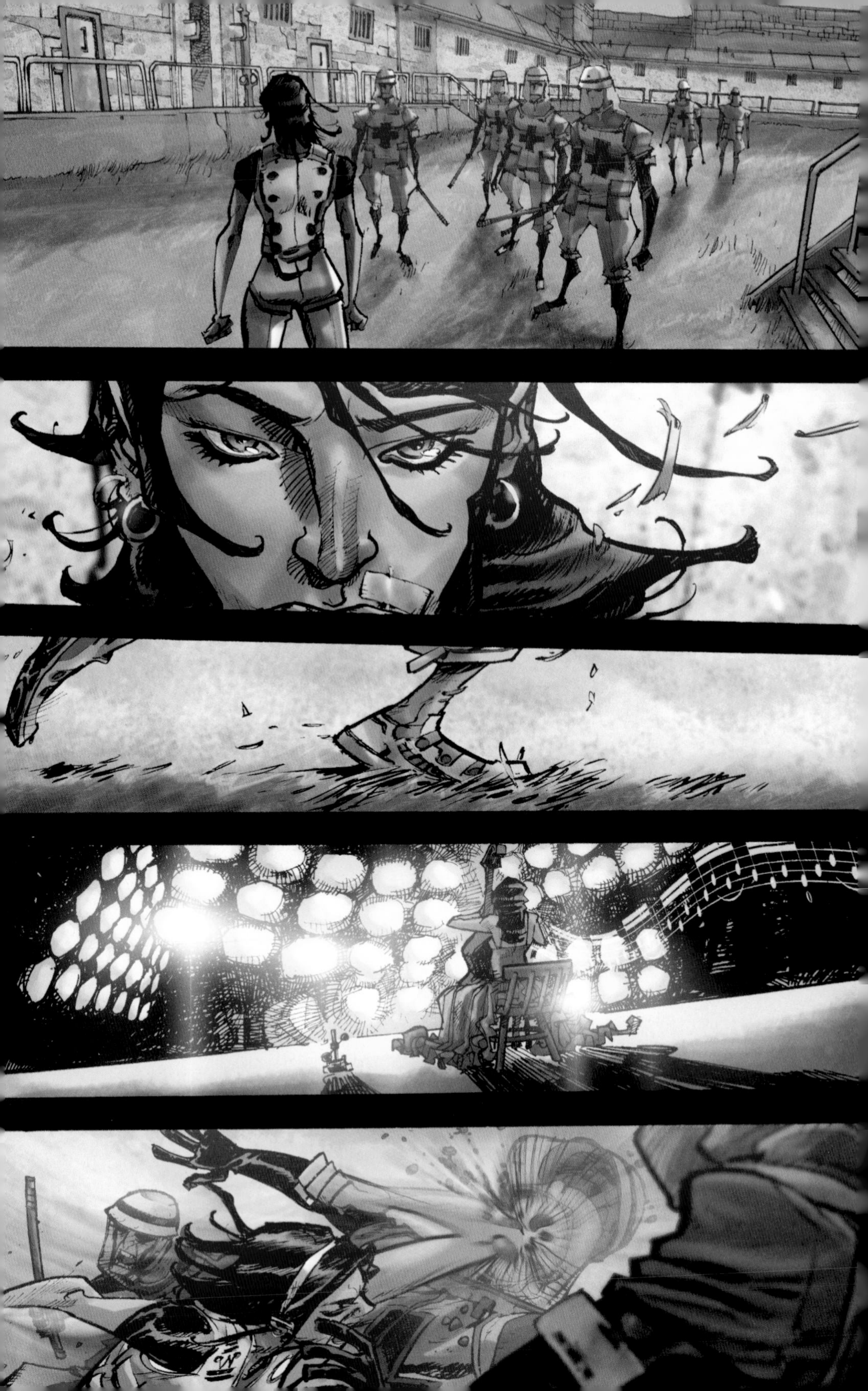

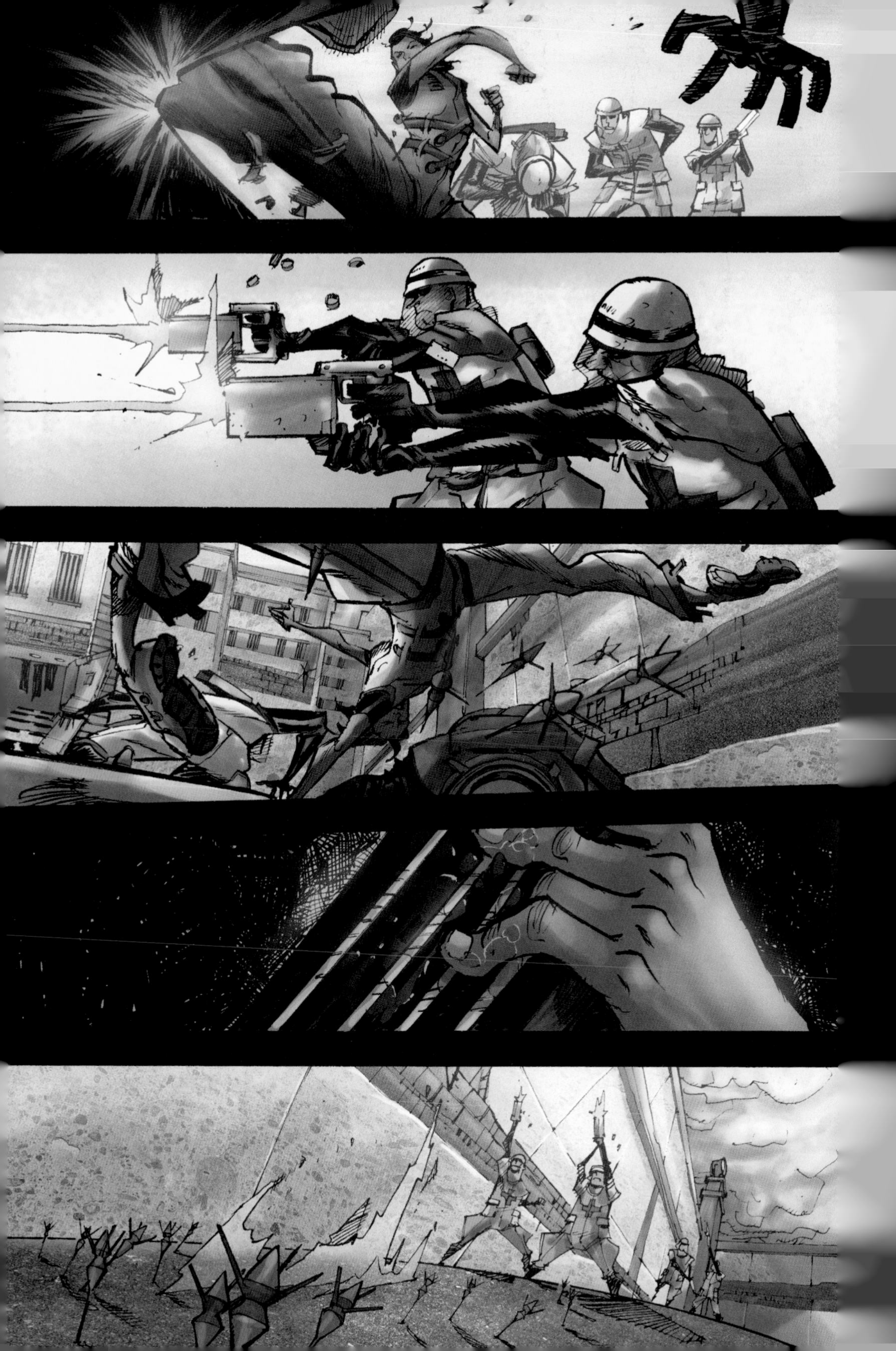

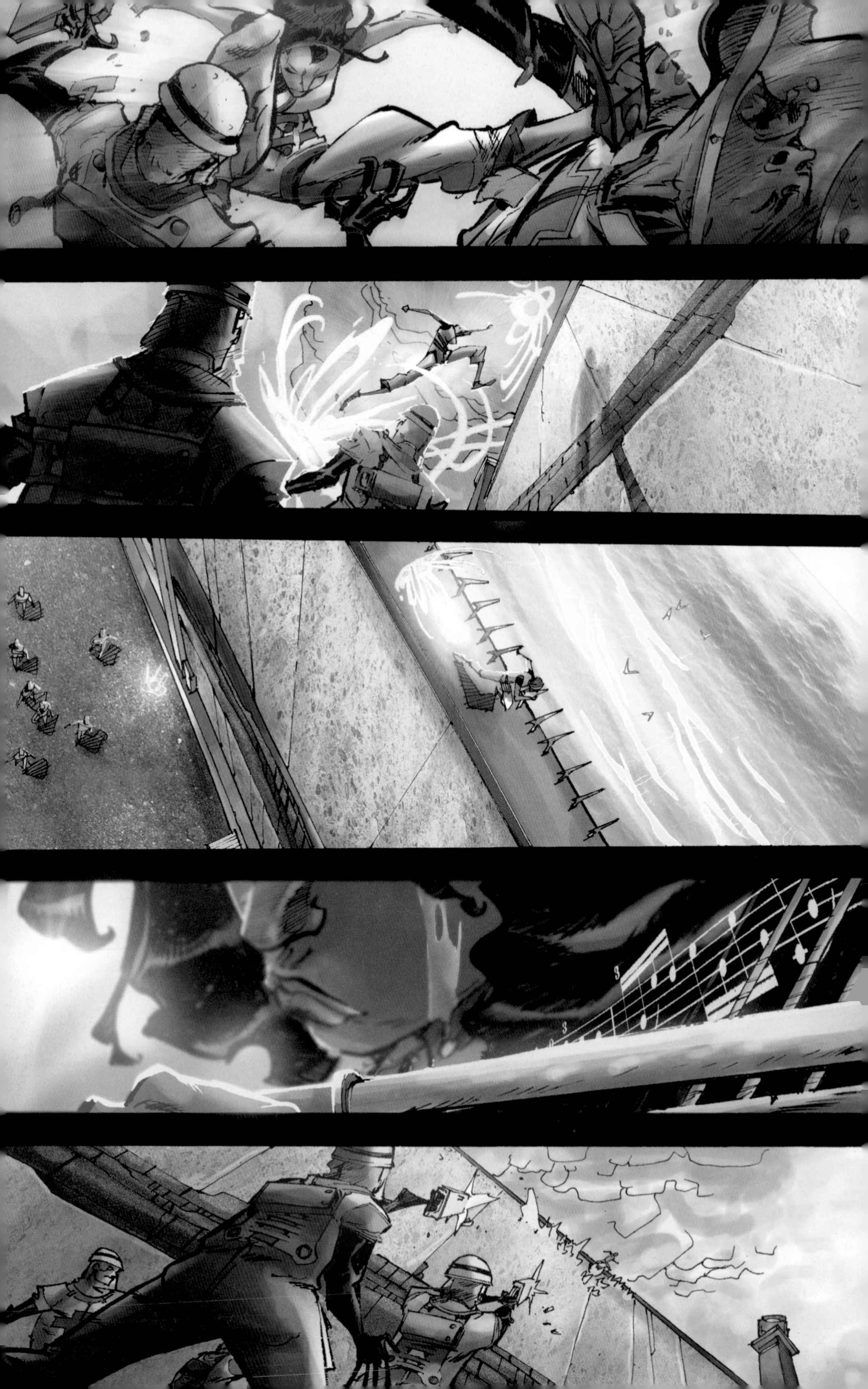

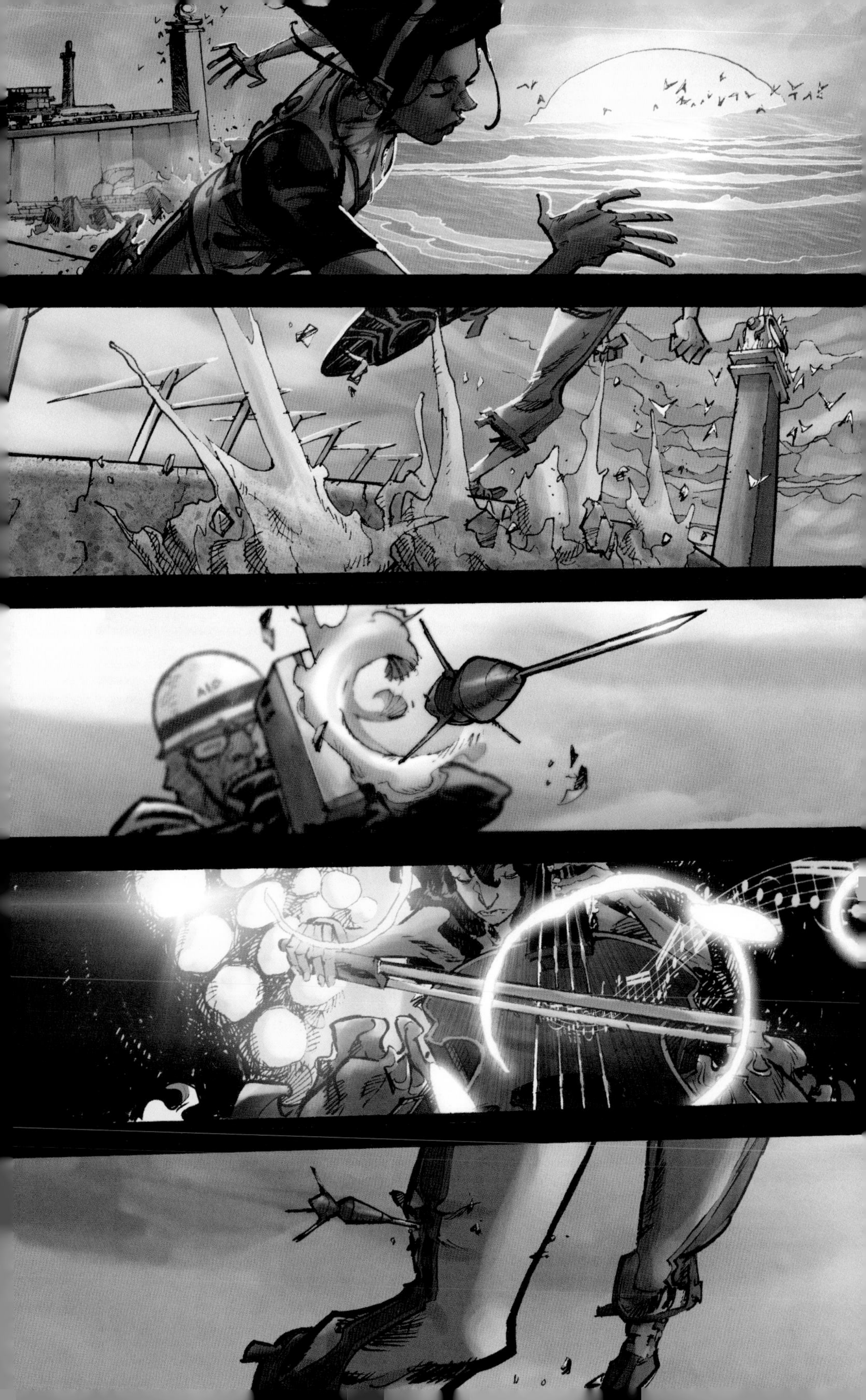

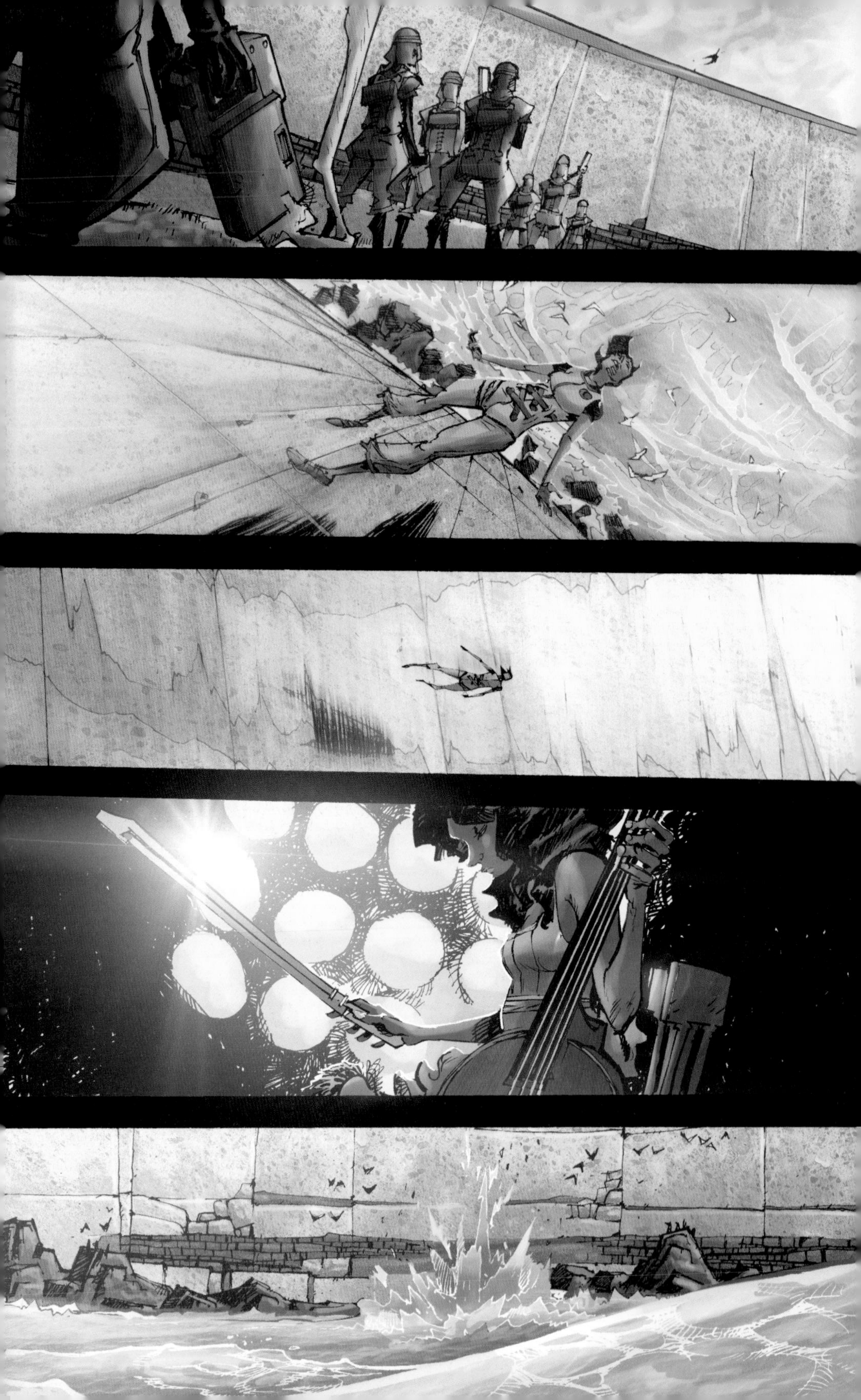

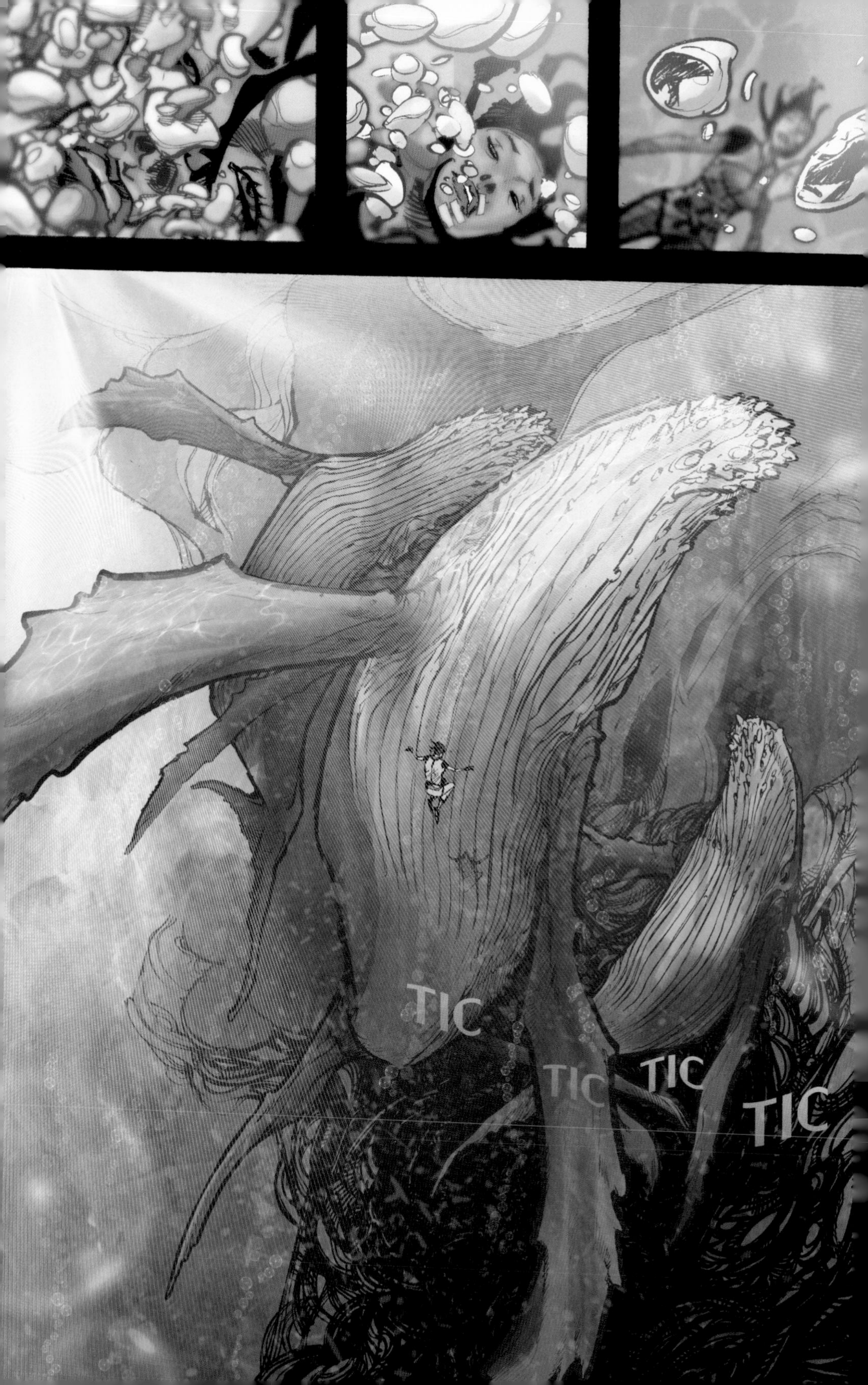
TIC
TIC
TIC
TIC

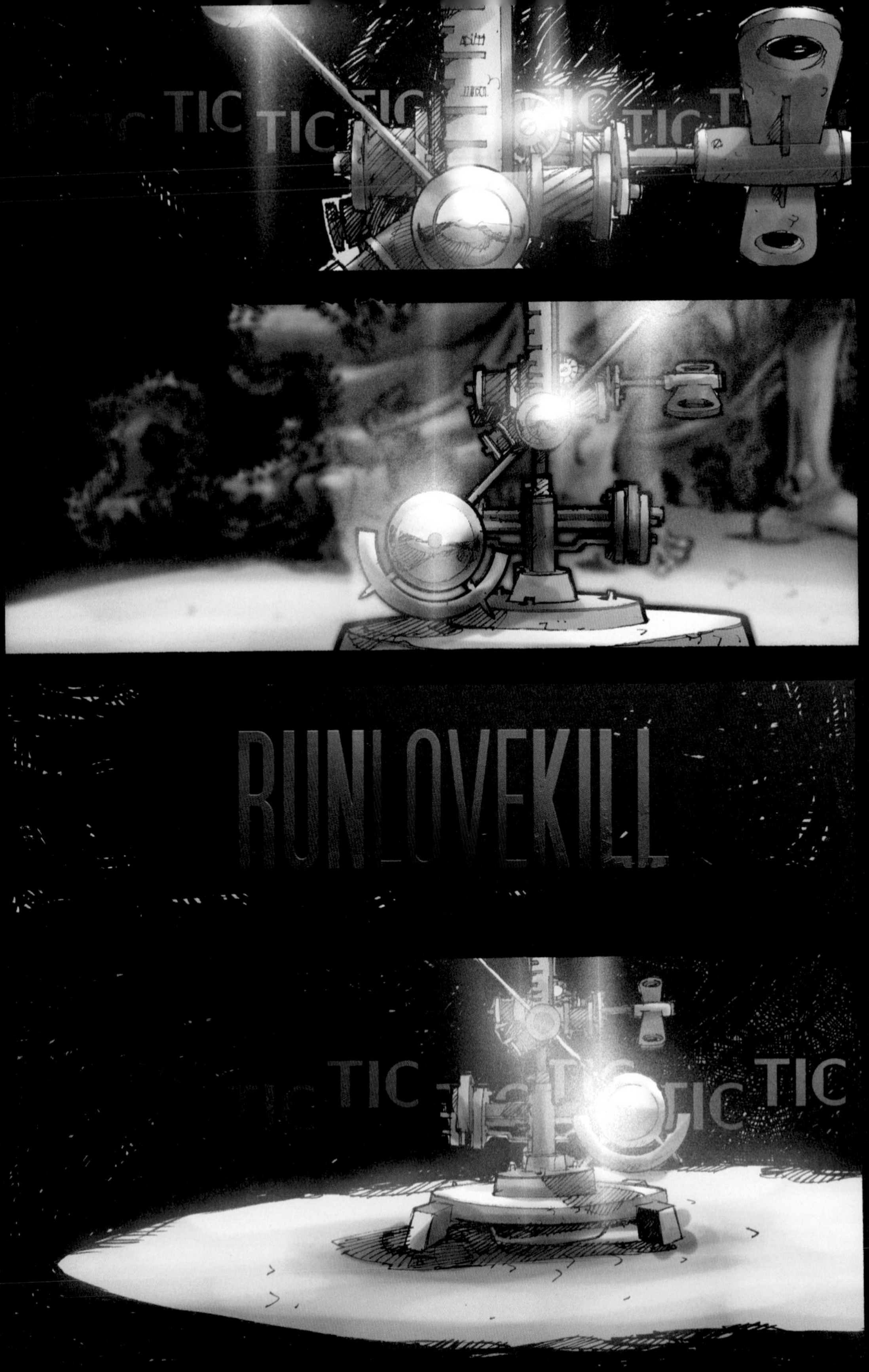
TIC
TIC
TIC
TIC
TIC
RUNLOVEKILL
TIC
TIC
TIC
TIC

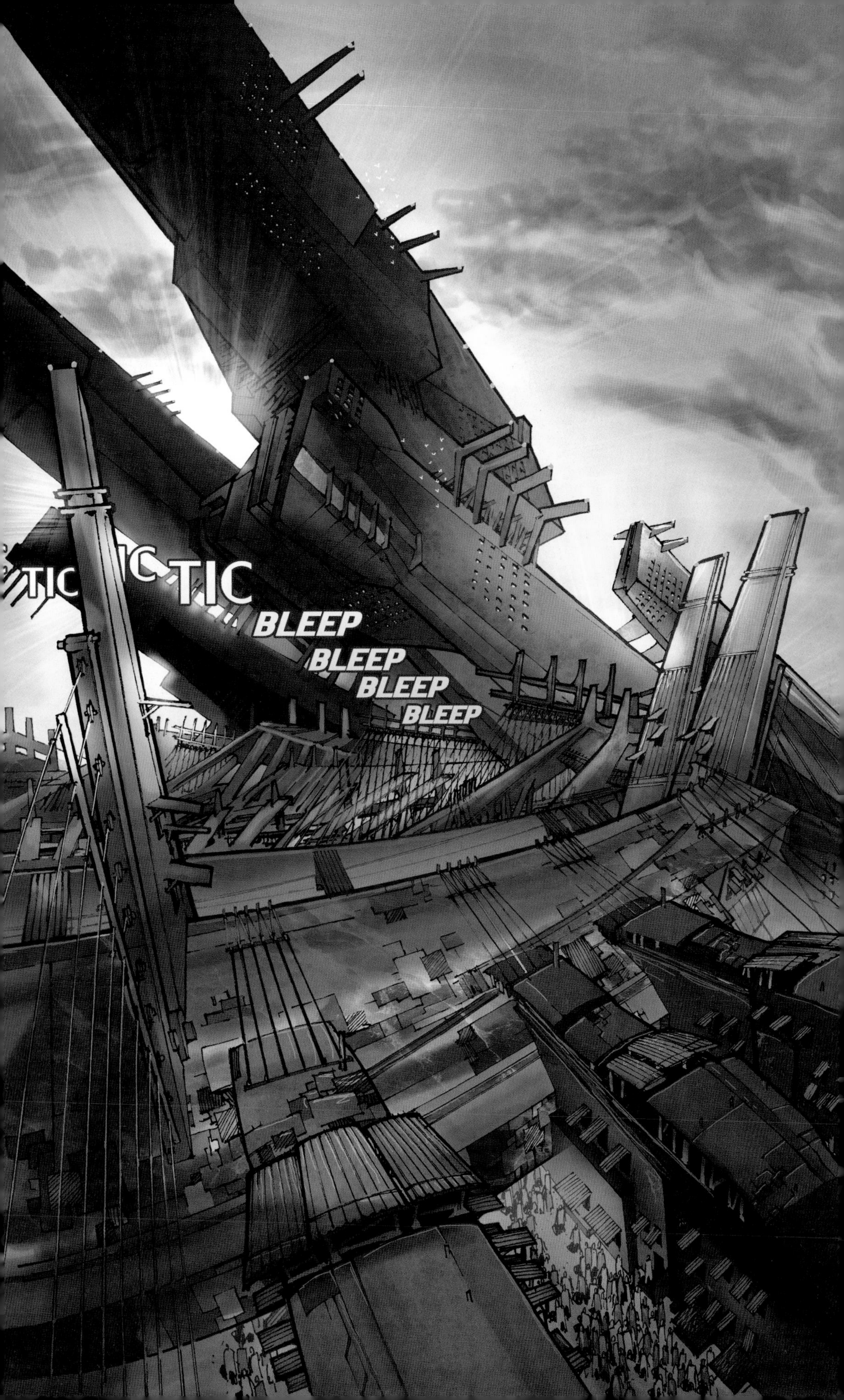
TIC
IC
TIC
BLEEP
BLEEP
BLEEP
BLEEP

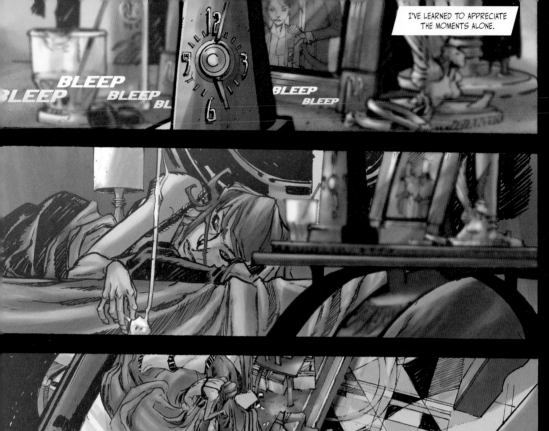

I'VE LEARNED TO APPRECIATE THE MOMENTS ALONE.

BLEEP
BLEEP
BLEEP
BL
BLEEP
BLEEP

NO SECRETS TO HIDE.

NO FEAR.

NO ONE TO RUN FROM.

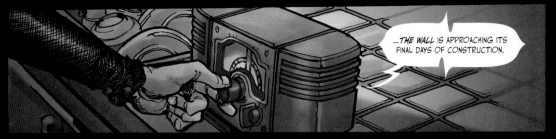

...*THE WALL* IS APPROACHING ITS FINAL DAYS OF CONSTRUCTION.

OUR DEFENSE MINISTRY, *THE ORIGAMI*, WISHES TO REASSURE THE GREAT CITIZENS OF *PRYGAT*...

...THAT THE COMPLETION OF THE WALL BRINGS US ONE STEP CLOSER...

...TO COMPLETE SECURITY FROM THE AGGRESSIVE NATURE OF OUR NEIGHBORING STATES.

THERE ISN'T MUCH ANY OF US CAN CALL OUR OWN. THE ORIGAMI CONTROLS IT ALL.

EVERYTHING FROM THE CITY'S DEFENSES TO THE FLOW OF INFORMATION.

AS LONG AS YOU LIVE IN PRYGAT, YOU'RE AT THEIR MERCY.

THAT'S WHY I NEED TO GET OUT.

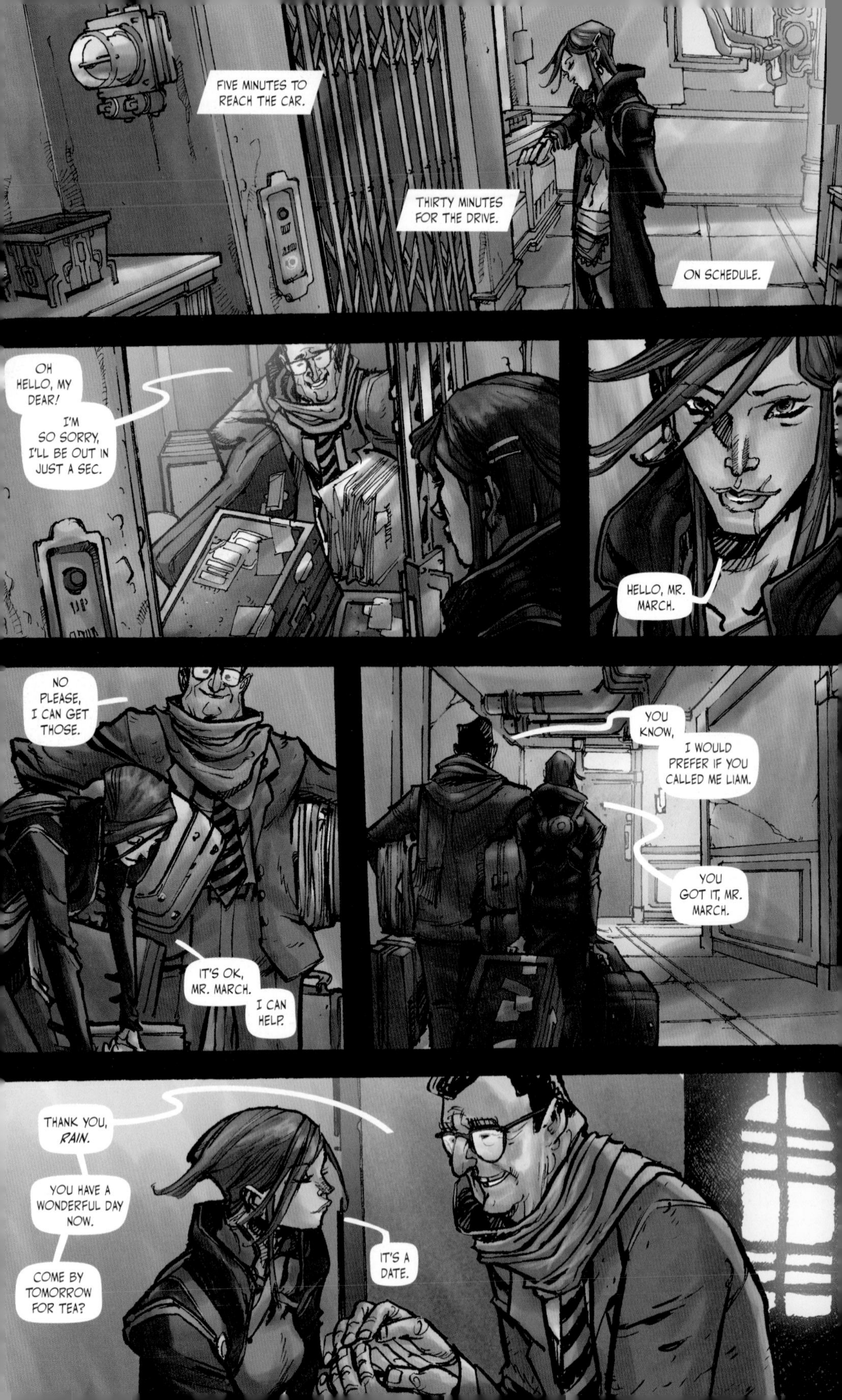

FIVE MINUTES TO REACH THE CAR.
THIRTY MINUTES FOR THE DRIVE.
ON SCHEDULE.
OH HELLO, MY DEAR!
I'M SO SORRY, I'LL BE OUT IN JUST A SEC.
HELLO, MR. MARCH.
NO PLEASE, I CAN GET THOSE.
IT'S OK, MR. MARCH.
I CAN HELP.
YOU KNOW,
I WOULD PREFER IF YOU CALLED ME LIAM.
YOU GOT IT, MR. MARCH.
THANK YOU, *RAIN.*
YOU HAVE A WONDERFUL DAY NOW.
COME BY TOMORROW FOR TEA?
IT'S A DATE.

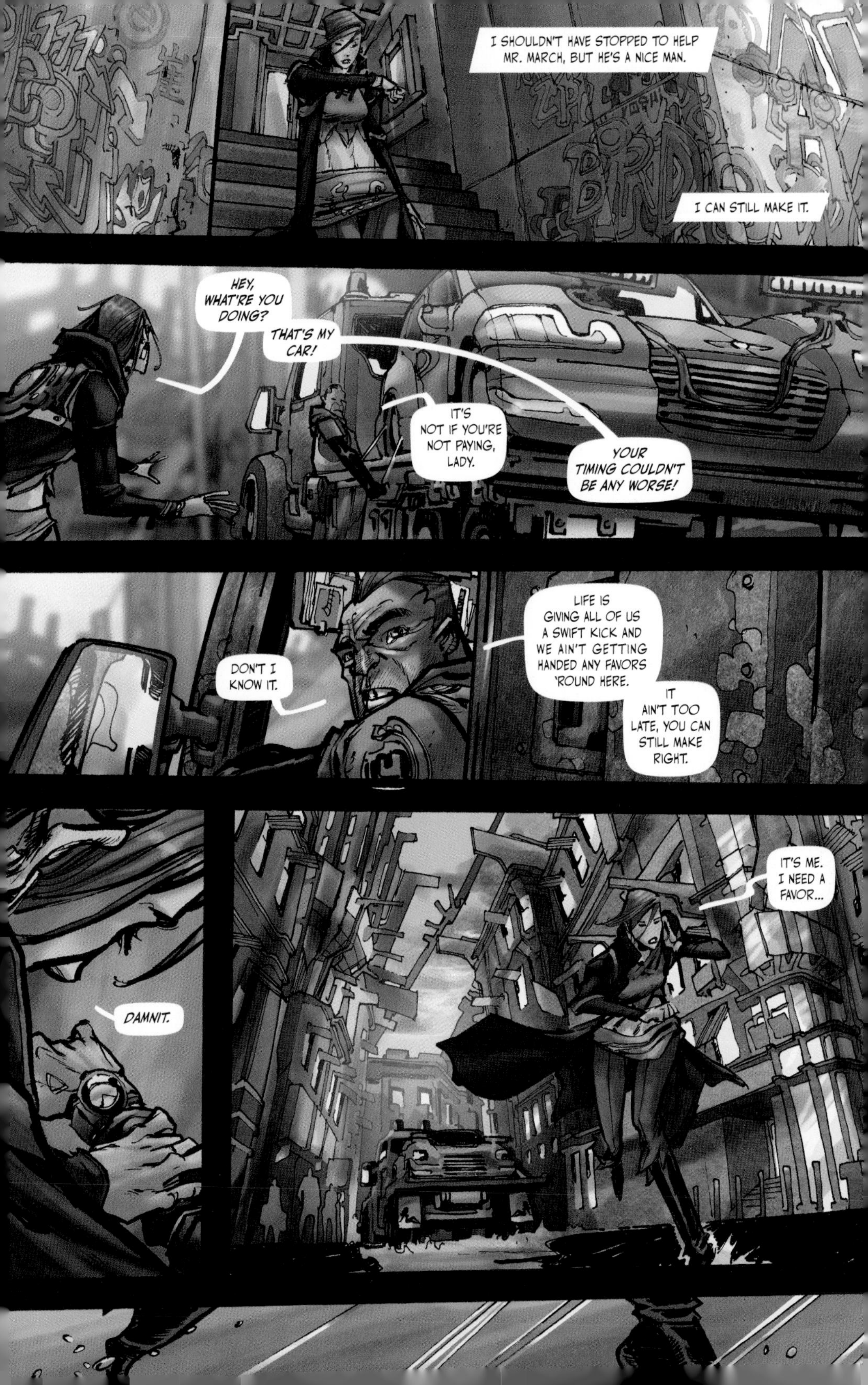
I SHOULDN'T HAVE STOPPED TO HELP MR. MARCH, BUT HE'S A NICE MAN.
I CAN STILL MAKE IT.
HEY, WHAT'RE YOU DOING?
THAT'S MY CAR!
IT'S NOT IF YOU'RE NOT PAYING, LADY.
YOUR TIMING COULDN'T BE ANY WORSE!
DON'T I KNOW IT.
LIFE IS GIVING ALL OF US A SWIFT KICK AND WE AIN'T GETTING HANDED ANY FAVORS 'ROUND HERE.
IT AIN'T TOO LATE, YOU CAN STILL MAKE RIGHT.
DAMNIT.
IT'S ME. I NEED A FAVOR...

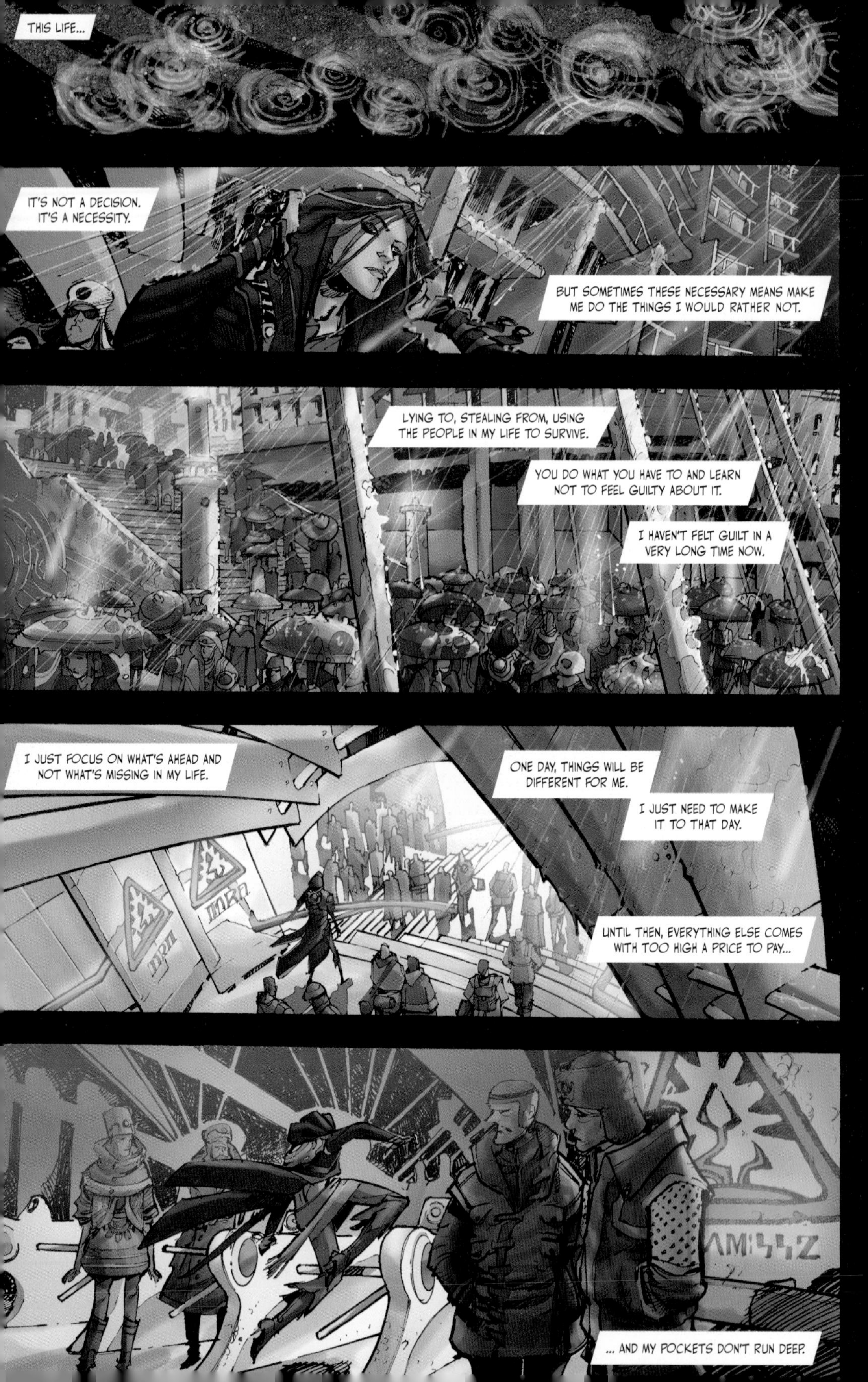
THIS LIFE...
IT'S NOT A DECISION. IT'S A NECESSITY.
BUT SOMETIMES THESE NECESSARY MEANS MAKE ME DO THE THINGS I WOULD RATHER NOT.
LYING TO, STEALING FROM, USING THE PEOPLE IN MY LIFE TO SURVIVE.
YOU DO WHAT YOU HAVE TO AND LEARN NOT TO FEEL GUILTY ABOUT IT.
I HAVEN'T FELT GUILT IN A VERY LONG TIME NOW.
I JUST FOCUS ON WHAT'S AHEAD AND NOT WHAT'S MISSING IN MY LIFE.
ONE DAY, THINGS WILL BE DIFFERENT FOR ME.
I JUST NEED TO MAKE IT TO THAT DAY.
UNTIL THEN, EVERYTHING ELSE COMES WITH TOO HIGH A PRICE TO PAY...
... AND MY POCKETS DON'T RUN DEEP.

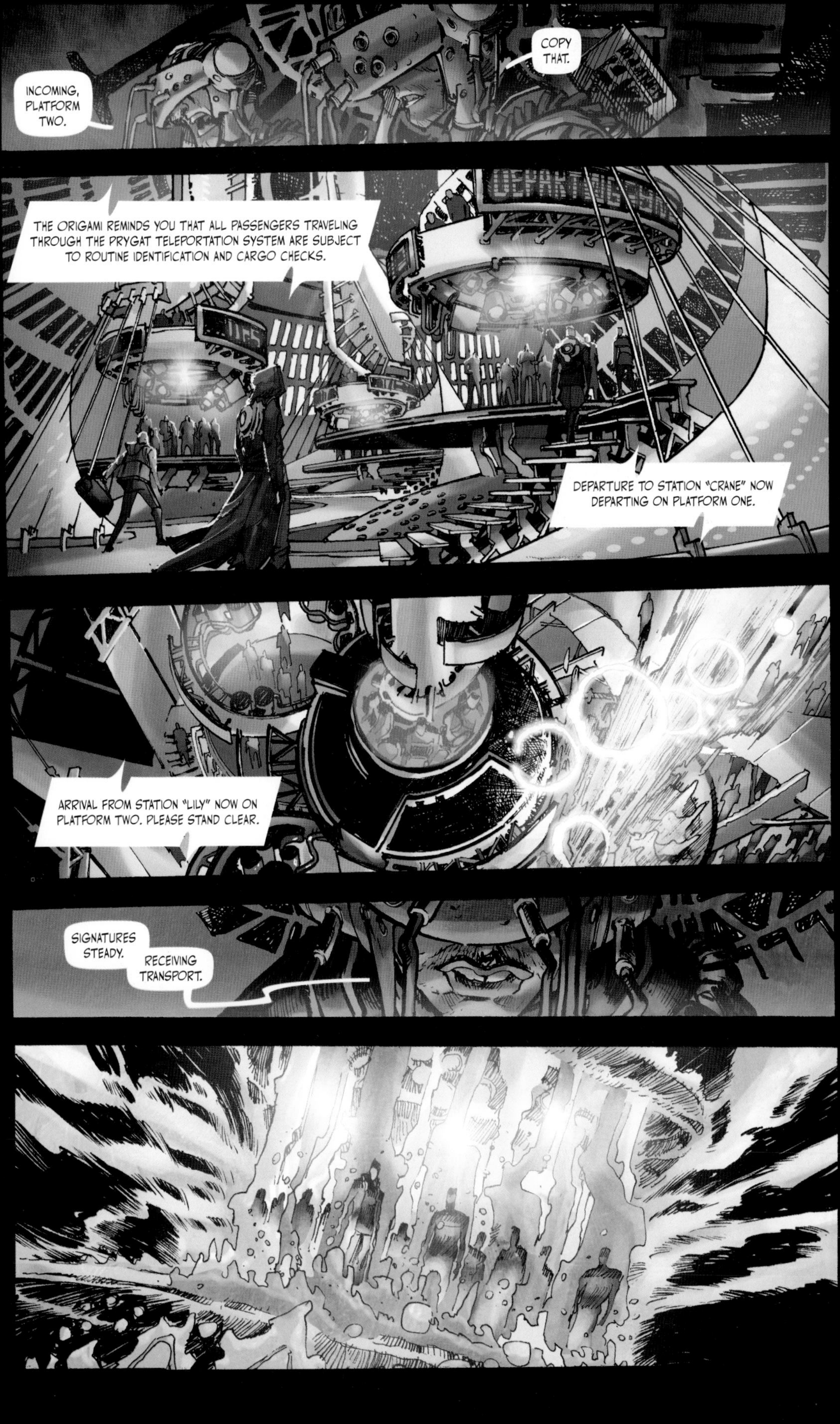

INCOMING, PLATFORM TWO.
COPY THAT.
THE ORIGAMI REMINDS YOU THAT ALL PASSENGERS TRAVELING THROUGH THE PRYGAT TELEPORTATION SYSTEM ARE SUBJECT TO ROUTINE IDENTIFICATION AND CARGO CHECKS.
DEPARTURE TO STATION "CRANE" NOW DEPARTING ON PLATFORM ONE.
ARRIVAL FROM STATION "LILY" NOW ON PLATFORM TWO. PLEASE STAND CLEAR.
SIGNATURES STEADY.
RECEIVING TRANSPORT.

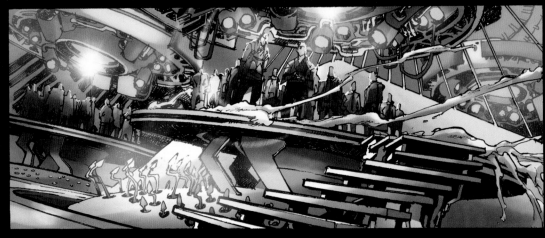

WELCOME TO
PRYGAT CENTRAL,
LADIES AND
GENTLEMEN.

I HOPE YOU
ENJOYED THE RIDE
AND PLEASE WATCH
YOUR STEP AS
YOU EXIT THE
PLATFORM.

AND YOU'RE
NOT EVEN
LISTENING...

DEYLIAD.

HELLO,
RAIN.

YOU LOOK
AS BEAUTIFUL
AS EVER.

READY TO
GET OUT OF
HERE?

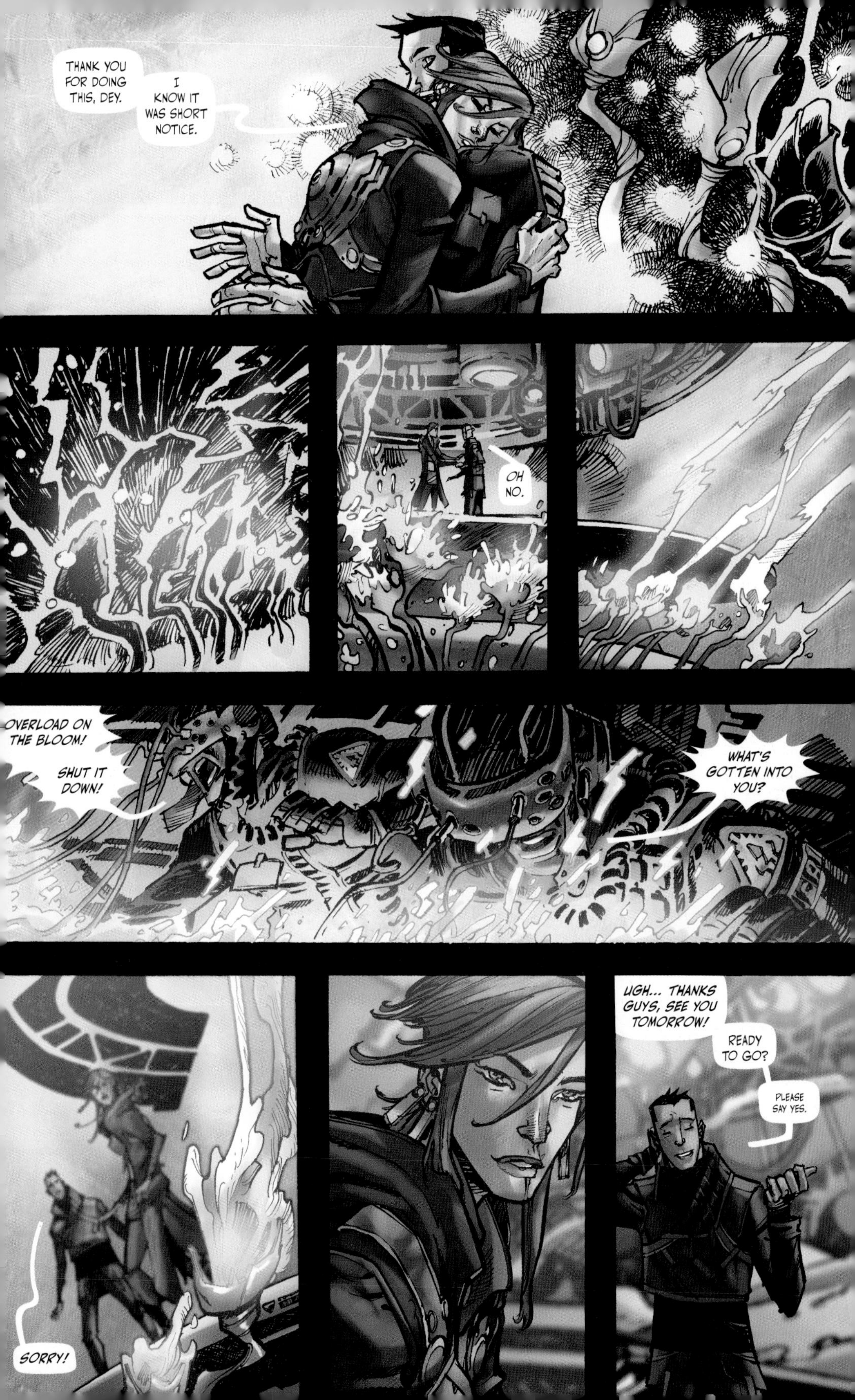
THANK YOU FOR DOING THIS, DEY.
I KNOW IT WAS SHORT NOTICE.
OH NO.
OVERLOAD ON THE BLOOM!
SHUT IT DOWN!
WHAT'S GOTTEN INTO YOU?
SORRY!
UGH... THANKS GUYS, SEE YOU TOMORROW!
READY TO GO?
PLEASE SAY YES.

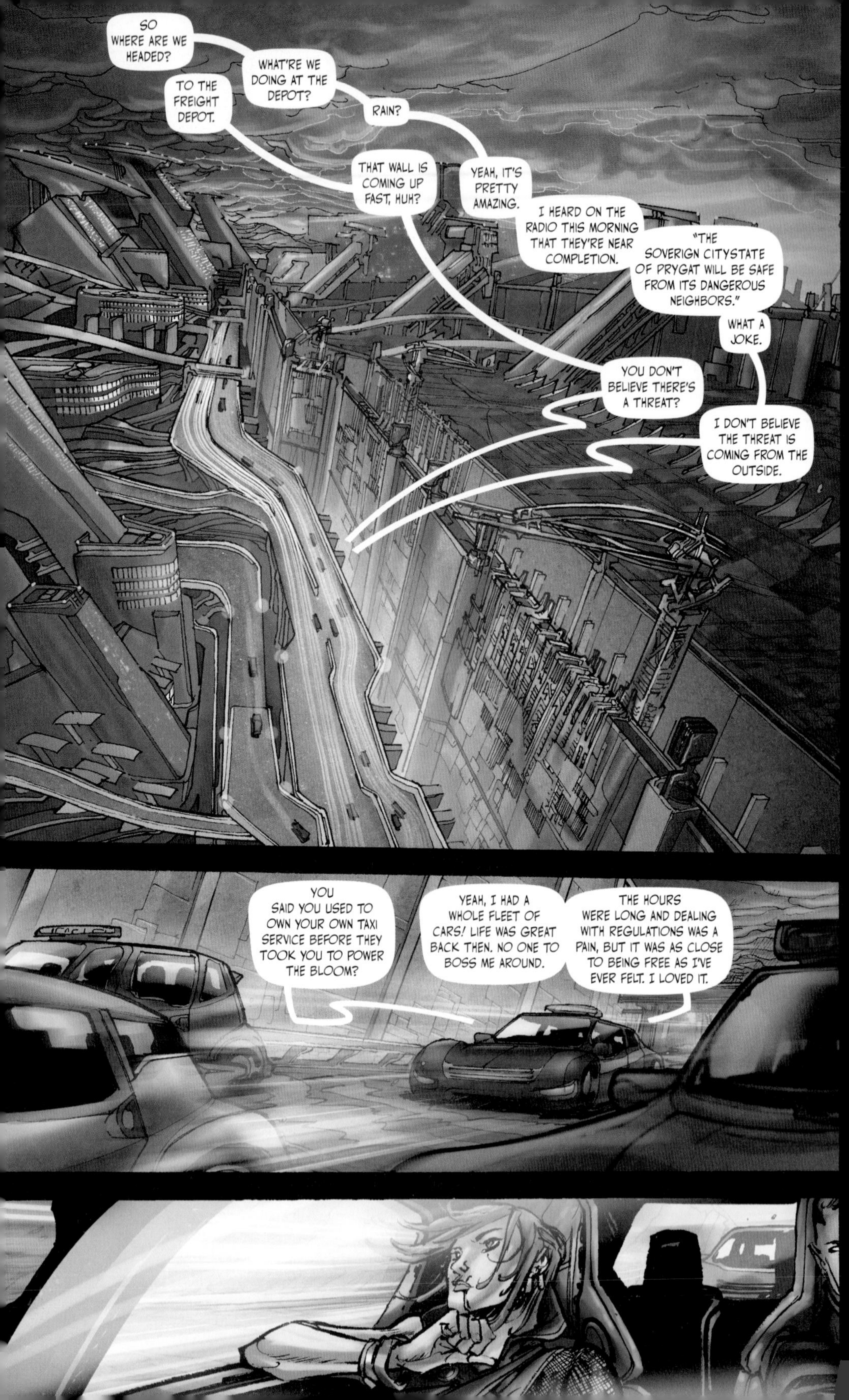
SO WHERE ARE WE HEADED?
TO THE FREIGHT DEPOT.
WHAT'RE WE DOING AT THE DEPOT?
RAIN?
THAT WALL IS COMING UP FAST, HUH?
YEAH, IT'S PRETTY AMAZING.
I HEARD ON THE RADIO THIS MORNING THAT THEY'RE NEAR COMPLETION.
"THE SOVERIGN CITYSTATE OF PRYGAT WILL BE SAFE FROM ITS DANGEROUS NEIGHBORS."
WHAT A JOKE.
YOU DON'T BELIEVE THERE'S A THREAT?
I DON'T BELIEVE THE THREAT IS COMING FROM THE OUTSIDE.
YOU SAID YOU USED TO OWN YOUR OWN TAXI SERVICE BEFORE THEY TOOK YOU TO POWER THE BLOOM?
YEAH, I HAD A WHOLE FLEET OF CARS! LIFE WAS GREAT BACK THEN. NO ONE TO BOSS ME AROUND.
THE HOURS WERE LONG AND DEALING WITH REGULATIONS WAS A PAIN, BUT IT WAS AS CLOSE TO BEING FREE AS I'VE EVER FELT. I LOVED IT.

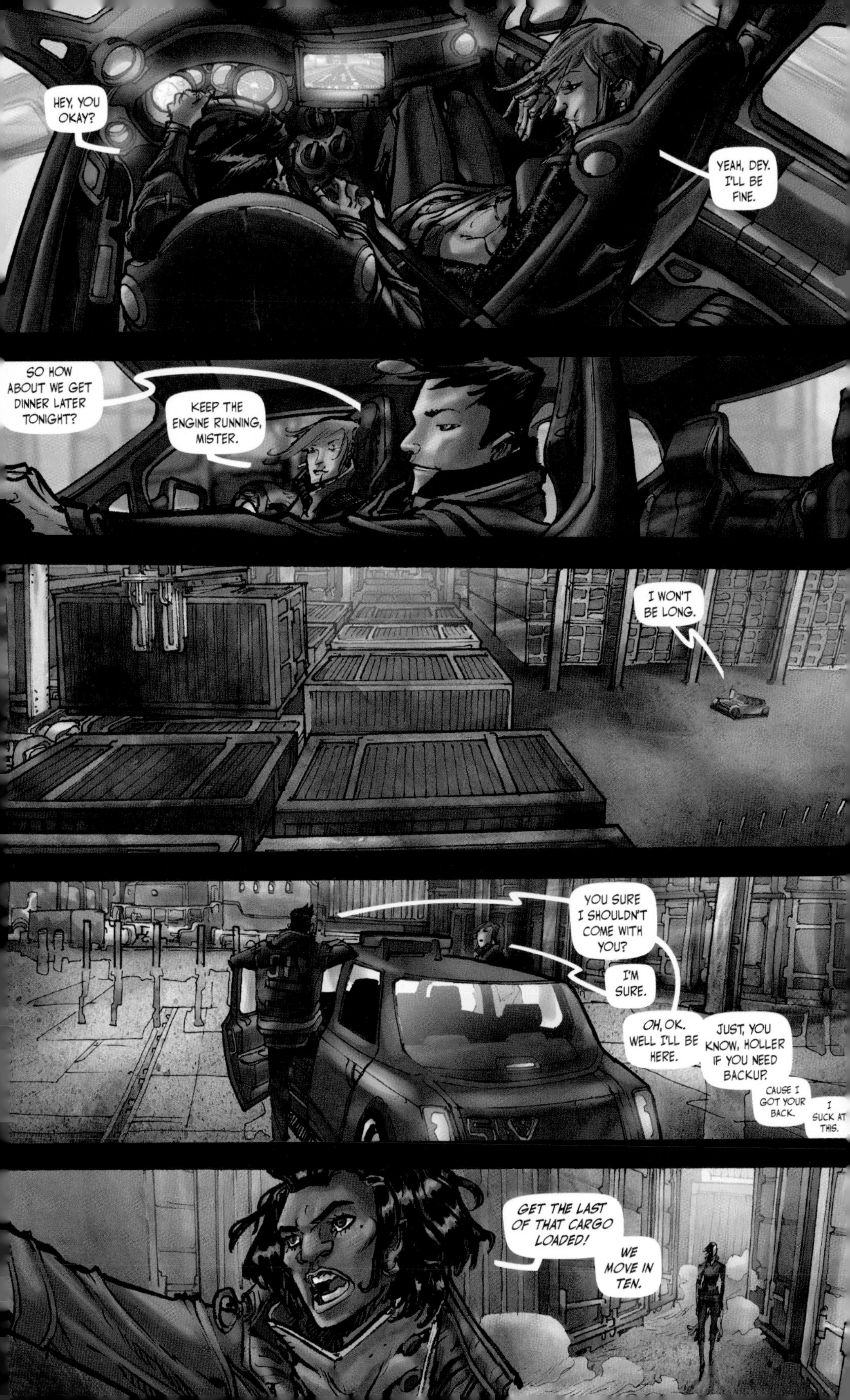
HEY, YOU OKAY?
YEAH, DEY. I'LL BE FINE.
SO HOW ABOUT WE GET DINNER LATER TONIGHT?
KEEP THE ENGINE RUNNING, MISTER.
I WON'T BE LONG.
YOU SURE I SHOULDN'T COME WITH YOU?
I'M SURE.
OH, OK. WELL I'LL BE HERE.
JUST, YOU KNOW, HOLLER IF YOU NEED BACKUP.
CAUSE I GOT YOUR BACK.
I SUCK AT THIS.
GET THE LAST OF THAT CARGO LOADED!
WE MOVE IN TEN.

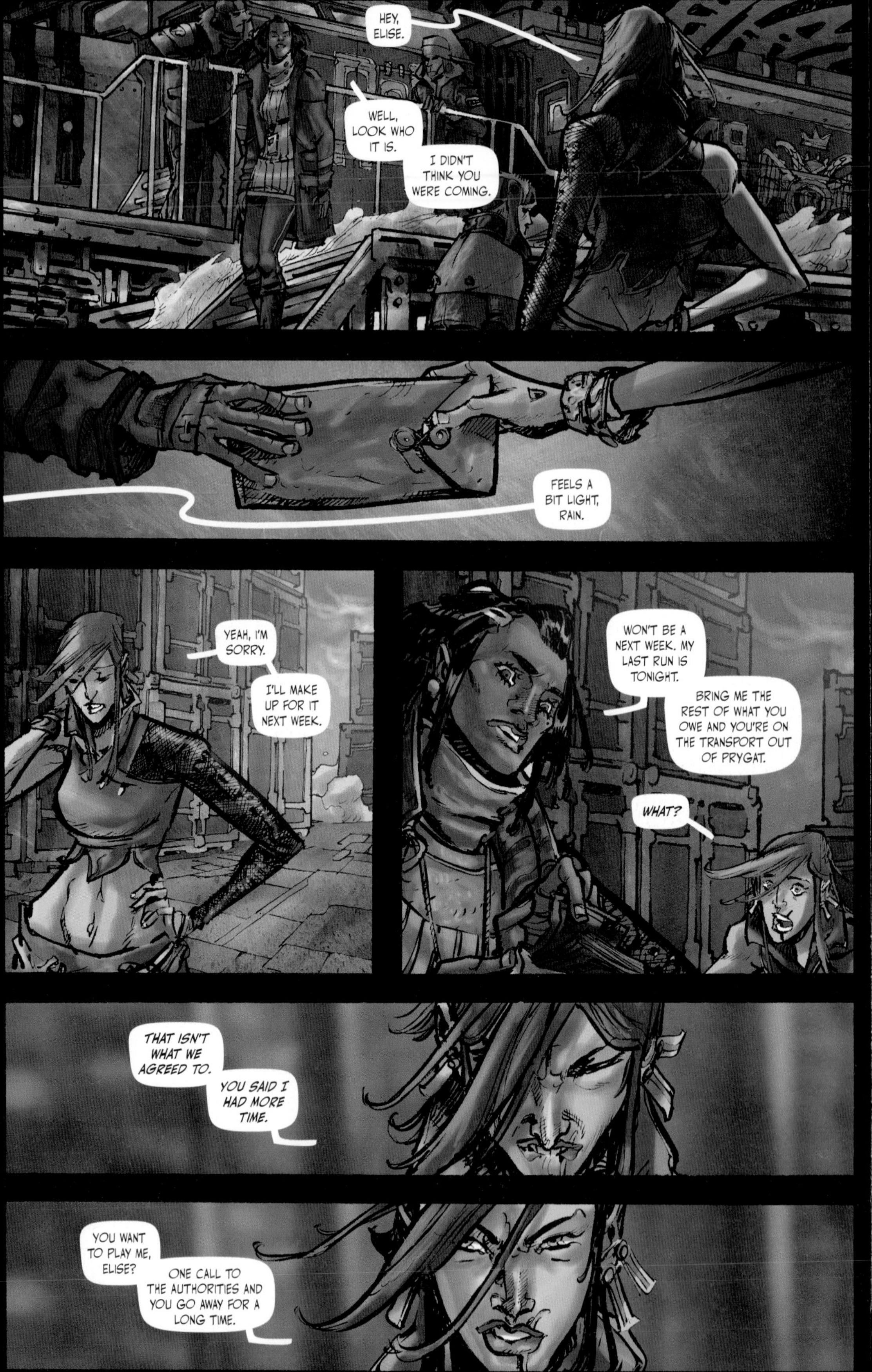
HEY, ELISE.
WELL, LOOK WHO IT IS.
I DIDN'T THINK YOU WERE COMING.
FEELS A BIT LIGHT, RAIN.
YEAH, I'M SORRY.
I'LL MAKE UP FOR IT NEXT WEEK.
WON'T BE A NEXT WEEK. MY LAST RUN IS TONIGHT.
BRING ME THE REST OF WHAT YOU OWE AND YOU'RE ON THE TRANSPORT OUT OF PRYGAT.
WHAT?
THAT ISN'T WHAT WE AGREED TO.
YOU SAID I HAD MORE TIME.
YOU WANT TO PLAY ME, ELISE?
ONE CALL TO THE AUTHORITIES AND YOU GO AWAY FOR A LONG TIME.

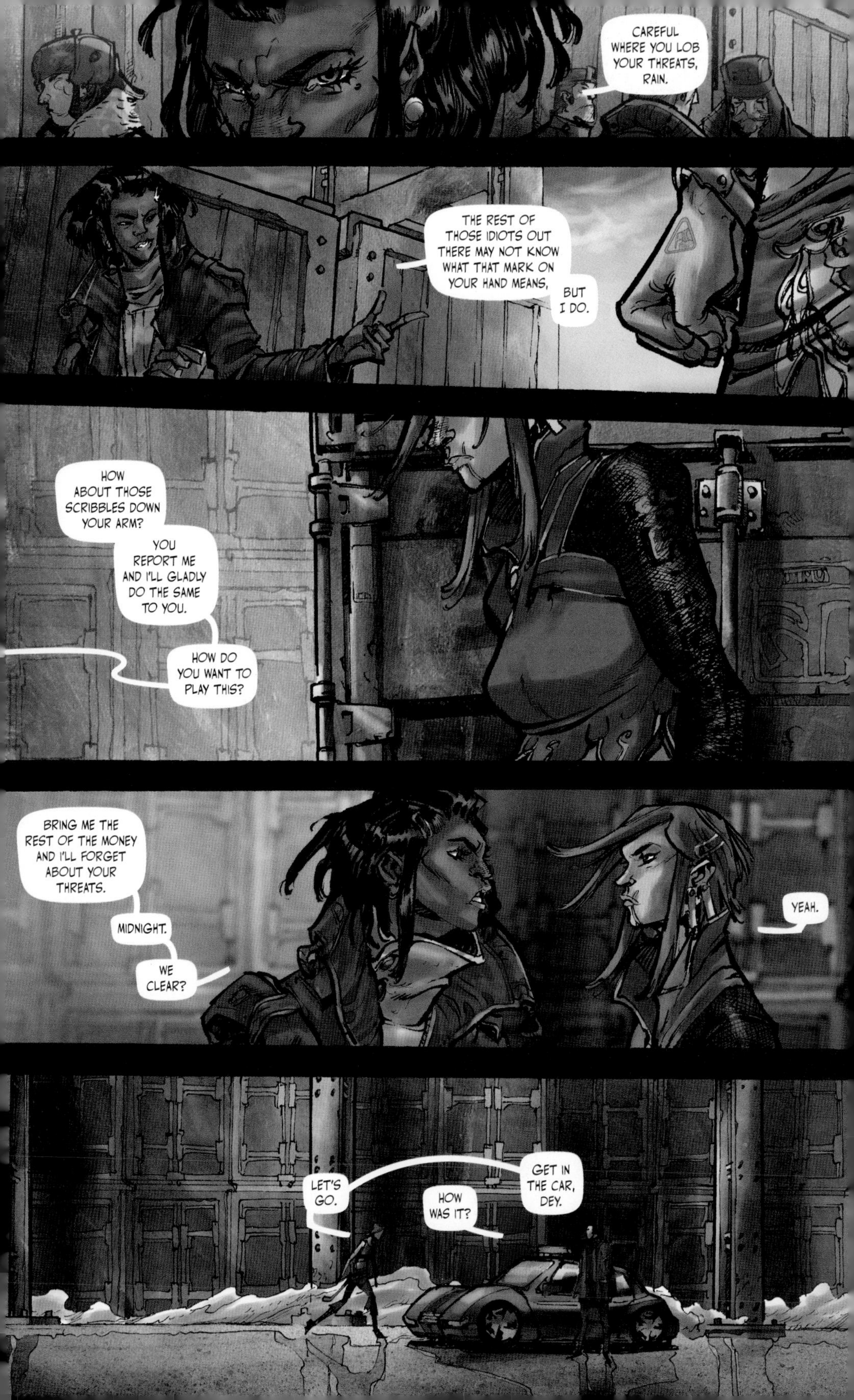
CAREFUL WHERE YOU LOB YOUR THREATS, RAIN.
THE REST OF THOSE IDIOTS OUT THERE MAY NOT KNOW WHAT THAT MARK ON YOUR HAND MEANS,
BUT I DO.
HOW ABOUT THOSE SCRIBBLES DOWN YOUR ARM?
YOU REPORT ME AND I'LL GLADLY DO THE SAME TO YOU.
HOW DO YOU WANT TO PLAY THIS?
BRING ME THE REST OF THE MONEY AND I'LL FORGET ABOUT YOUR THREATS.
MIDNIGHT.
WE CLEAR?
YEAH.
LET'S GO.
GET IN THE CAR, DEY.
HOW WAS IT?

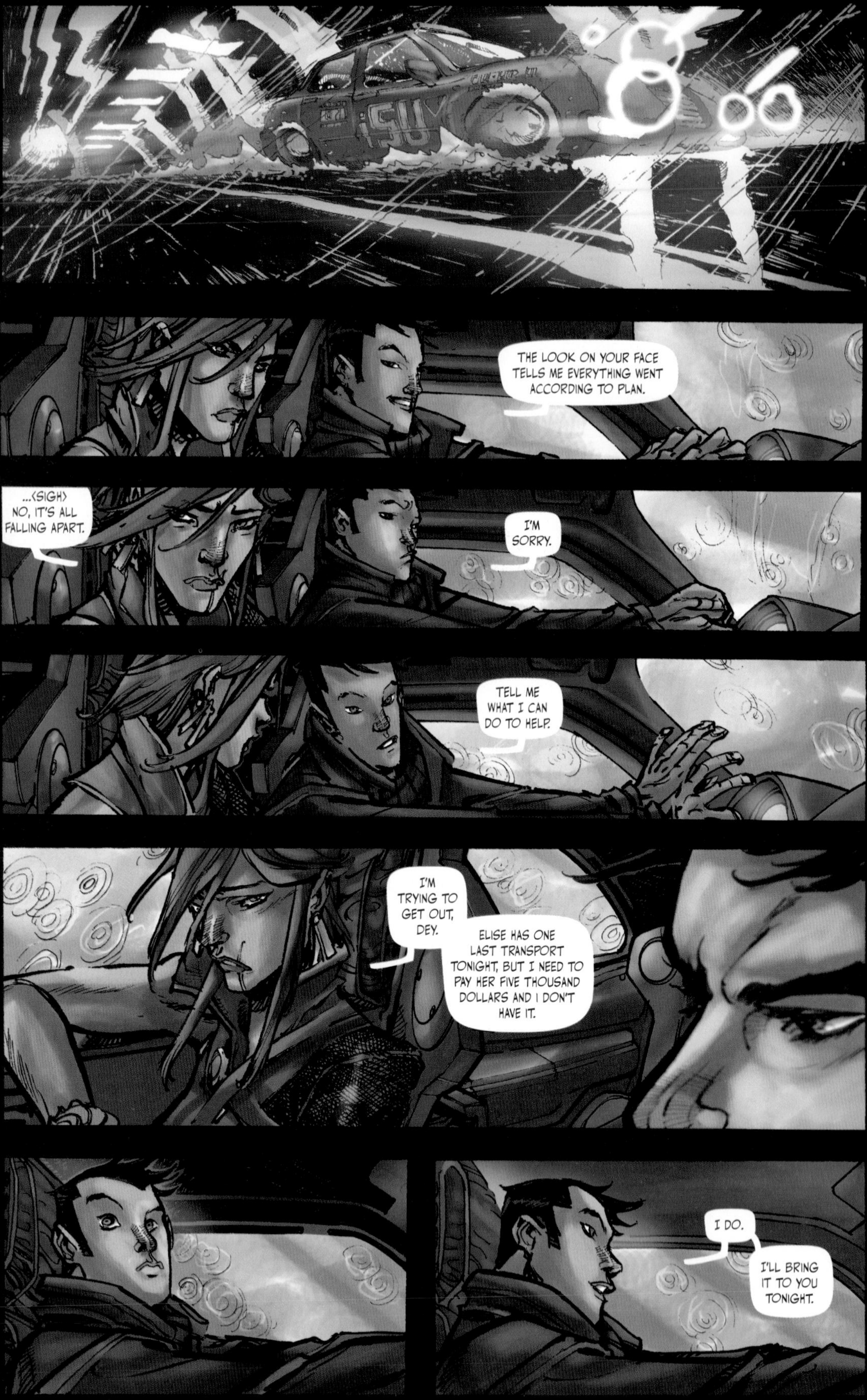
THE LOOK ON YOUR FACE TELLS ME EVERYTHING WENT ACCORDING TO PLAN.
...<SIGH> NO, IT'S ALL FALLING APART.
I'M SORRY.
TELL ME WHAT I CAN DO TO HELP.
I'M TRYING TO GET OUT, DEY.
ELISE HAS ONE LAST TRANSPORT TONIGHT, BUT I NEED TO PAY HER FIVE THOUSAND DOLLARS AND I DON'T HAVE IT.
I DO.
I'LL BRING IT TO YOU TONIGHT.

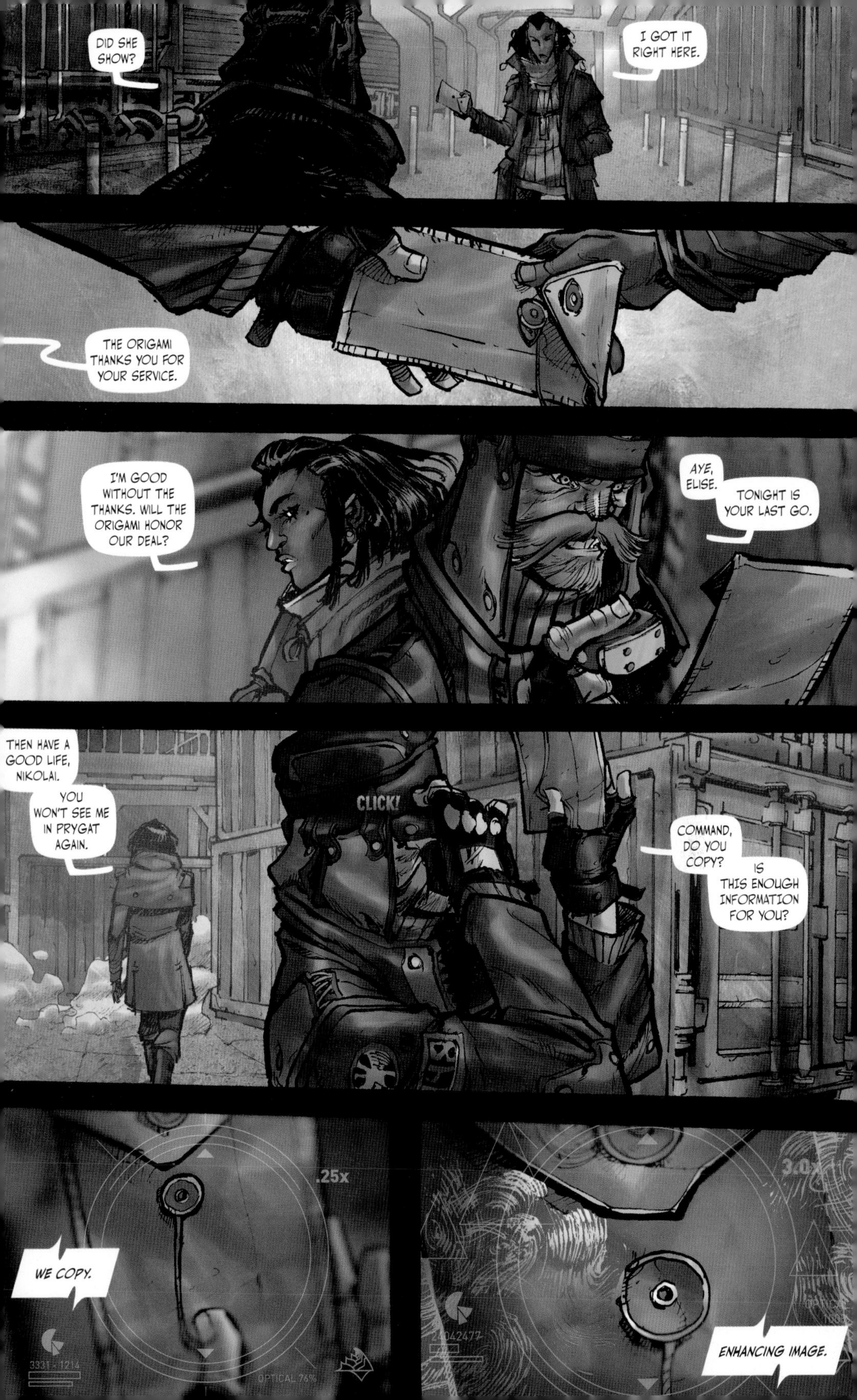
DID SHE SHOW?
I GOT IT RIGHT HERE.
THE ORIGAMI THANKS YOU FOR YOUR SERVICE.
I'M GOOD WITHOUT THE THANKS. WILL THE ORIGAMI HONOR OUR DEAL?
AYE, ELISE.
TONIGHT IS YOUR LAST GO.
THEN HAVE A GOOD LIFE, NIKOLAI.
YOU WON'T SEE ME IN PRYGAT AGAIN.
CLICK!
COMMAND, DO YOU COPY?
IS THIS ENOUGH INFORMATION FOR YOU?
.25x
WE COPY.
3.0x
ENHANCING IMAGE.

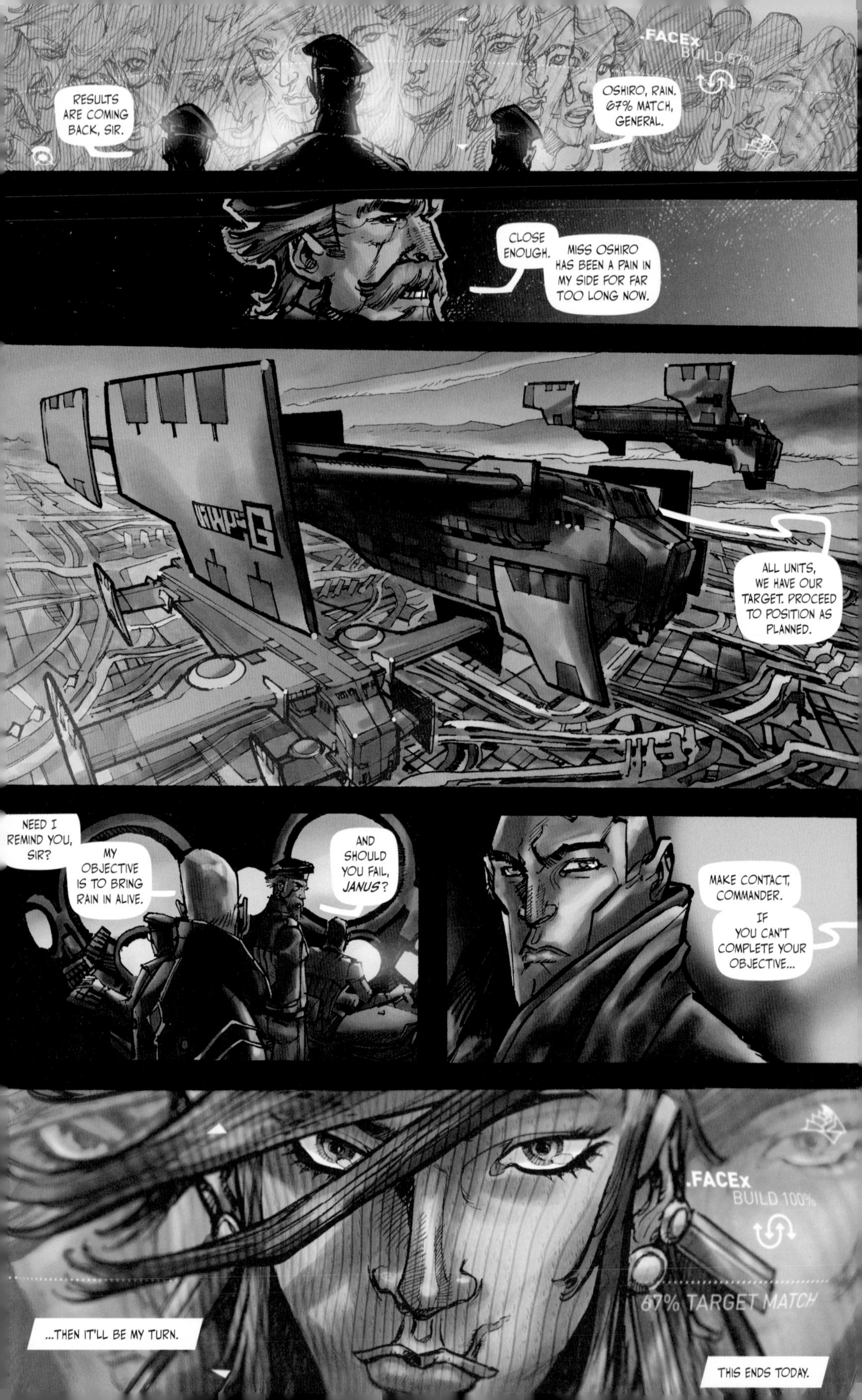
.FACEx
BUILD 57%
RESULTS ARE COMING BACK, SIR.
OSHIRO, RAIN. 67% MATCH, GENERAL.
CLOSE ENOUGH.
MISS OSHIRO HAS BEEN A PAIN IN MY SIDE FOR FAR TOO LONG NOW.
ALL UNITS, WE HAVE OUR TARGET. PROCEED TO POSITION AS PLANNED.
NEED I REMIND YOU, SIR?
MY OBJECTIVE IS TO BRING RAIN IN ALIVE.
AND SHOULD YOU FAIL, JANUS?
MAKE CONTACT, COMMANDER.
IF YOU CAN'T COMPLETE YOUR OBJECTIVE...
...THEN IT'LL BE MY TURN.
.FACEx
BUILD 100%
67% TARGET MATCH
THIS ENDS TODAY.

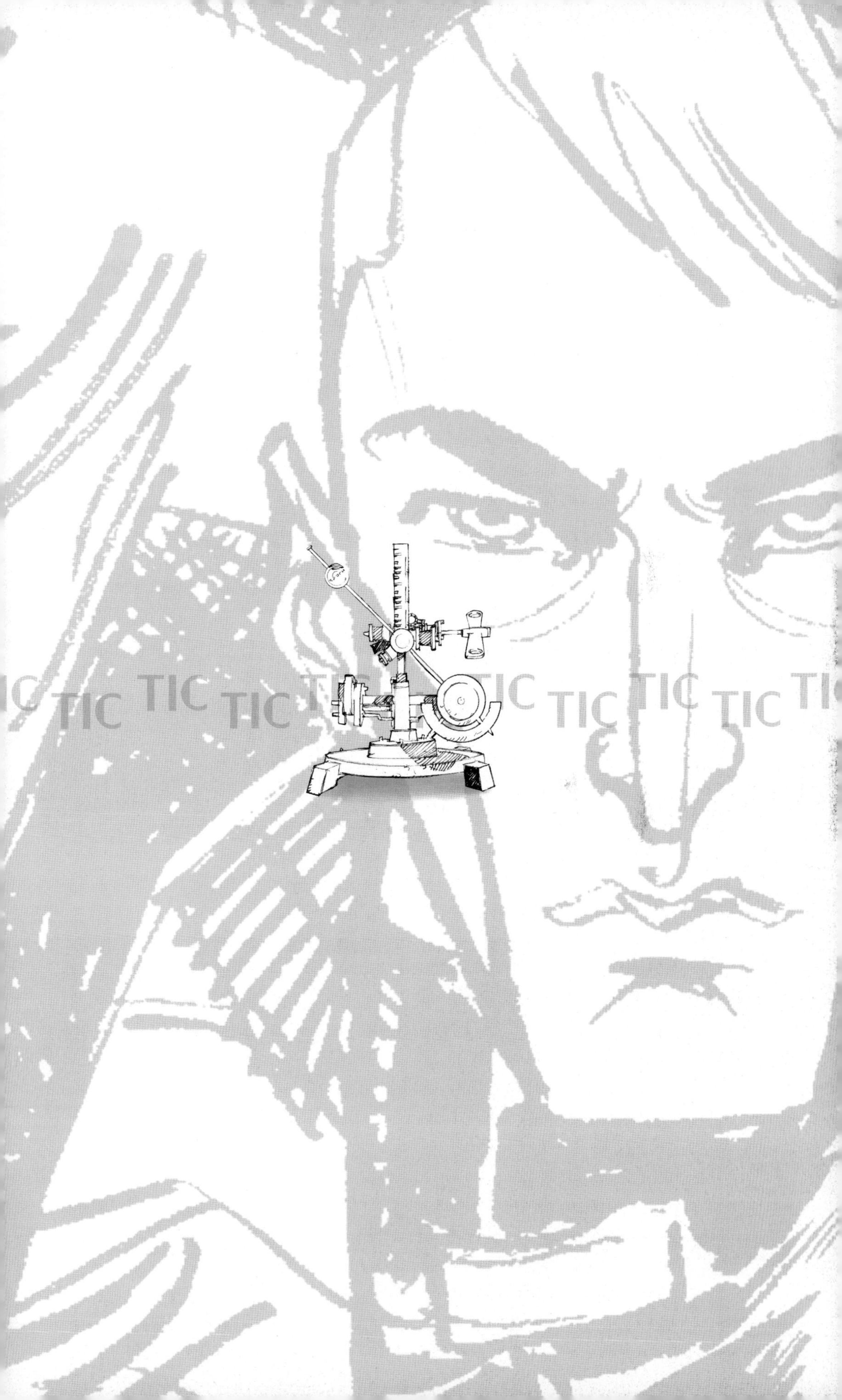
TIC TIC TIC TIC TIC TIC TIC

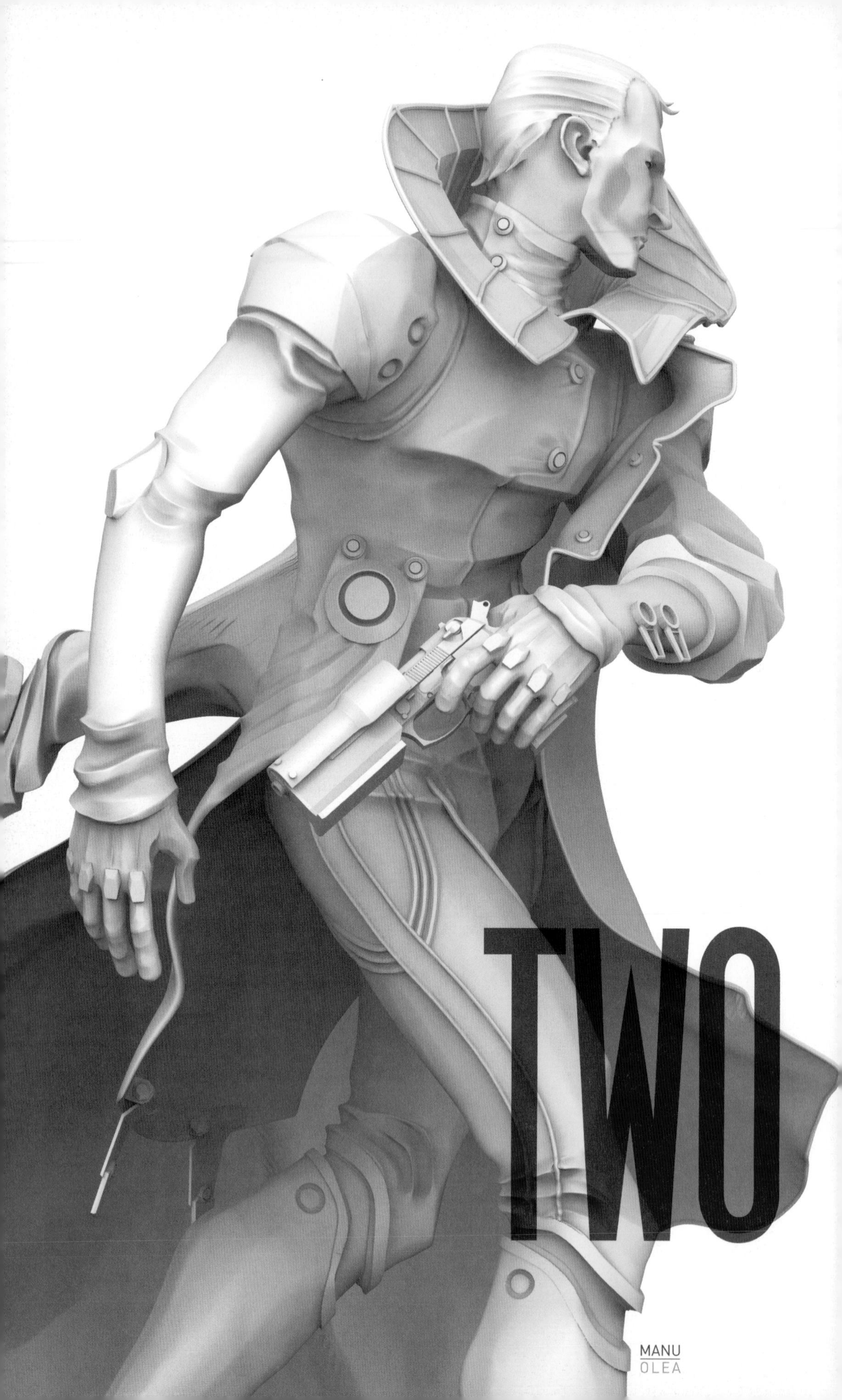
TWO
MANU
OLEA

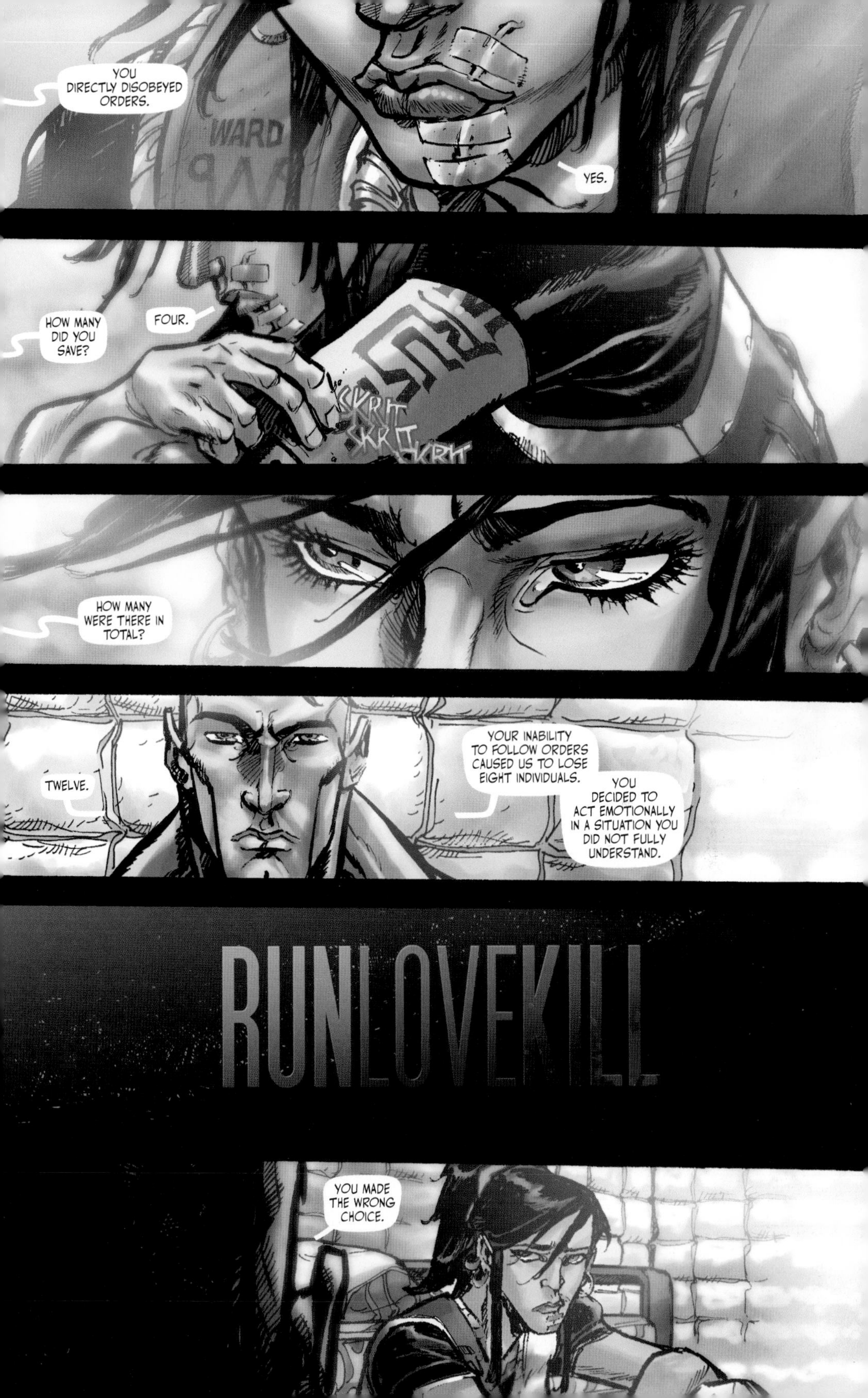
YOU DIRECTLY DISOBEYED ORDERS.
WARD
YES.
HOW MANY DID YOU SAVE?
FOUR.
SKRIT SKRIT SKRIT
HOW MANY WERE THERE IN TOTAL?
TWELVE.
YOUR INABILITY TO FOLLOW ORDERS CAUSED US TO LOSE EIGHT INDIVIDUALS.
YOU DECIDED TO ACT EMOTIONALLY IN A SITUATION YOU DID NOT FULLY UNDERSTAND.
RUNLOVEKILL
YOU MADE THE WRONG CHOICE.

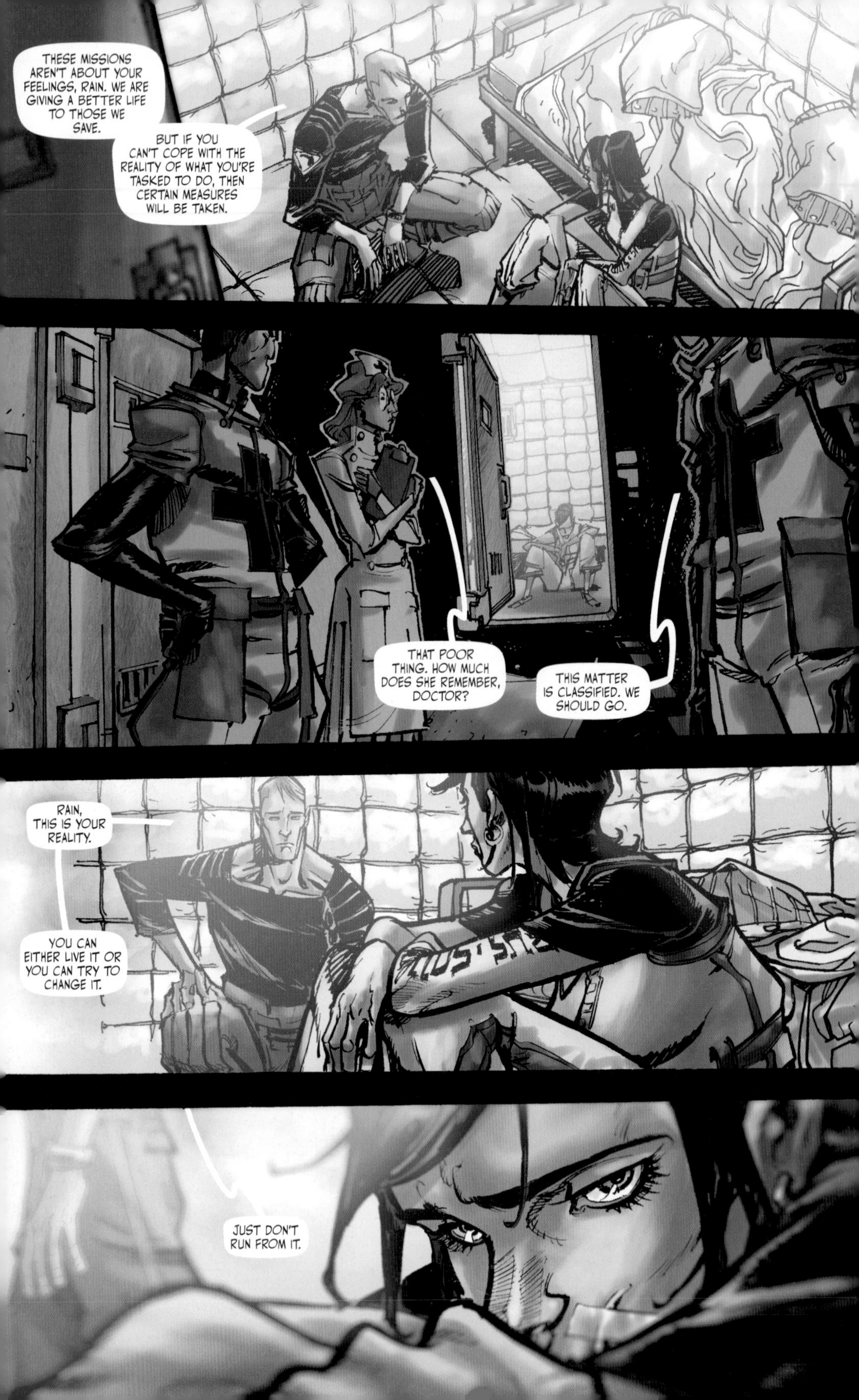
THESE MISSIONS AREN'T ABOUT YOUR FEELINGS, RAIN. WE ARE GIVING A BETTER LIFE TO THOSE WE SAVE.
BUT IF YOU CAN'T COPE WITH THE REALITY OF WHAT YOU'RE TASKED TO DO, THEN CERTAIN MEASURES WILL BE TAKEN.
THAT POOR THING. HOW MUCH DOES SHE REMEMBER, DOCTOR?
THIS MATTER IS CLASSIFIED. WE SHOULD GO.
RAIN, THIS IS YOUR REALITY.
YOU CAN EITHER LIVE IT OR YOU CAN TRY TO CHANGE IT.
JUST DON'T RUN FROM IT.

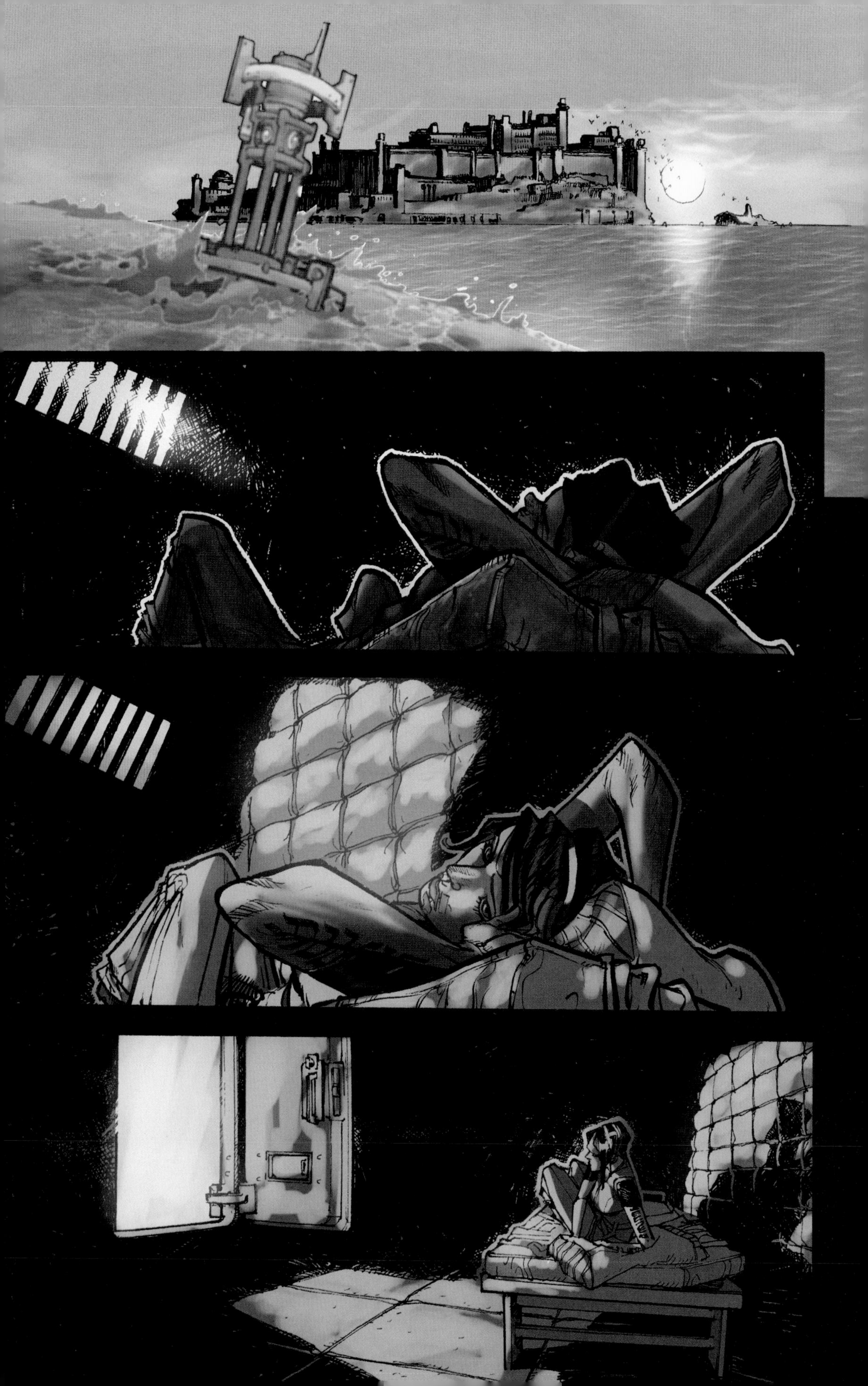

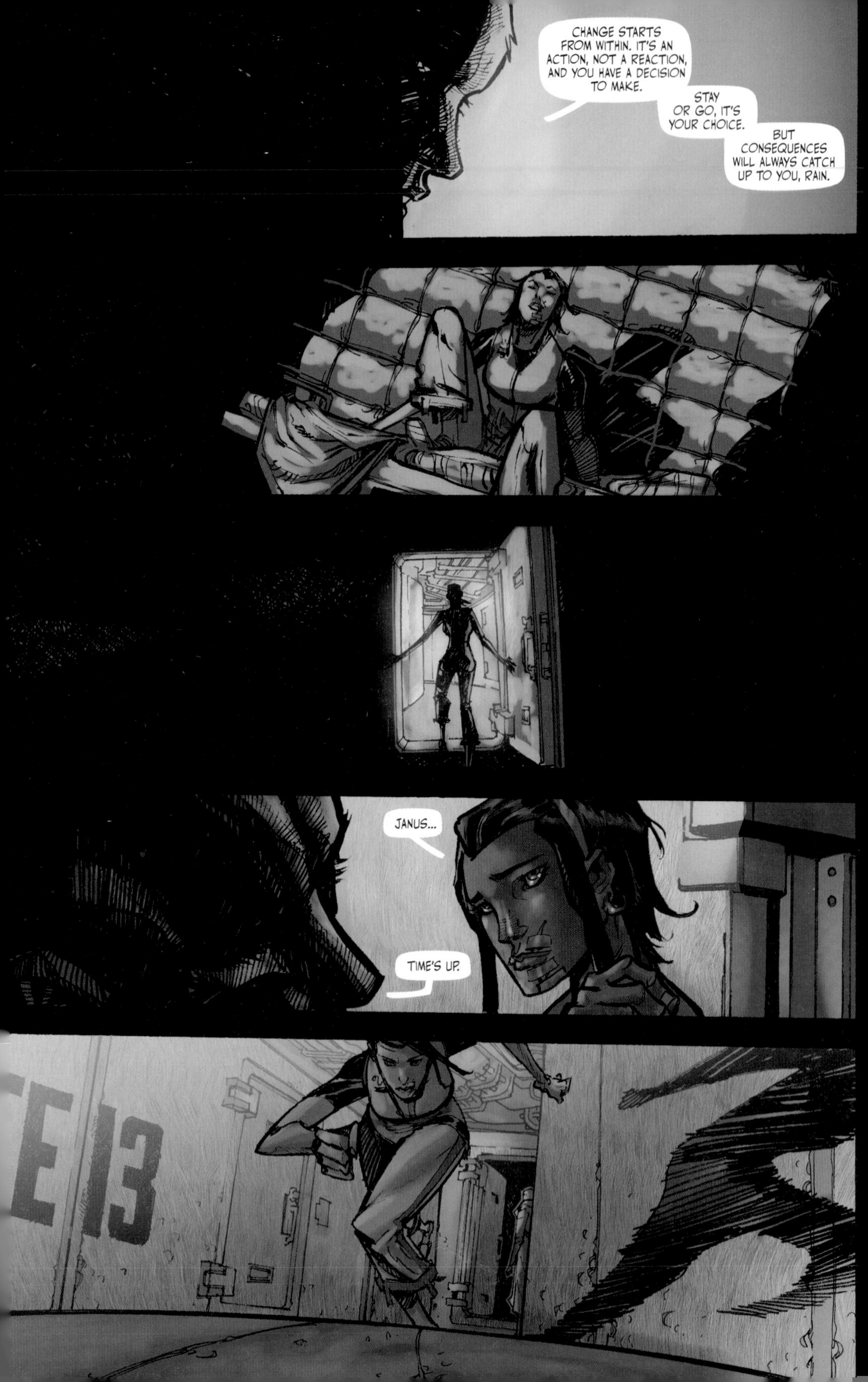
CHANGE STARTS FROM WITHIN. IT'S AN ACTION, NOT A REACTION, AND YOU HAVE A DECISION TO MAKE.
STAY OR GO, IT'S YOUR CHOICE.
BUT CONSEQUENCES WILL ALWAYS CATCH UP TO YOU, RAIN.
JANUS...
TIME'S UP.
E13

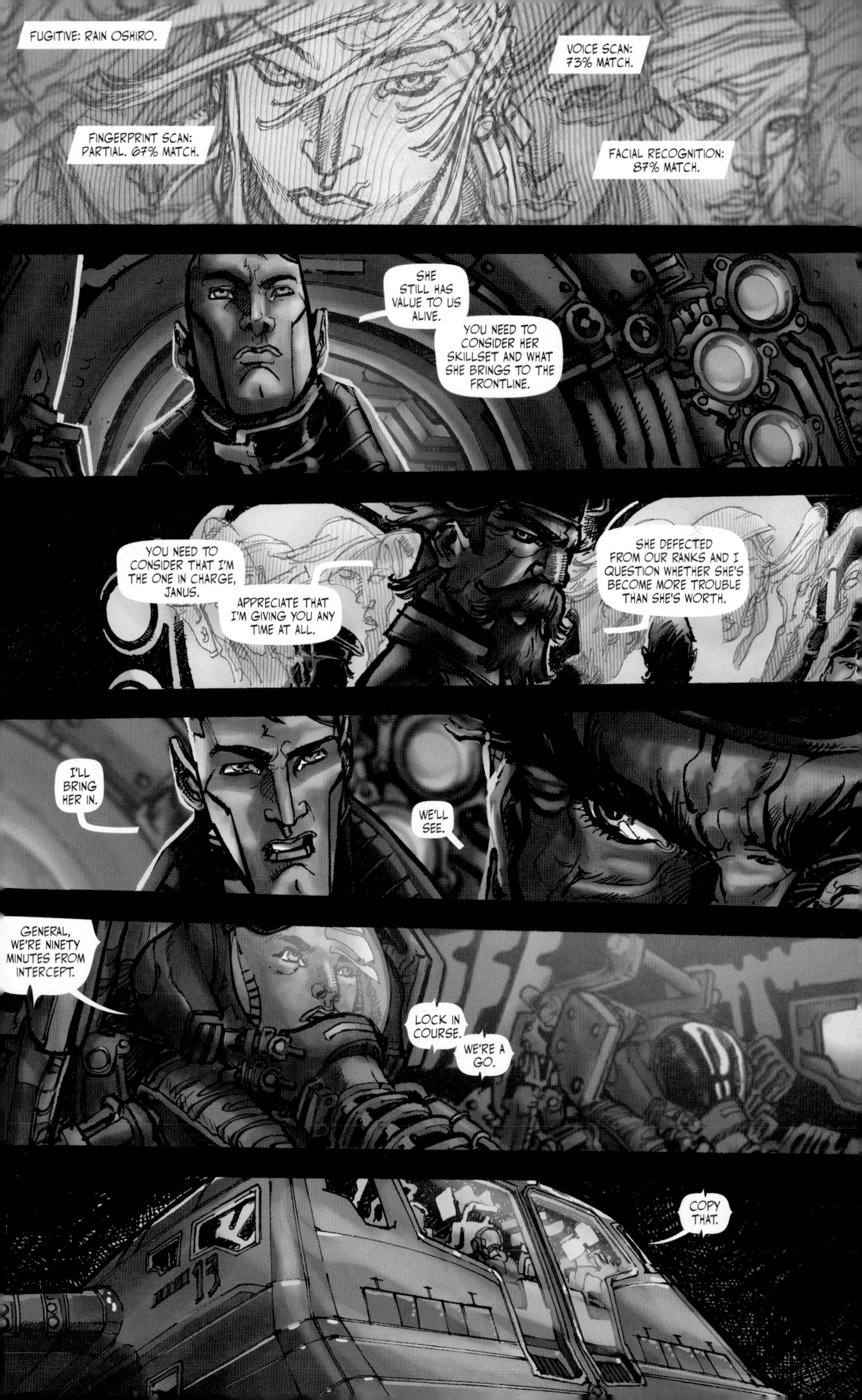
FUGITIVE: RAIN OSHIRO.
VOICE SCAN: 73% MATCH.
FINGERPRINT SCAN: PARTIAL. 67% MATCH.
FACIAL RECOGNITION: 87% MATCH.
SHE STILL HAS VALUE TO US ALIVE.
YOU NEED TO CONSIDER HER SKILLSET AND WHAT SHE BRINGS TO THE FRONTLINE.
SHE DEFECTED FROM OUR RANKS AND I QUESTION WHETHER SHE'S BECOME MORE TROUBLE THAN SHE'S WORTH.
YOU NEED TO CONSIDER THAT I'M THE ONE IN CHARGE, JANUS.
APPRECIATE THAT I'M GIVING YOU ANY TIME AT ALL.
I'LL BRING HER IN.
WE'LL SEE.
GENERAL, WE'RE NINETY MINUTES FROM INTERCEPT.
LOCK IN COURSE.
WE'RE A GO.
COPY THAT.

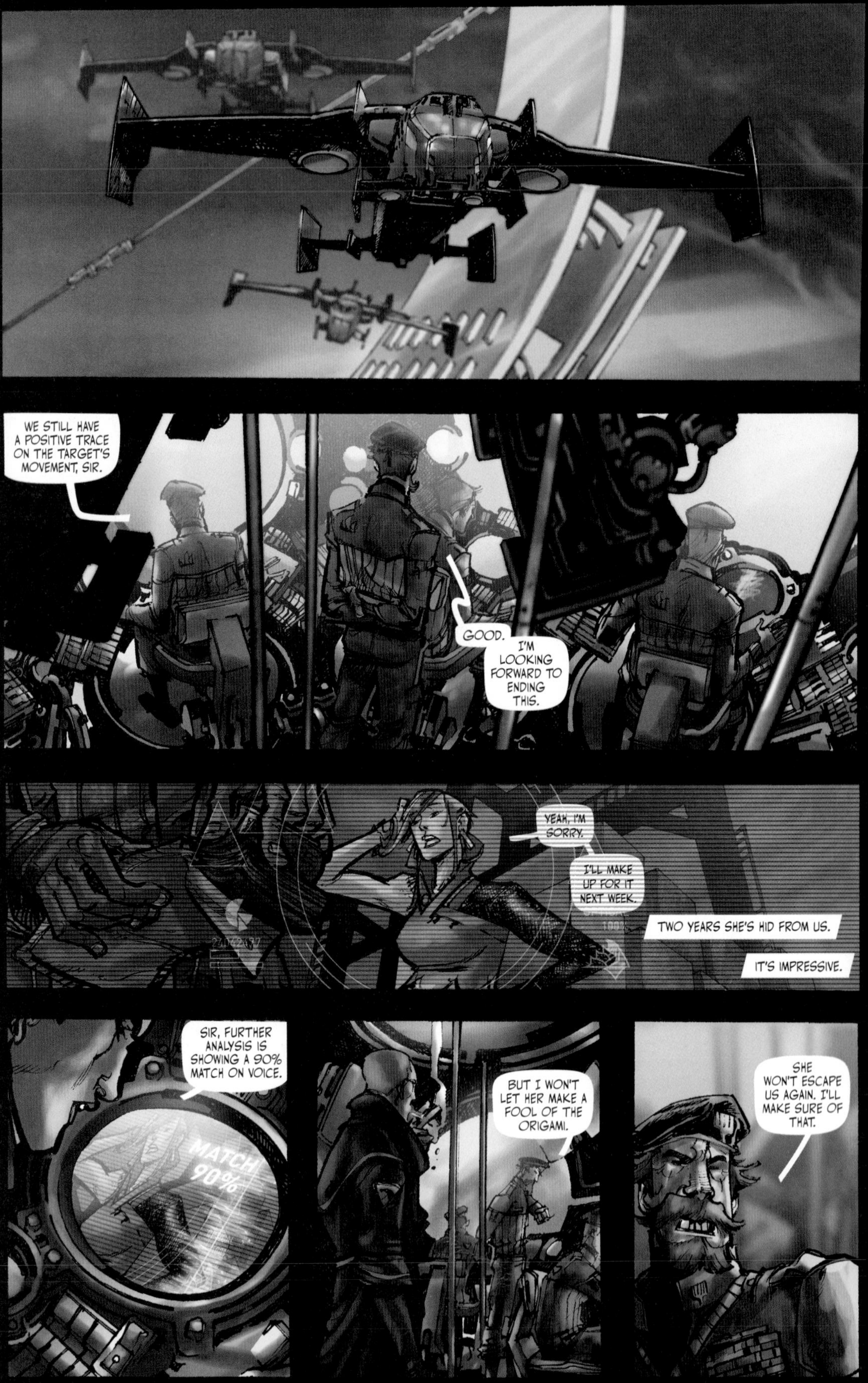

WE STILL HAVE A POSITIVE TRACE ON THE TARGET'S MOVEMENT, SIR.
GOOD. I'M LOOKING FORWARD TO ENDING THIS.
YEAH, I'M SORRY.
I'LL MAKE UP FOR IT NEXT WEEK.
TWO YEARS SHE'S HID FROM US.
IT'S IMPRESSIVE.
SIR, FURTHER ANALYSIS IS SHOWING A 90% MATCH ON VOICE.
MATCH 90%
BUT I WON'T LET HER MAKE A FOOL OF THE ORIGAMI.
SHE WON'T ESCAPE US AGAIN. I'LL MAKE SURE OF THAT.

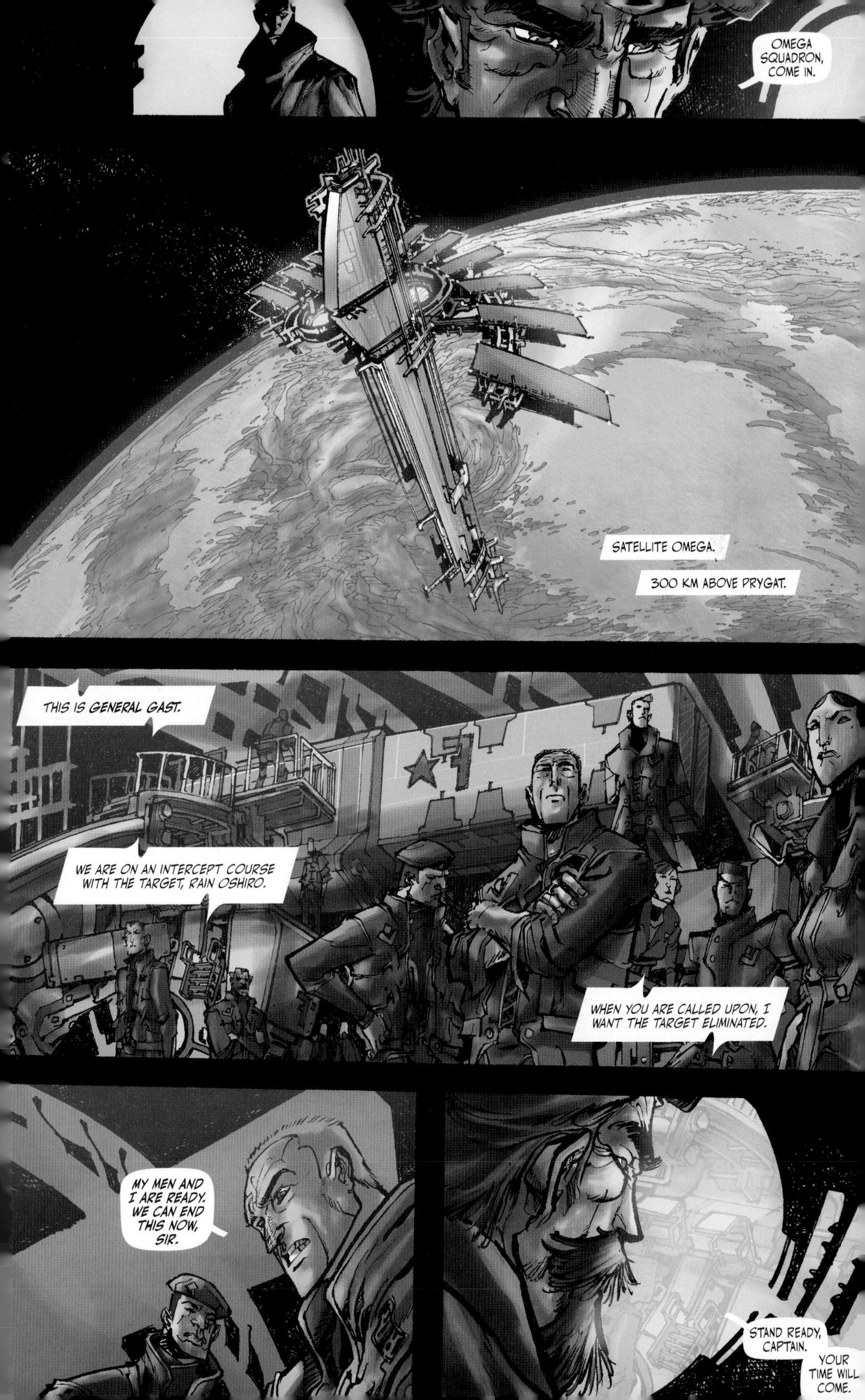
OMEGA SQUADRON, COME IN.
SATELLITE OMEGA.
300 KM ABOVE PRYGAT.
THIS IS GENERAL GAST.
WE ARE ON AN INTERCEPT COURSE WITH THE TARGET, RAIN OSHIRO.
WHEN YOU ARE CALLED UPON, I WANT THE TARGET ELIMINATED.
MY MEN AND I ARE READY. WE CAN END THIS NOW, SIR.
STAND READY, CAPTAIN.
YOUR TIME WILL COME.

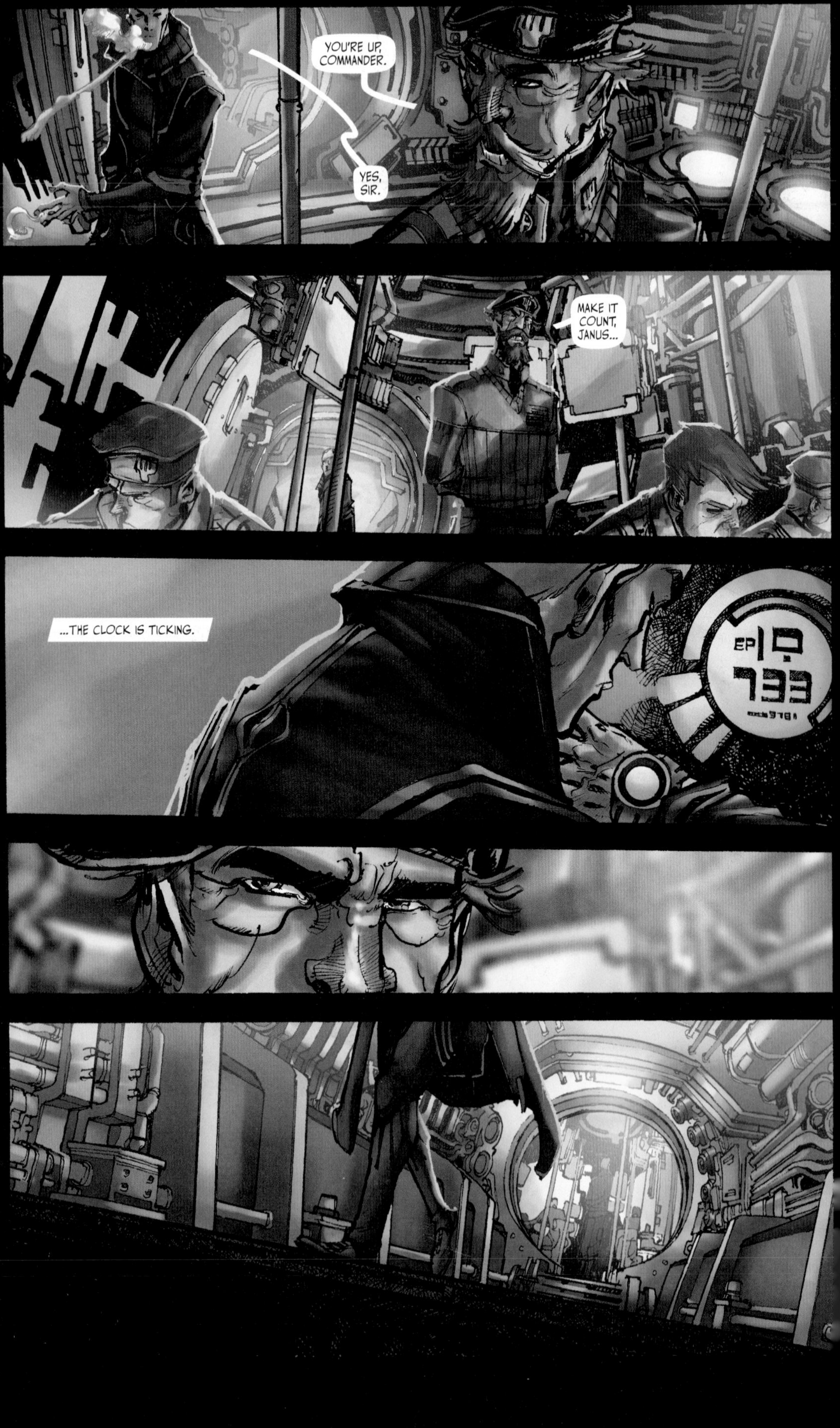
YOU'RE UP, COMMANDER.
YES, SIR.
MAKE IT COUNT, JANUS...
...THE CLOCK IS TICKING.

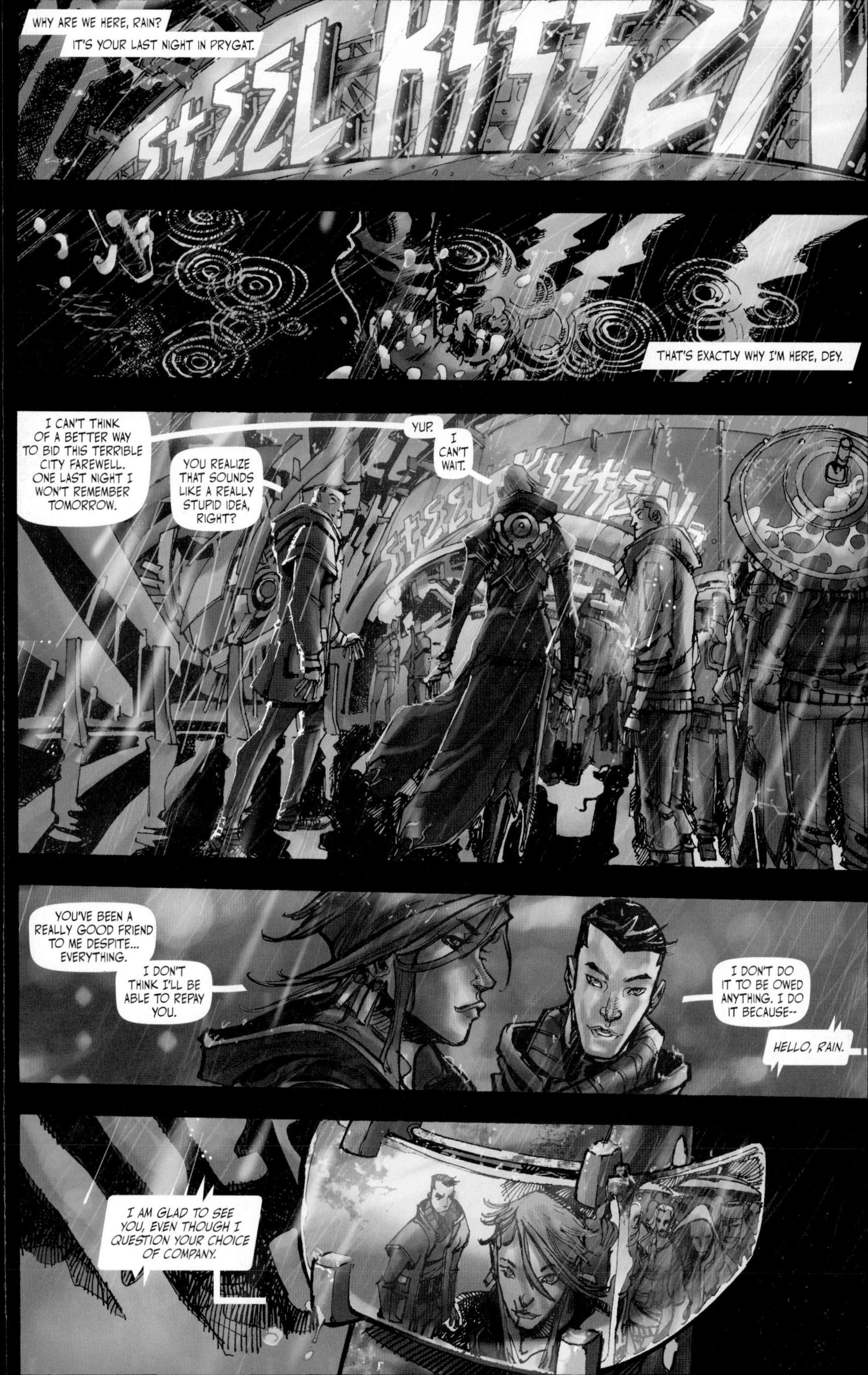
WHY ARE WE HERE, RAIN?
IT'S YOUR LAST NIGHT IN PRYGAT.
THAT'S EXACTLY WHY I'M HERE, DEY.
I CAN'T THINK OF A BETTER WAY TO BID THIS TERRIBLE CITY FAREWELL. ONE LAST NIGHT I WON'T REMEMBER TOMORROW.
YOU REALIZE THAT SOUNDS LIKE A REALLY STUPID IDEA, RIGHT?
YUP. I CAN'T WAIT.
YOU'VE BEEN A REALLY GOOD FRIEND TO ME DESPITE... EVERYTHING.
I DON'T THINK I'LL BE ABLE TO REPAY YOU.
I DON'T DO IT TO BE OWED ANYTHING. I DO IT BECAUSE--
HELLO, RAIN.
I AM GLAD TO SEE YOU, EVEN THOUGH I QUESTION YOUR CHOICE OF COMPANY.

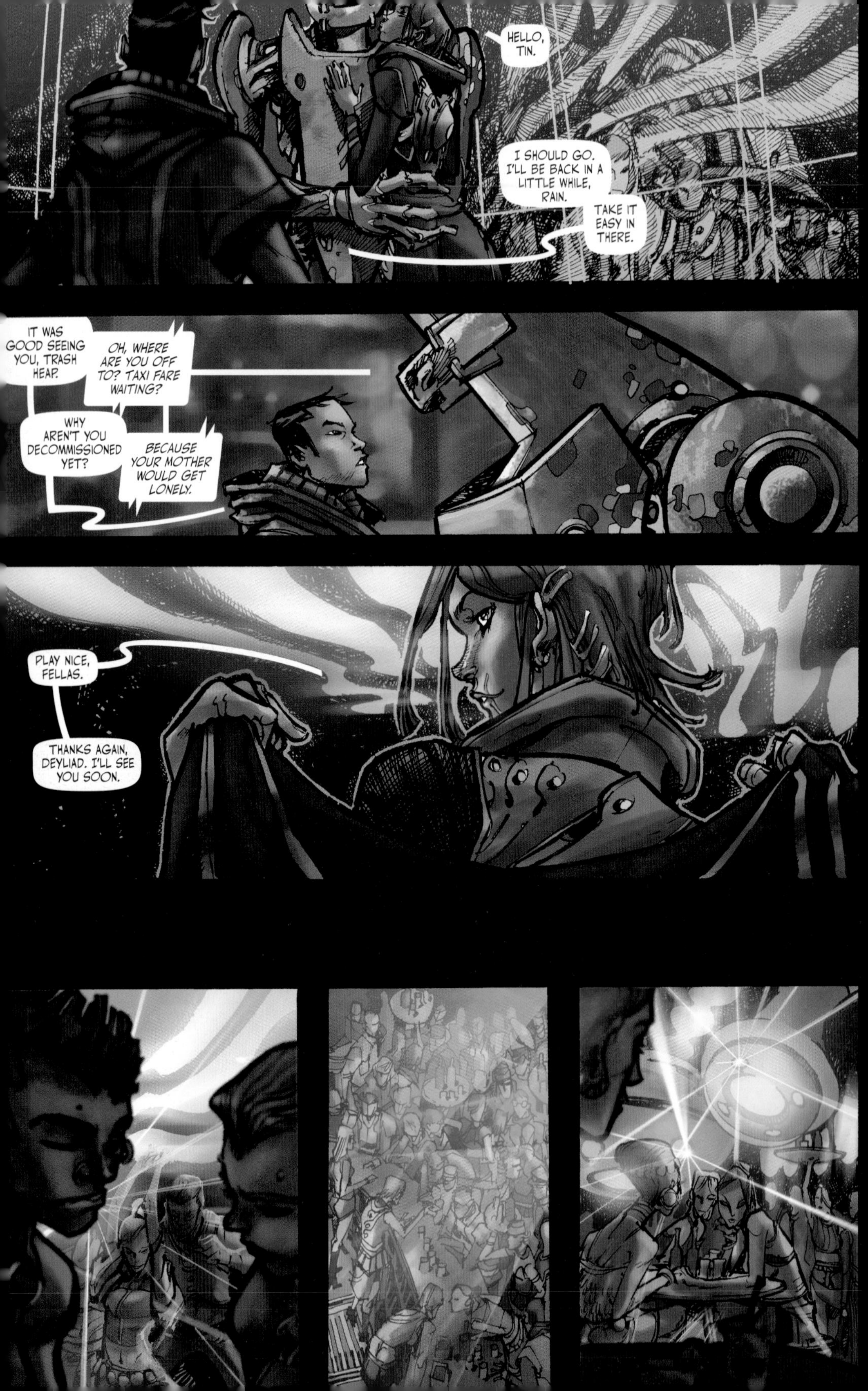
HELLO, TIN.
I SHOULD GO. I'LL BE BACK IN A LITTLE WHILE, RAIN.
TAKE IT EASY IN THERE.
IT WAS GOOD SEEING YOU, TRASH HEAP.
OH, WHERE ARE YOU OFF TO? TAXI FARE WAITING?
WHY AREN'T YOU DECOMMISSIONED YET?
BECAUSE YOUR MOTHER WOULD GET LONELY.
PLAY NICE, FELLAS.
THANKS AGAIN, DEYLIAD. I'LL SEE YOU SOON.

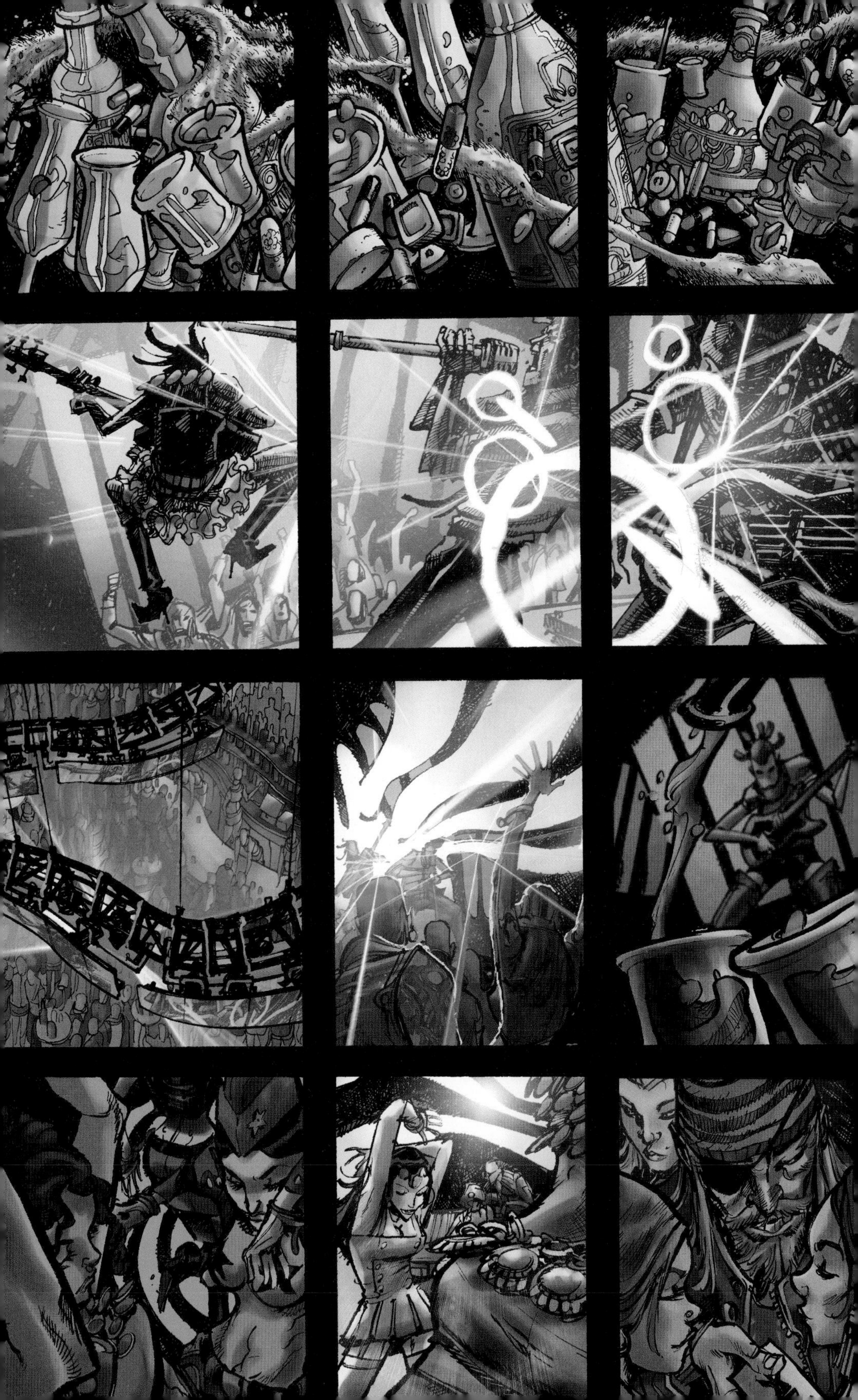

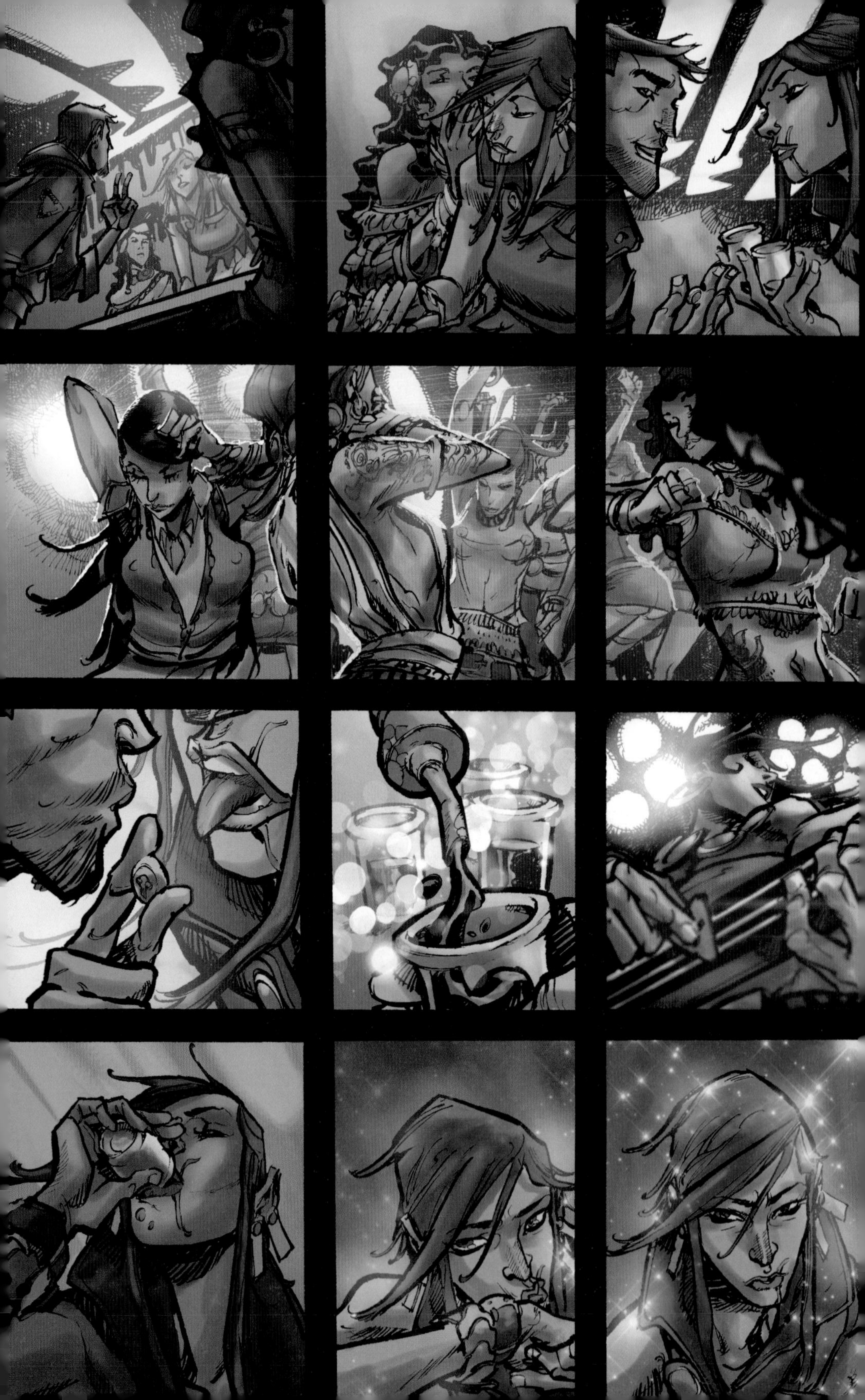

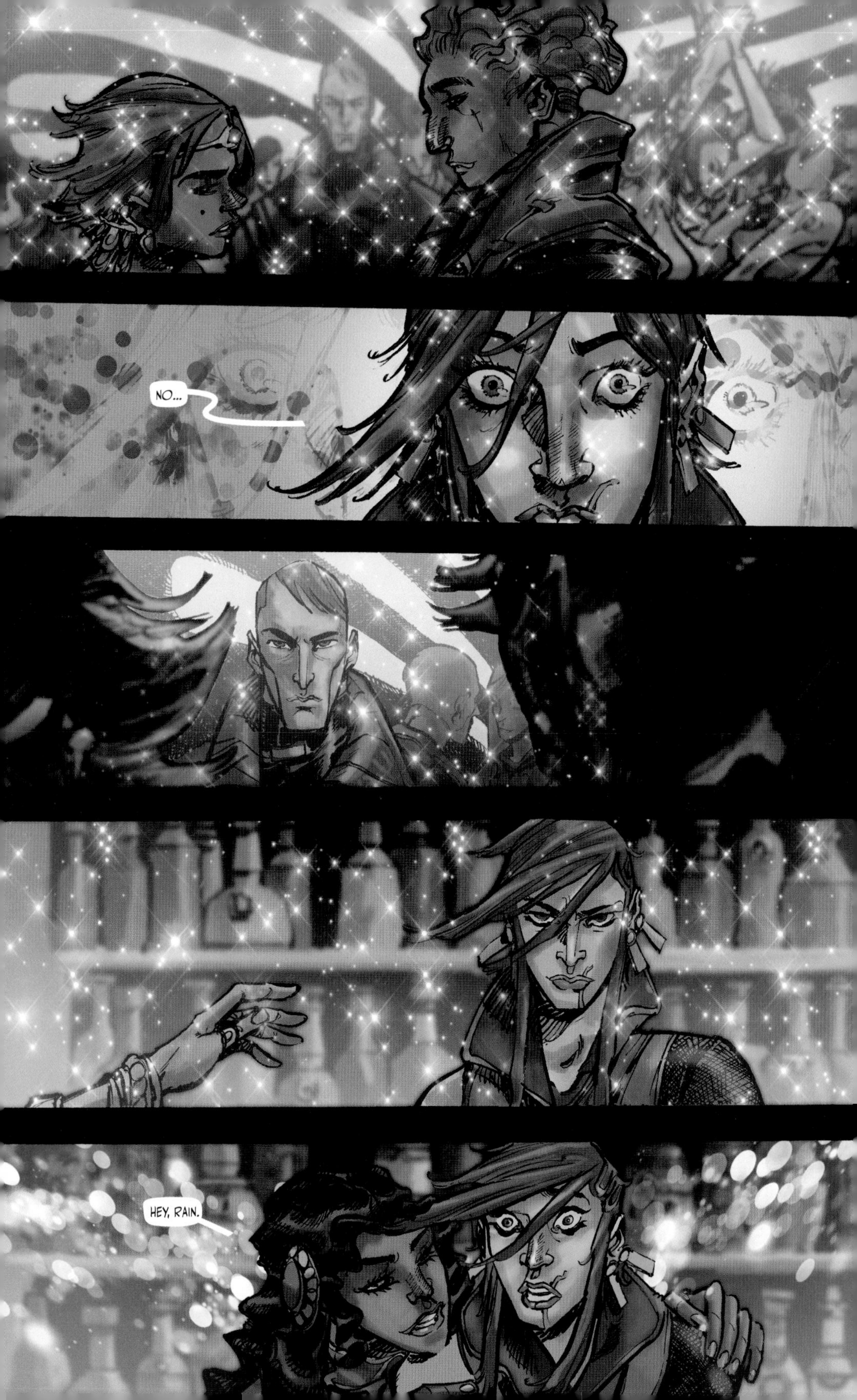
NO...
HEY, RAIN.

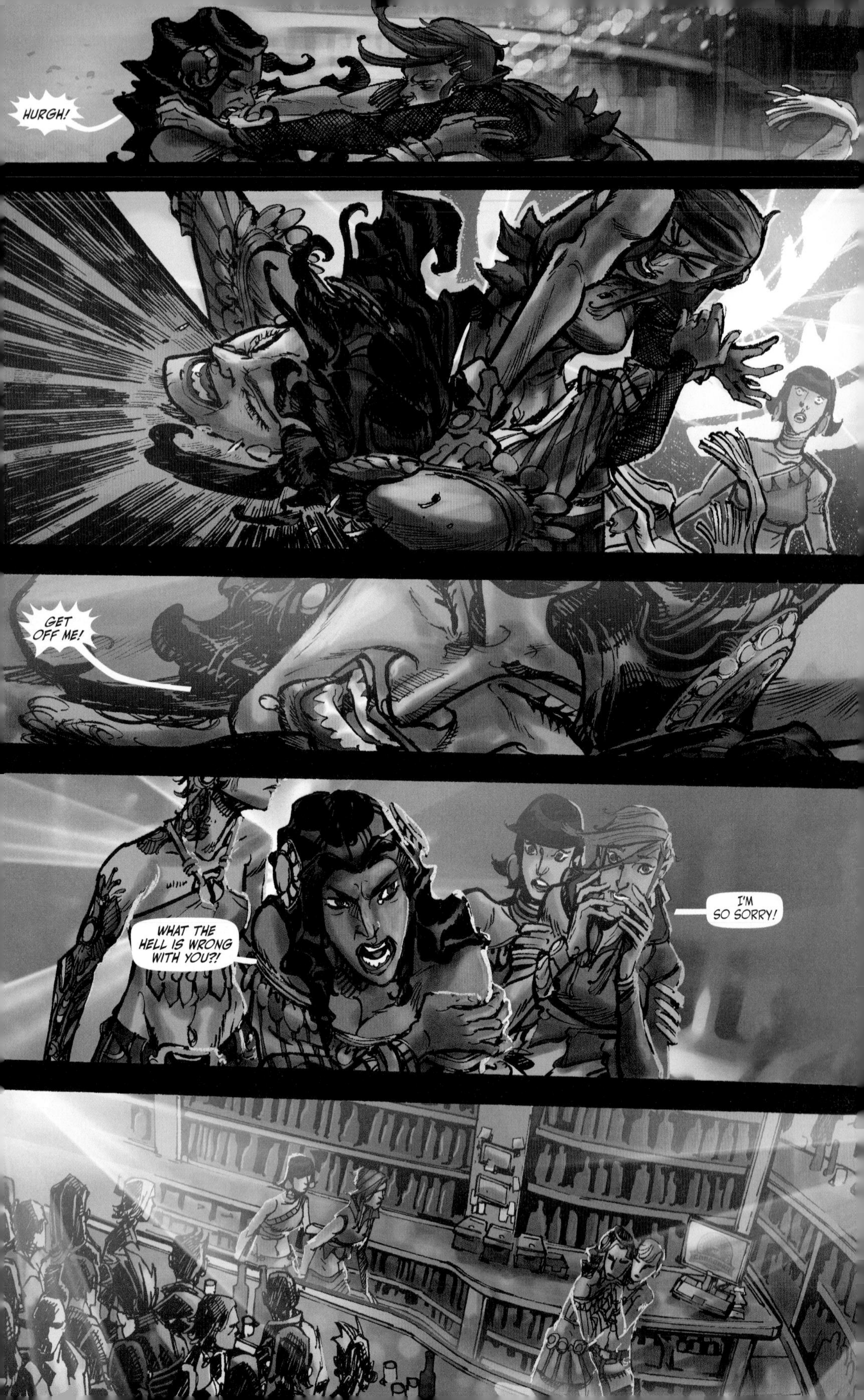
HURGH!
GET OFF ME!
WHAT THE HELL IS WRONG WITH YOU?!
I'M SO SORRY!

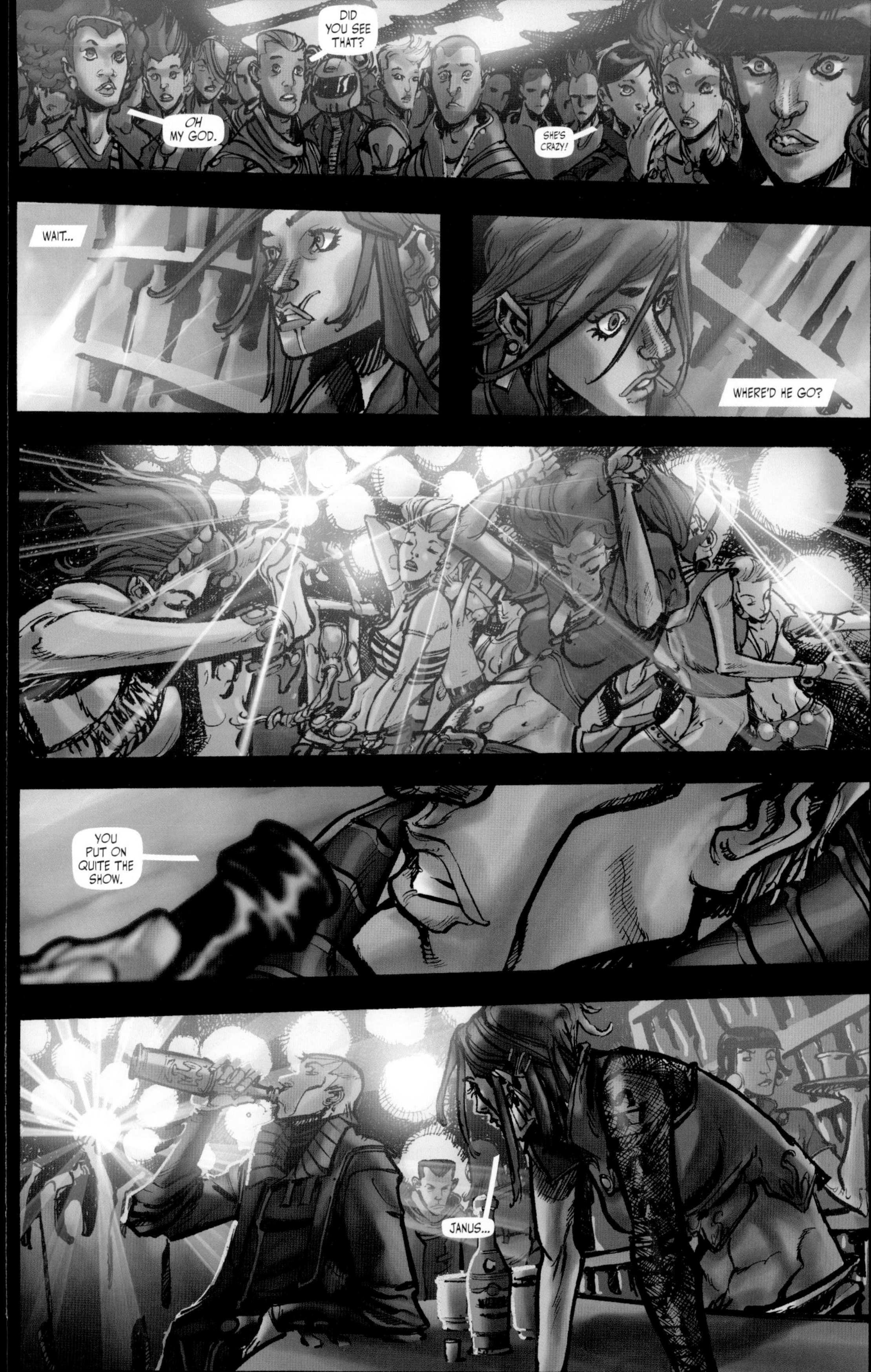
DID YOU SEE THAT?
OH MY GOD.
SHE'S CRAZY!
WAIT...
WHERE'D HE GO?
YOU PUT ON QUITE THE SHOW.
JANUS...

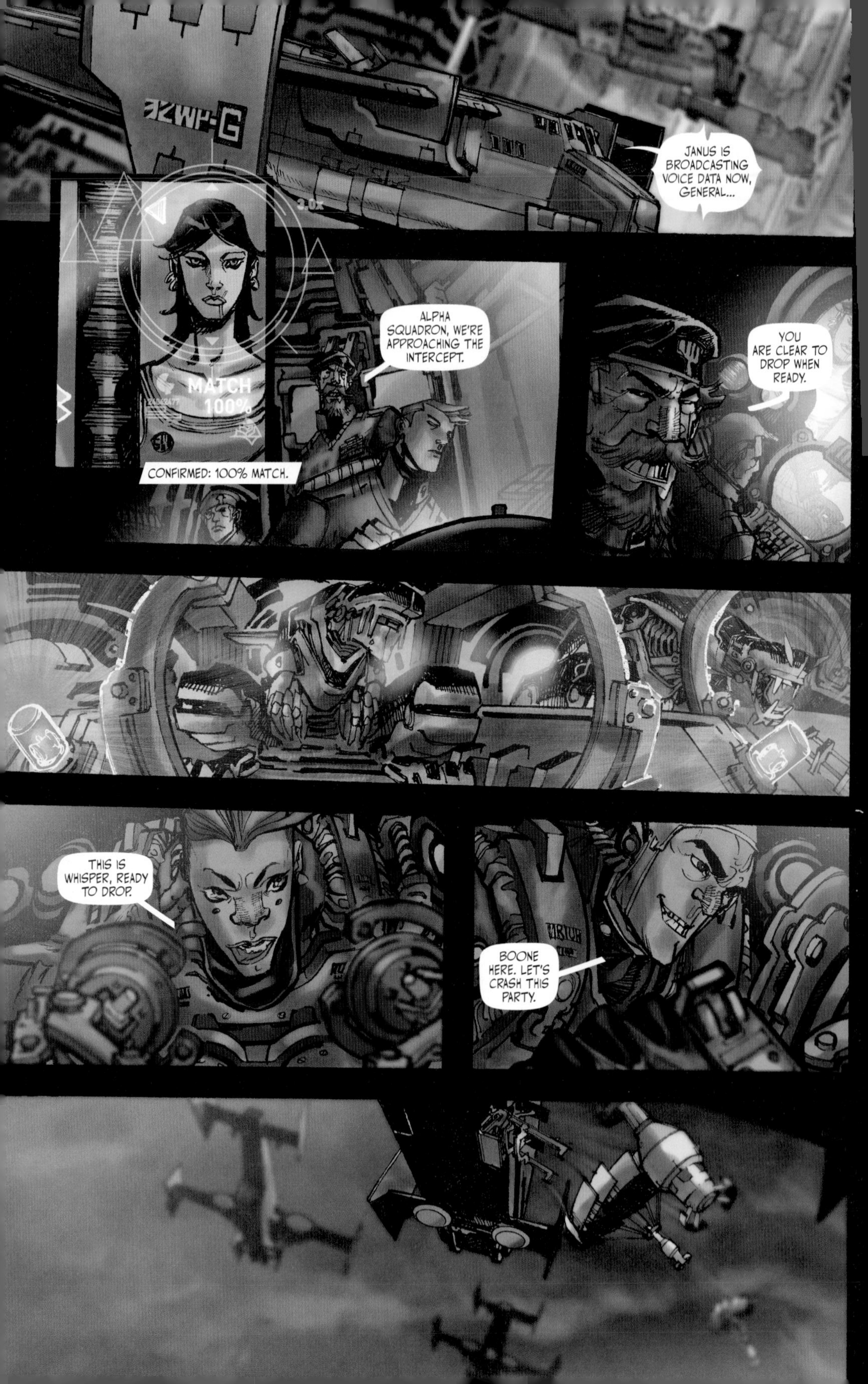
JANUS IS BROADCASTING VOICE DATA NOW, GENERAL...
MATCH 100%
CONFIRMED: 100% MATCH.
ALPHA SQUADRON, WE'RE APPROACHING THE INTERCEPT.
YOU ARE CLEAR TO DROP WHEN READY.
THIS IS WHISPER, READY TO DROP.
BOONE HERE. LET'S CRASH THIS PARTY.

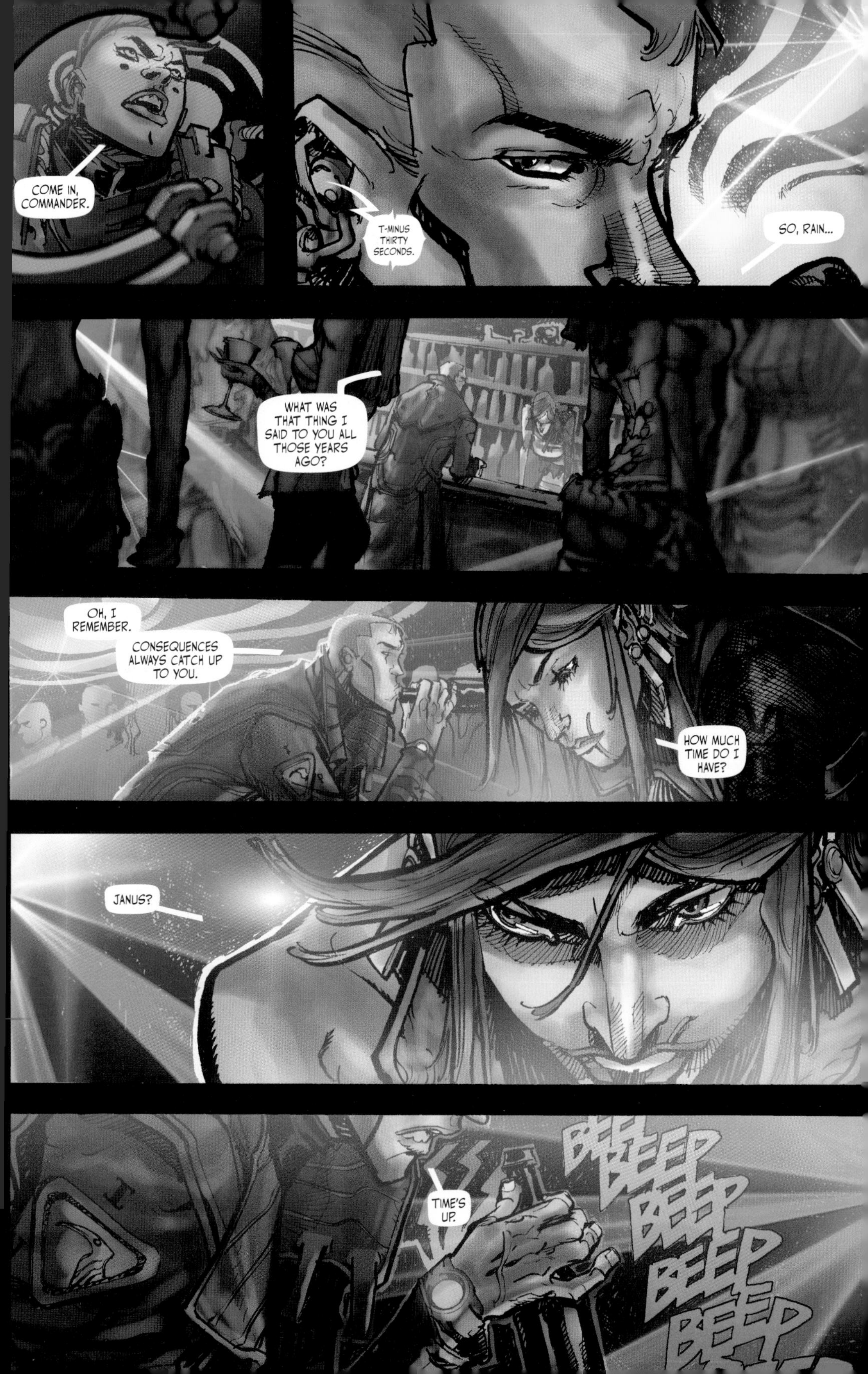

COME IN, COMMANDER.
T-MINUS THIRTY SECONDS.
SO, RAIN...
WHAT WAS THAT THING I SAID TO YOU ALL THOSE YEARS AGO?
OH, I REMEMBER.
CONSEQUENCES ALWAYS CATCH UP TO YOU.
HOW MUCH TIME DO I HAVE?
JANUS?
TIME'S UP.
BEEP BEEP BEEP BEEP BEEP

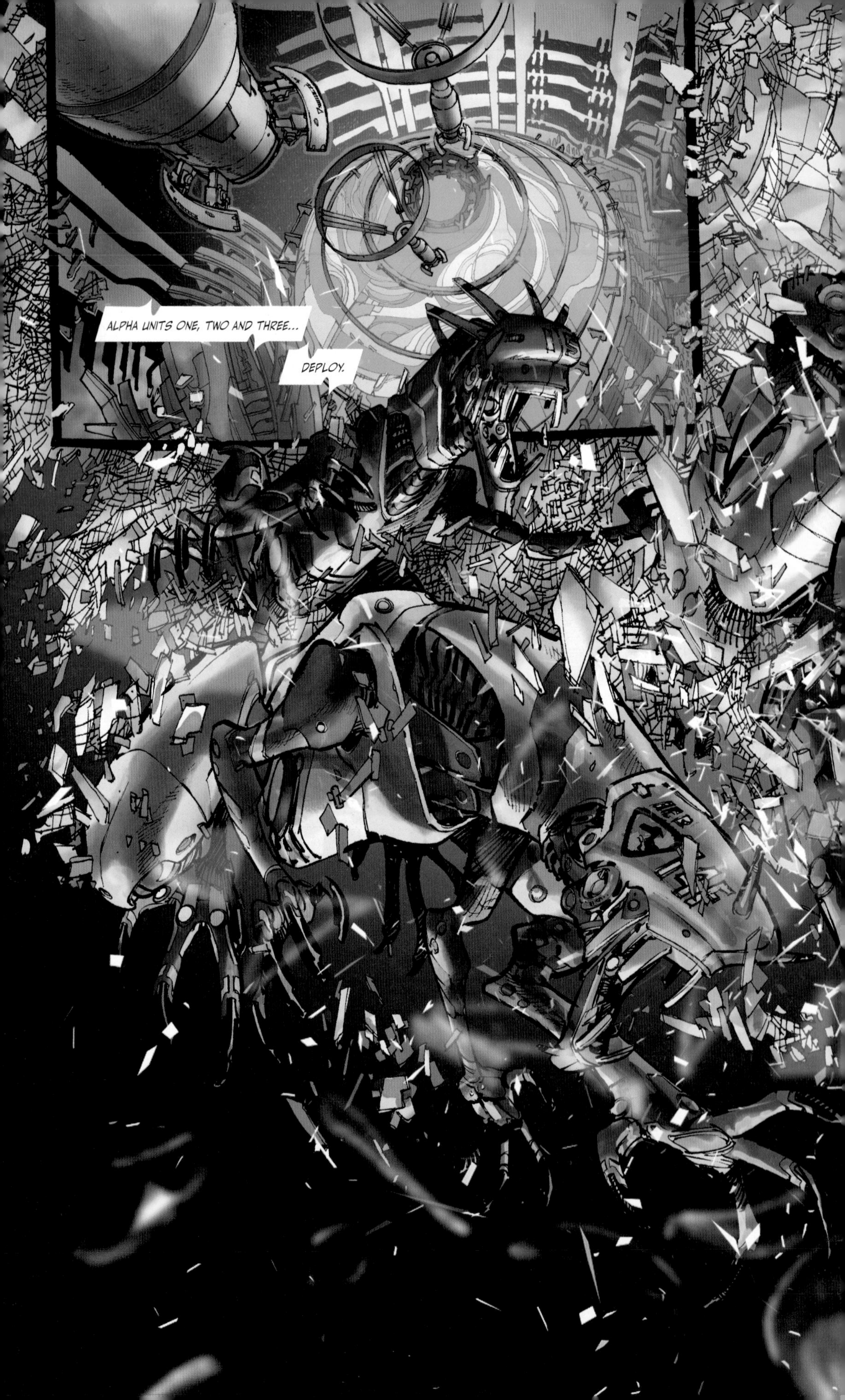
ALPHA UNITS ONE, TWO AND THREE...
DEPLOY.

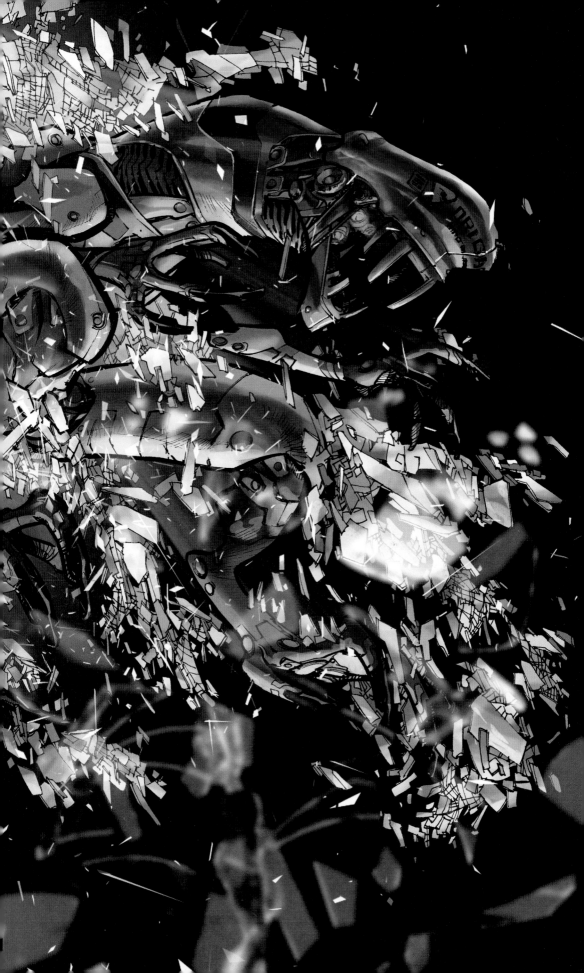

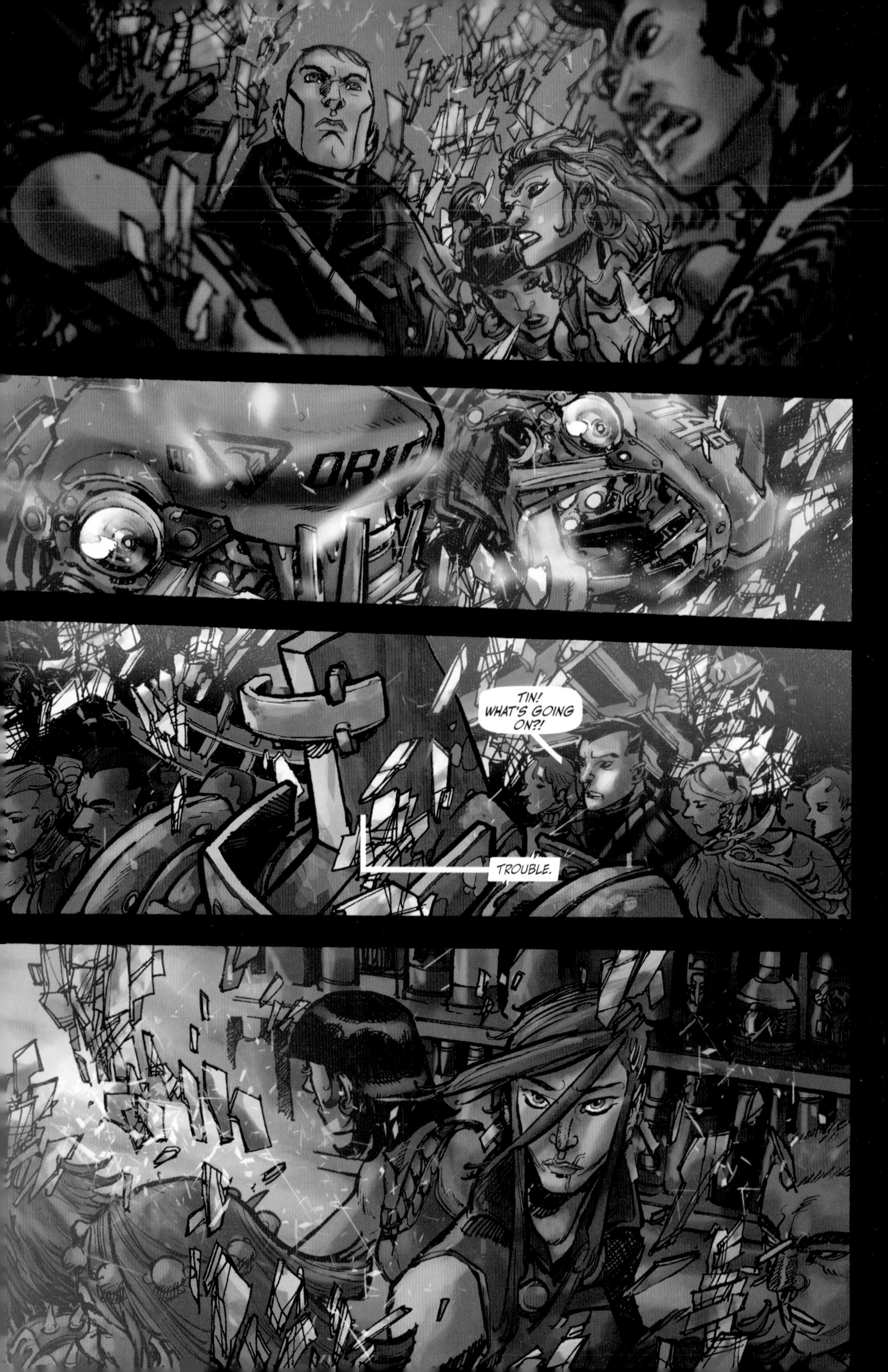
TIN! WHAT'S GOING ON?!
TROUBLE.

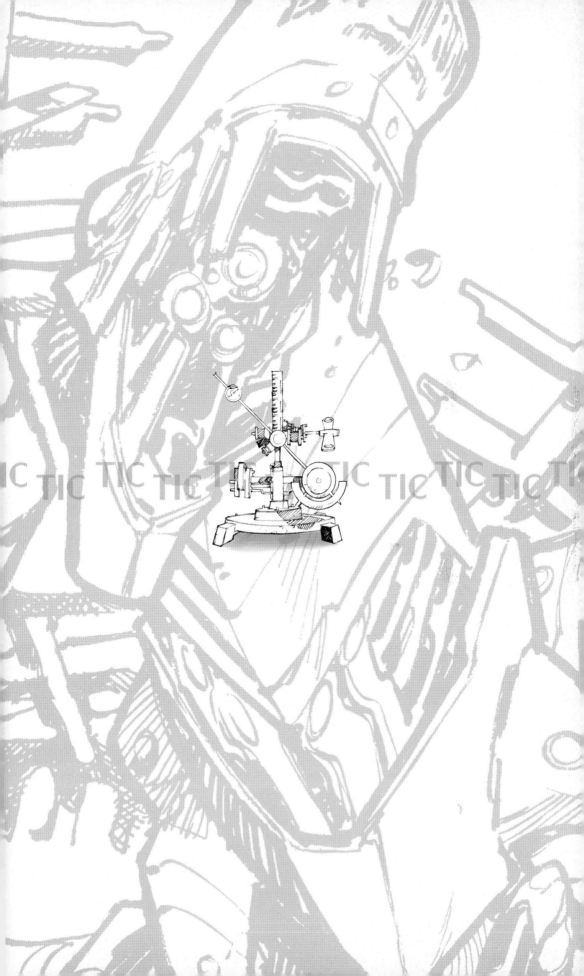

ORIGI

CANETE
INDUSTRIALS
M-450

THREE

MANU
OLEA

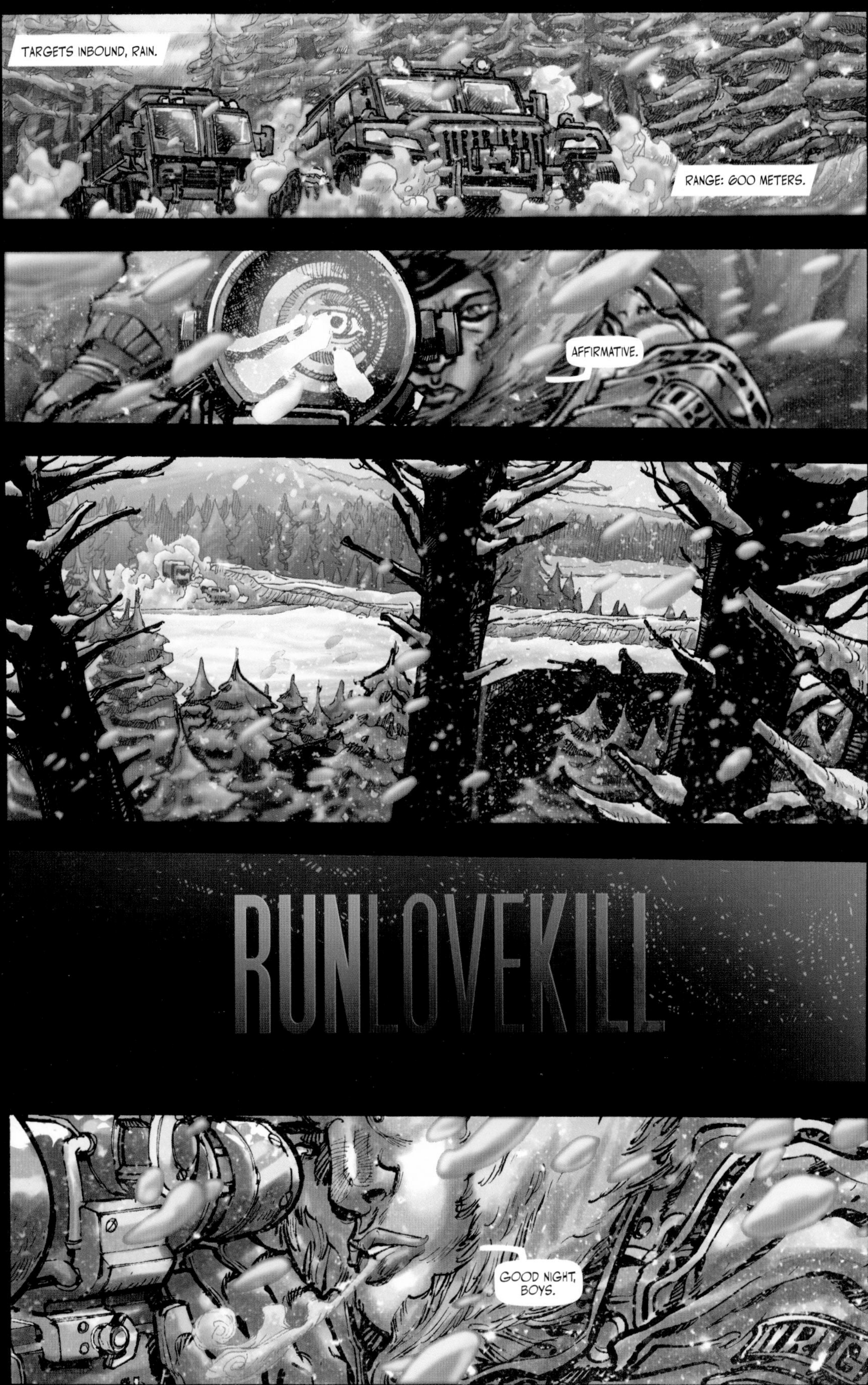
TARGETS INBOUND, RAIN.
RANGE: 600 METERS.
AFFIRMATIVE.
RUNLOVEKILL
GOOD NIGHT, BOYS.

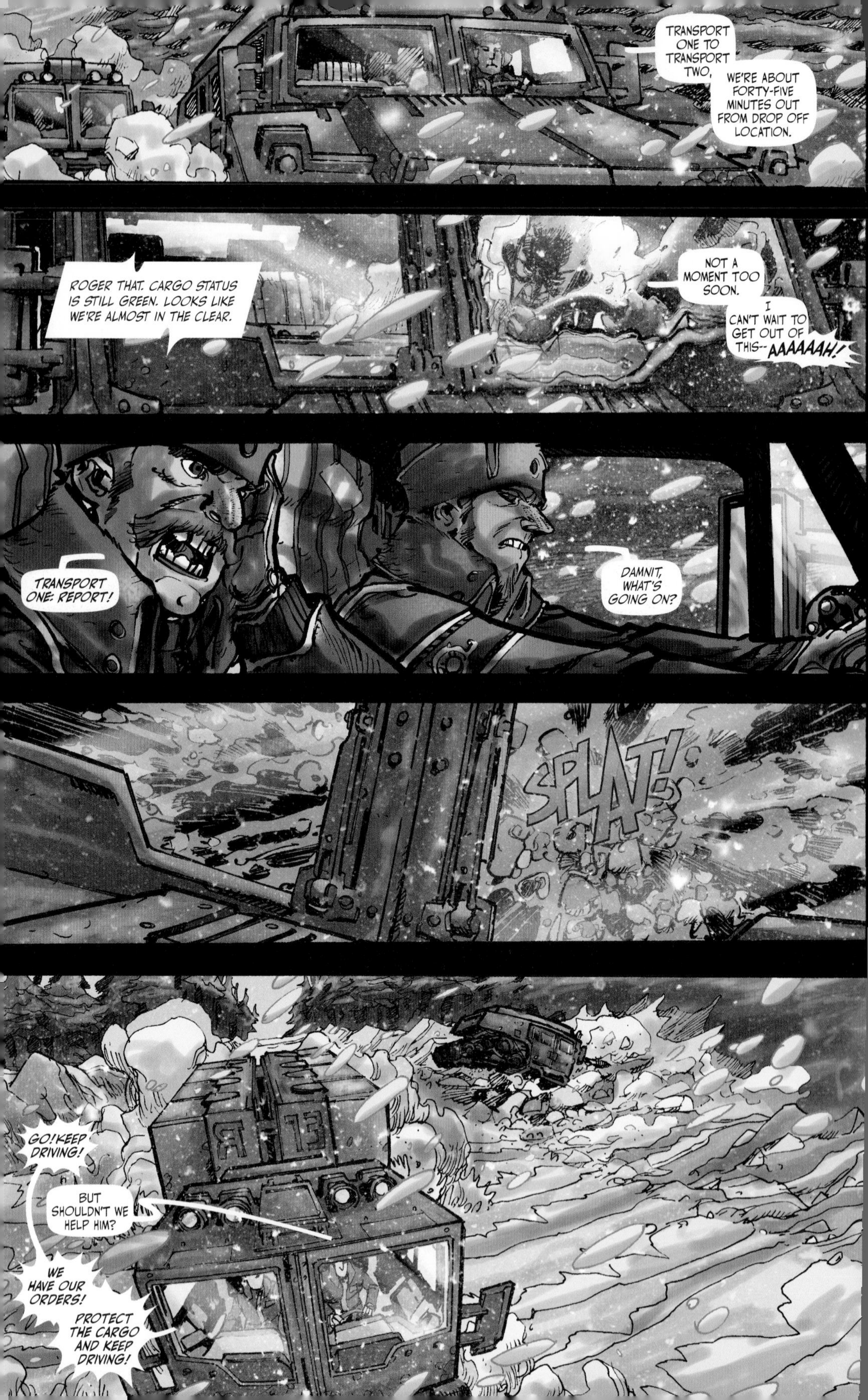
TRANSPORT ONE TO TRANSPORT TWO,
WE'RE ABOUT FORTY-FIVE MINUTES OUT FROM DROP OFF LOCATION.
ROGER THAT. CARGO STATUS IS STILL GREEN. LOOKS LIKE WE'RE ALMOST IN THE CLEAR.
NOT A MOMENT TOO SOON.
I CAN'T WAIT TO GET OUT OF THIS--AAAAAAH!
TRANSPORT ONE: REPORT!
DAMNIT, WHAT'S GOING ON?
SPLAT!
GO! KEEP DRIVING!
BUT SHOULDN'T WE HELP HIM?
WE HAVE OUR ORDERS!
PROTECT THE CARGO AND KEEP DRIVING!

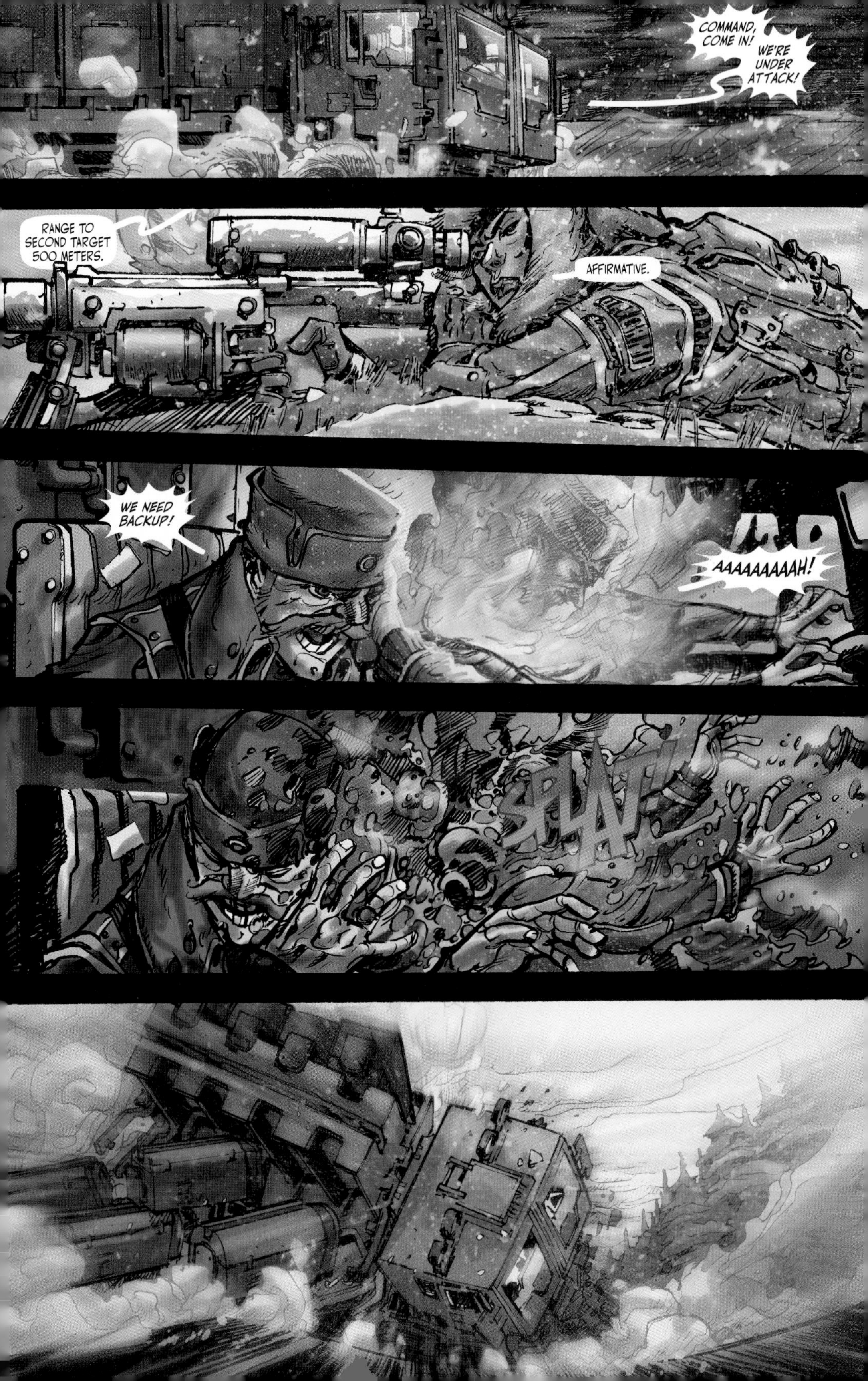
COMMAND, COME IN!
WE'RE UNDER ATTACK!
RANGE TO SECOND TARGET 500 METERS.
AFFIRMATIVE.
WE NEED BACKUP!
AAAAAAAAAH!
SPLAT!

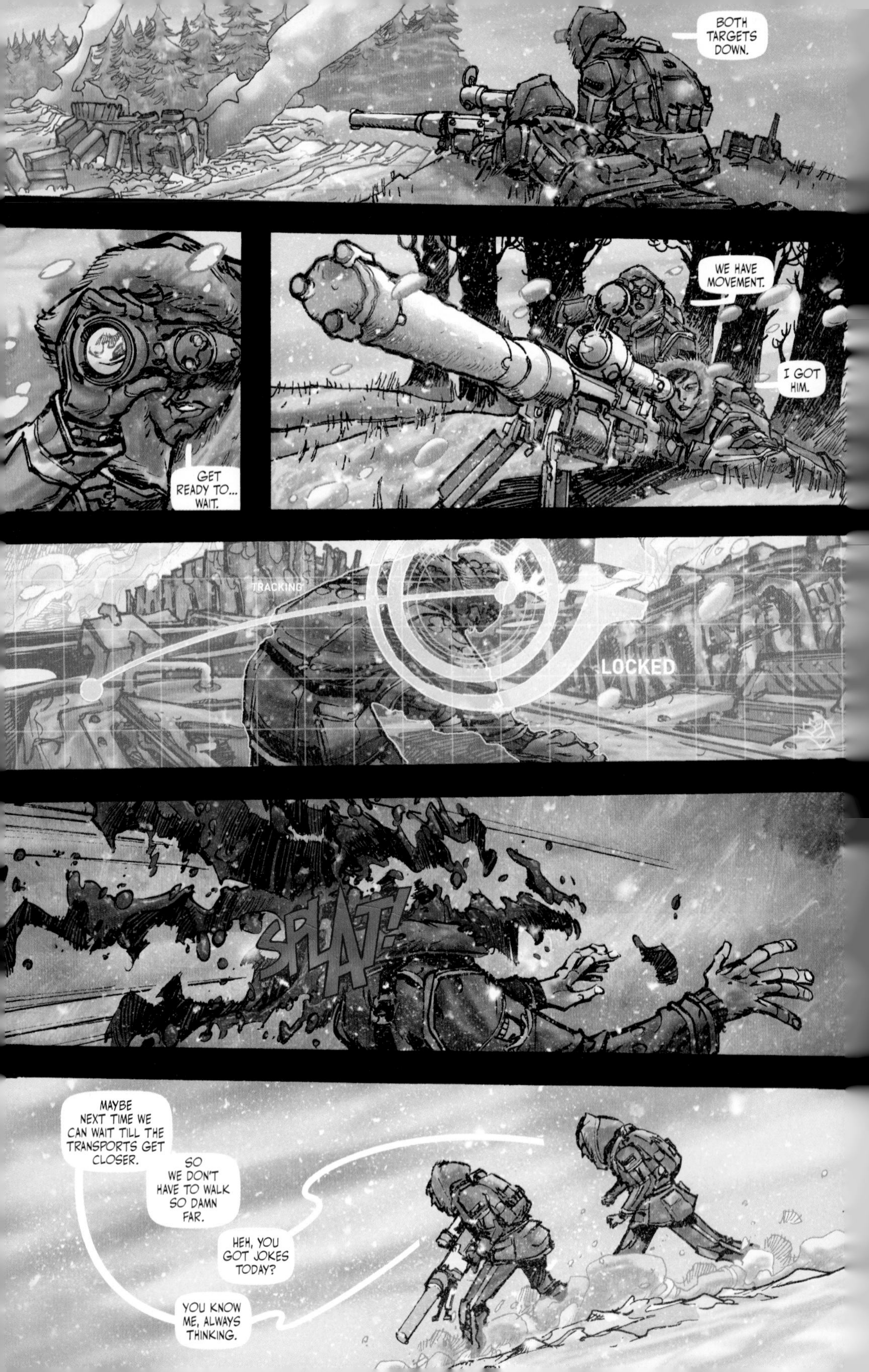
BOTH TARGETS DOWN.
GET READY TO... WAIT.
WE HAVE MOVEMENT.
I GOT HIM.
TRACKING
LOCKED
SPLAT!
MAYBE NEXT TIME WE CAN WAIT TILL THE TRANSPORTS GET CLOSER.
SO WE DON'T HAVE TO WALK SO DAMN FAR.
HEH, YOU GOT JOKES TODAY?
YOU KNOW ME, ALWAYS THINKING.

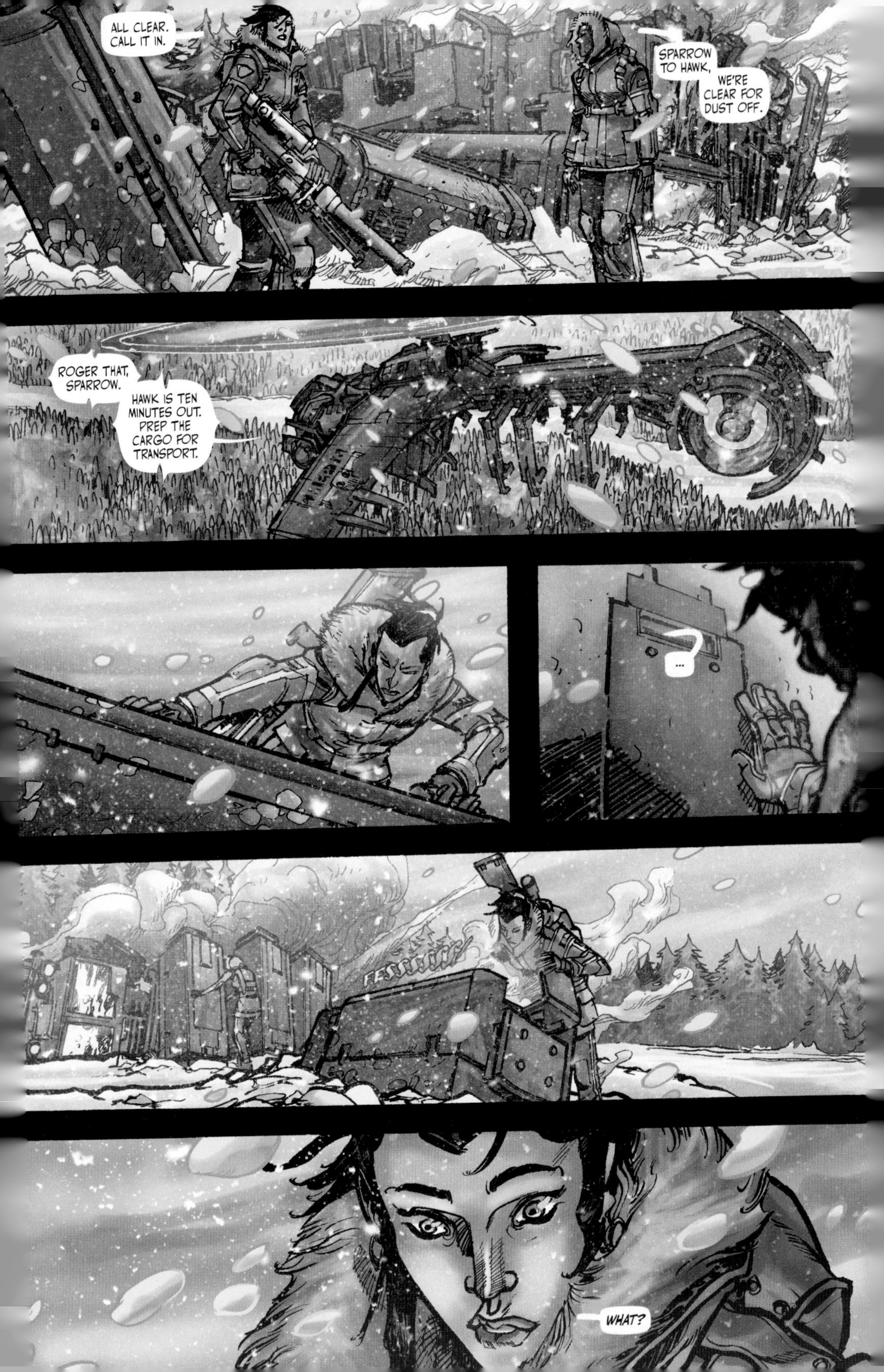
ALL CLEAR. CALL IT IN.
SPARROW TO HAWK,
WE'RE CLEAR FOR DUST OFF.
ROGER THAT, SPARROW.
HAWK IS TEN MINUTES OUT. PREP THE CARGO FOR TRANSPORT.
...
WHAT?

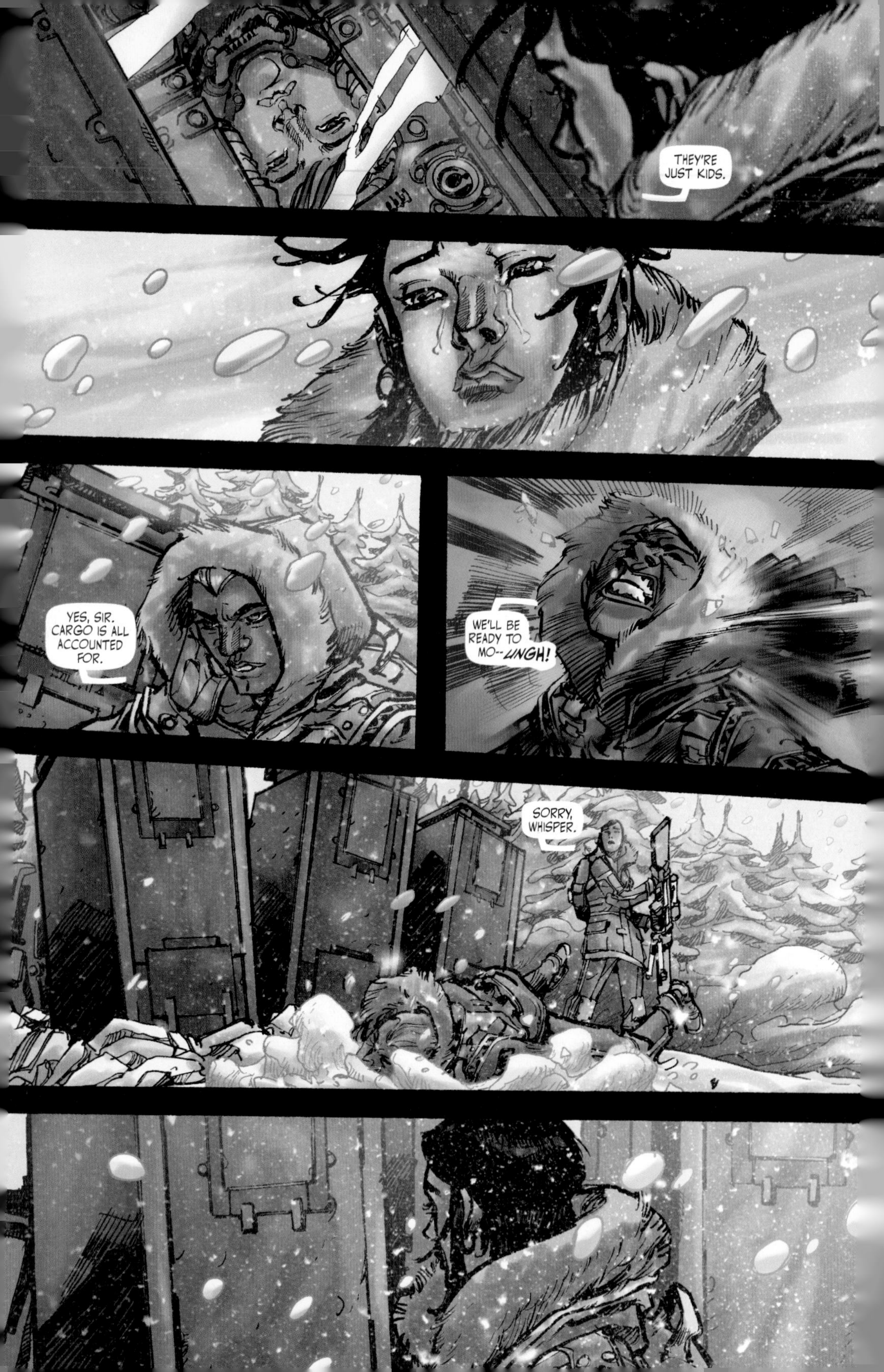
THEY'RE JUST KIDS.
YES, SIR. CARGO IS ALL ACCOUNTED FOR.
WE'LL BE READY TO MO--UNGH!
SORRY, WHISPER.

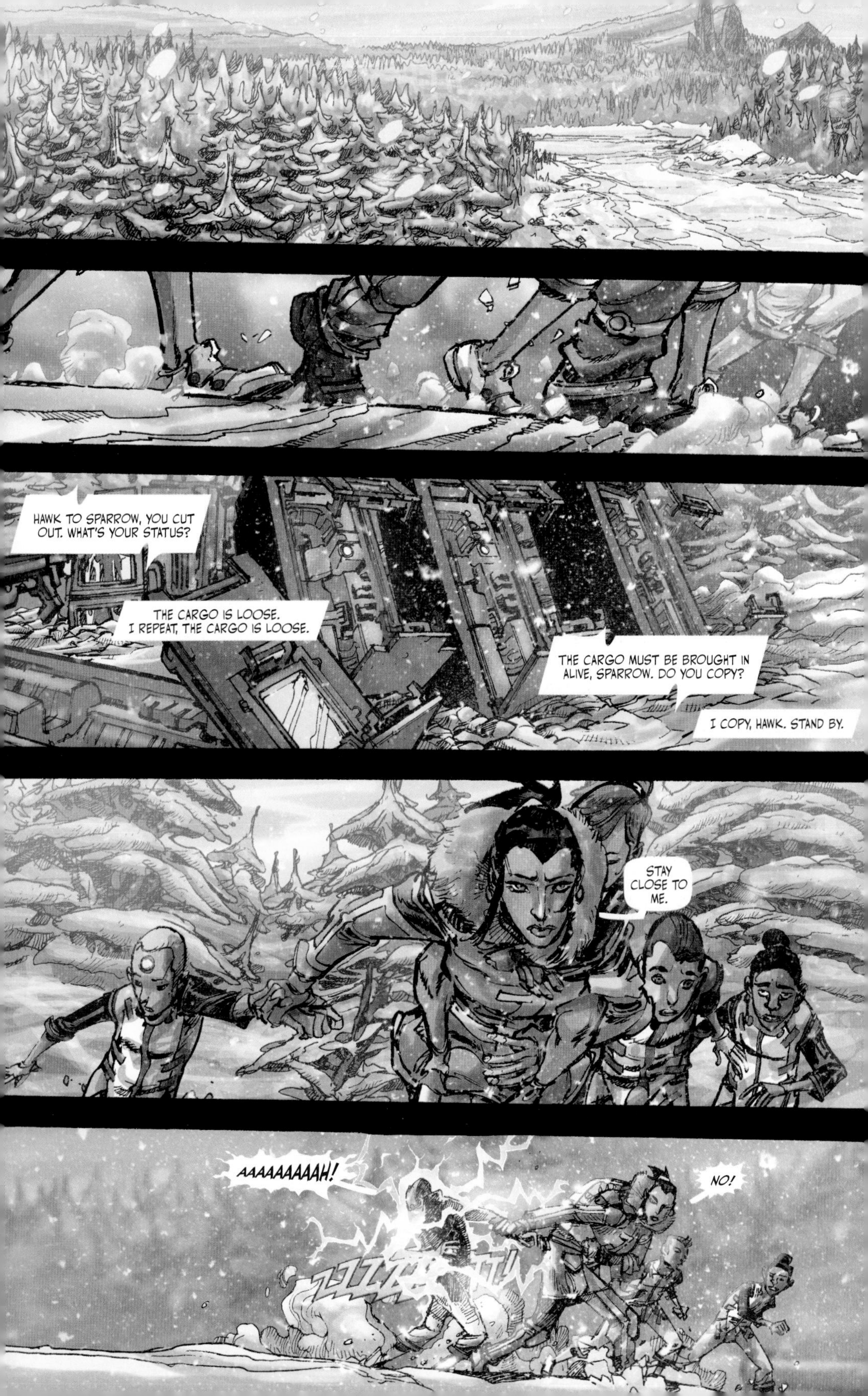
HAWK TO SPARROW, YOU CUT OUT. WHAT'S YOUR STATUS?
THE CARGO IS LOOSE. I REPEAT, THE CARGO IS LOOSE.
THE CARGO MUST BE BROUGHT IN ALIVE, SPARROW. DO YOU COPY?
I COPY, HAWK. STAND BY.
STAY CLOSE TO ME.
AAAAAAAAAH!
NO!

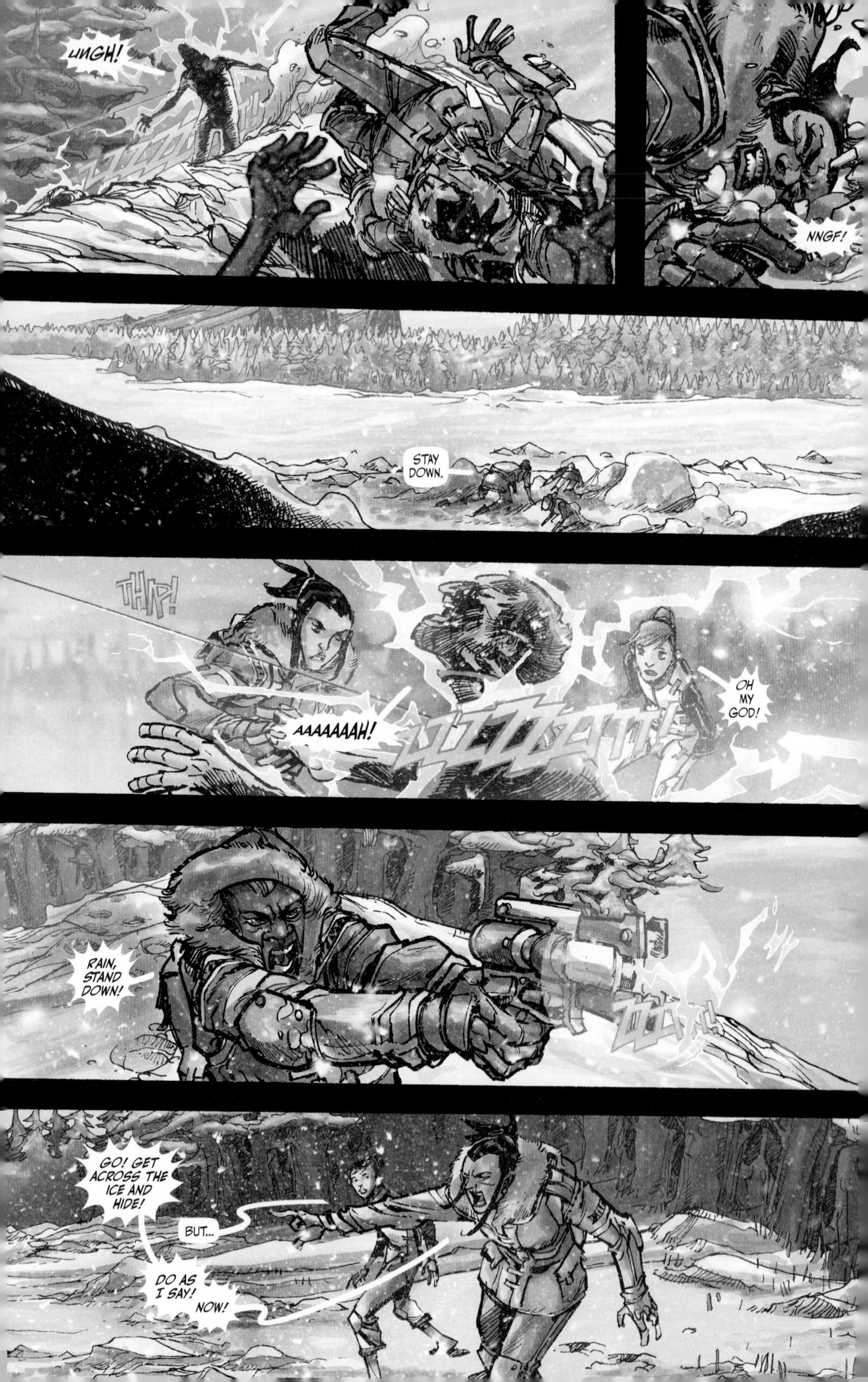
UNGH!
NNGF!
STAY DOWN.
THIP!
AAAAAAAH!
OH MY GOD!
RAIN, STAND DOWN!
GO! GET ACROSS THE ICE AND HIDE!
BUT...
DO AS I SAY!
NOW!

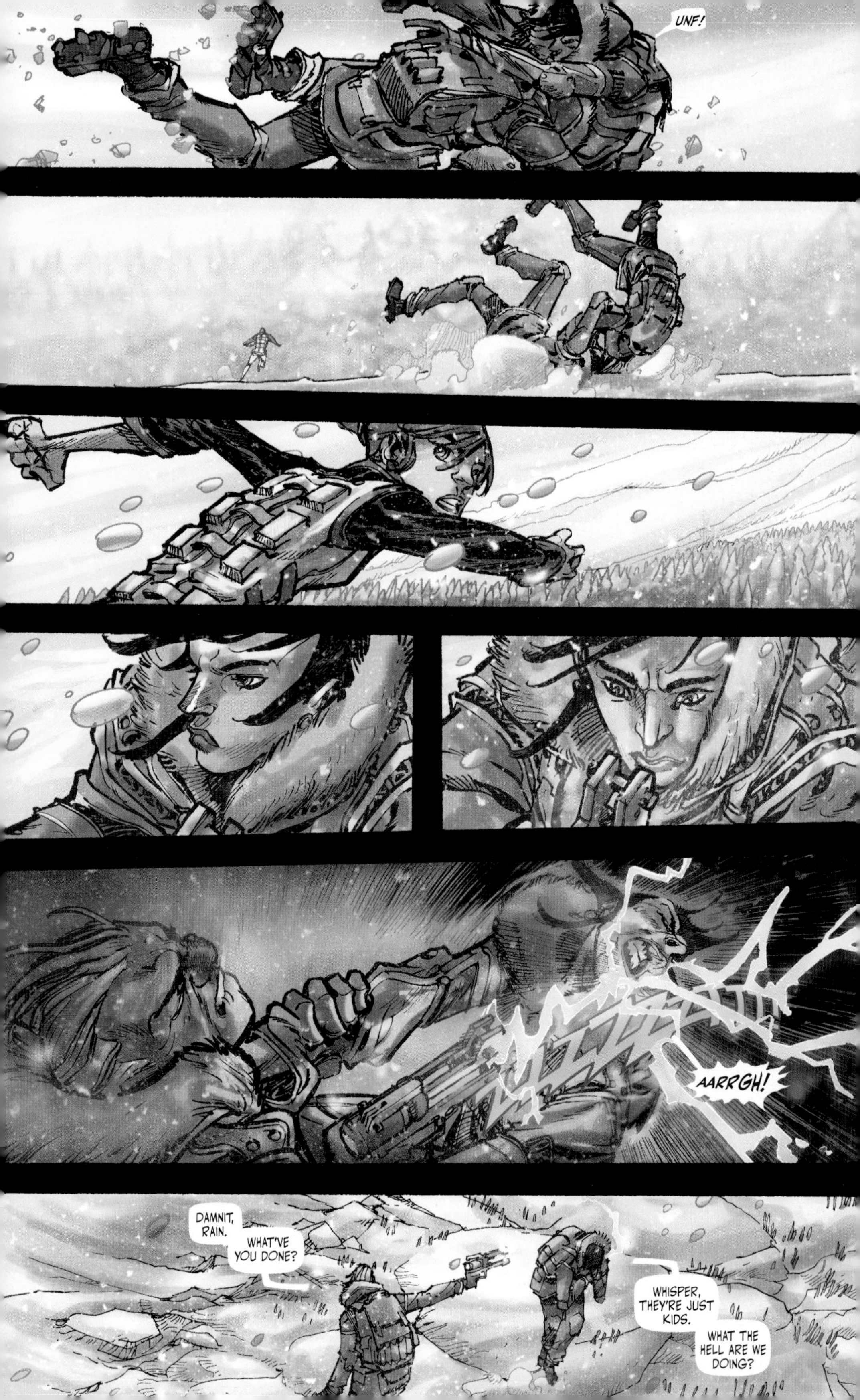
UNF!
AARRGH!
DAMNIT, RAIN.
WHAT'VE YOU DONE?
WHISPER, THEY'RE JUST KIDS.
WHAT THE HELL ARE WE DOING?

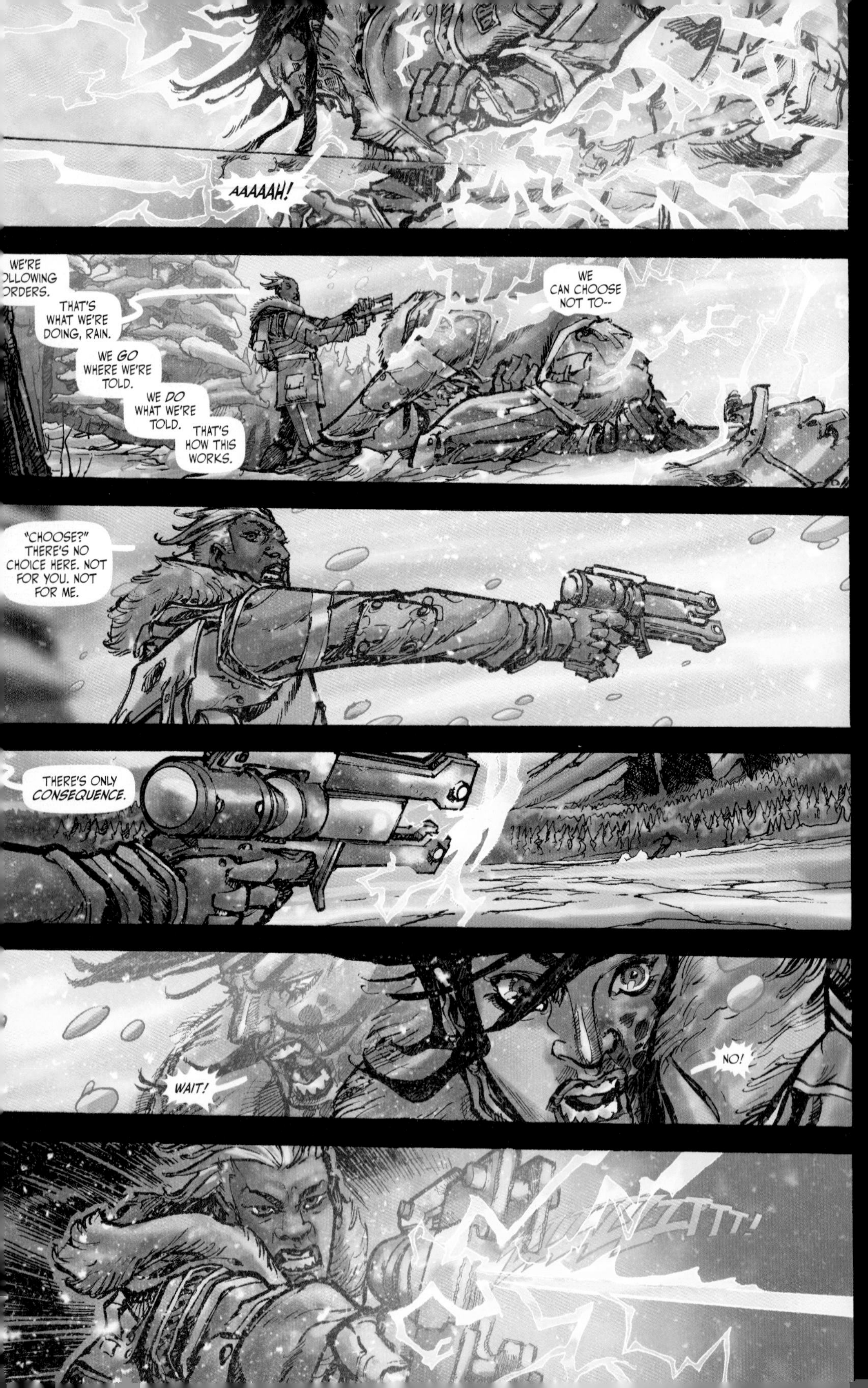
AAAAAH!
WE'RE FOLLOWING ORDERS.
THAT'S WHAT WE'RE DOING, RAIN.
WE GO WHERE WE'RE TOLD.
WE DO WHAT WE'RE TOLD.
THAT'S HOW THIS WORKS.
WE CAN CHOOSE NOT TO--
"CHOOSE?" THERE'S NO CHOICE HERE. NOT FOR YOU. NOT FOR ME.
THERE'S ONLY CONSEQUENCE.
WAIT!
NO!
ZZTTT!

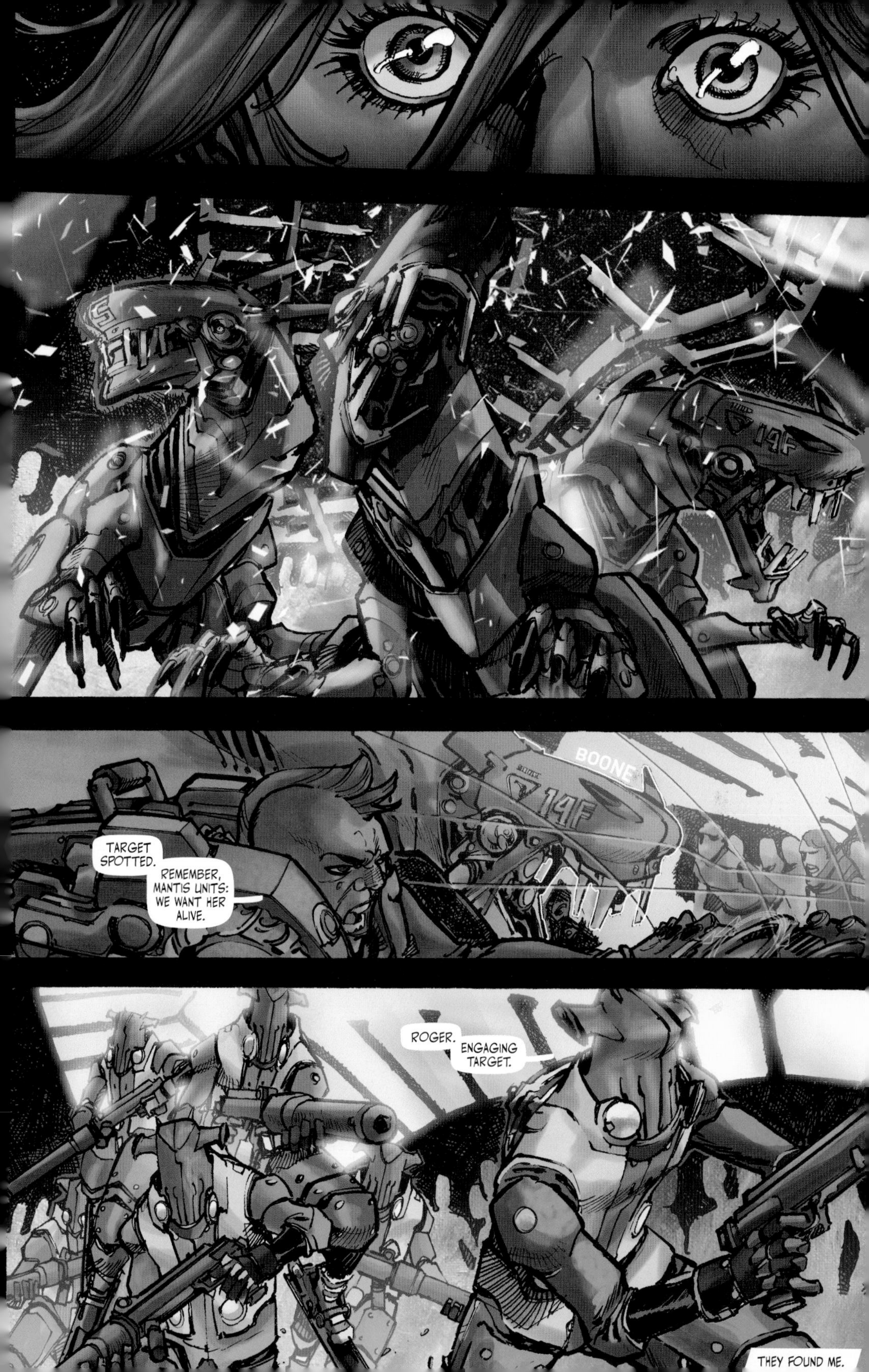

BOONE
14F
TARGET SPOTTED.
REMEMBER, MANTIS UNITS: WE WANT HER ALIVE.
ROGER.
ENGAGING TARGET.
THEY FOUND ME.

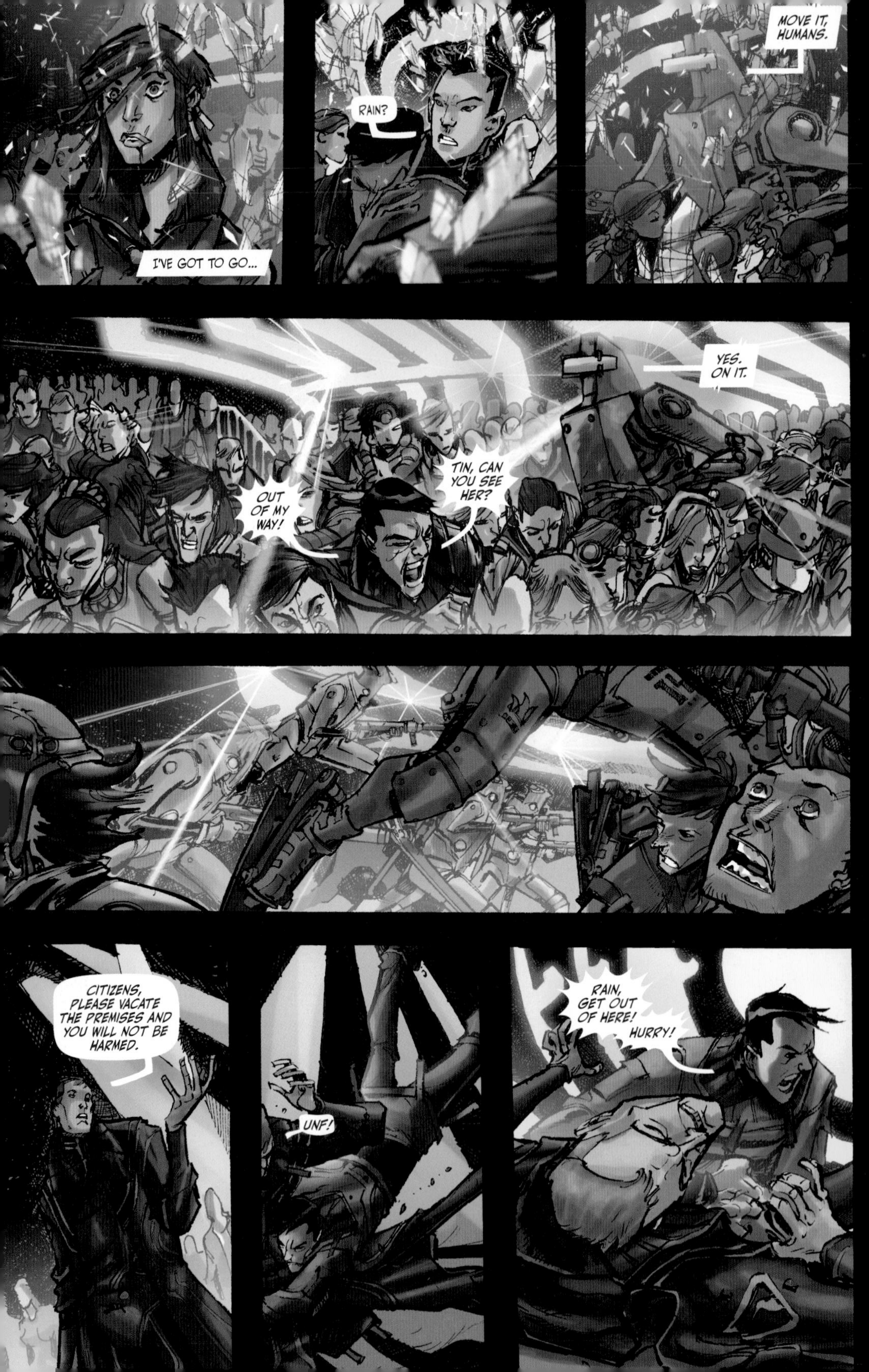
I'VE GOT TO GO...
RAIN?
MOVE IT, HUMANS.
YES. ON IT.
OUT OF MY WAY!
TIN, CAN YOU SEE HER?
CITIZENS, PLEASE VACATE THE PREMISES AND YOU WILL NOT BE HARMED.
UNF!
RAIN, GET OUT OF HERE!
HURRY!

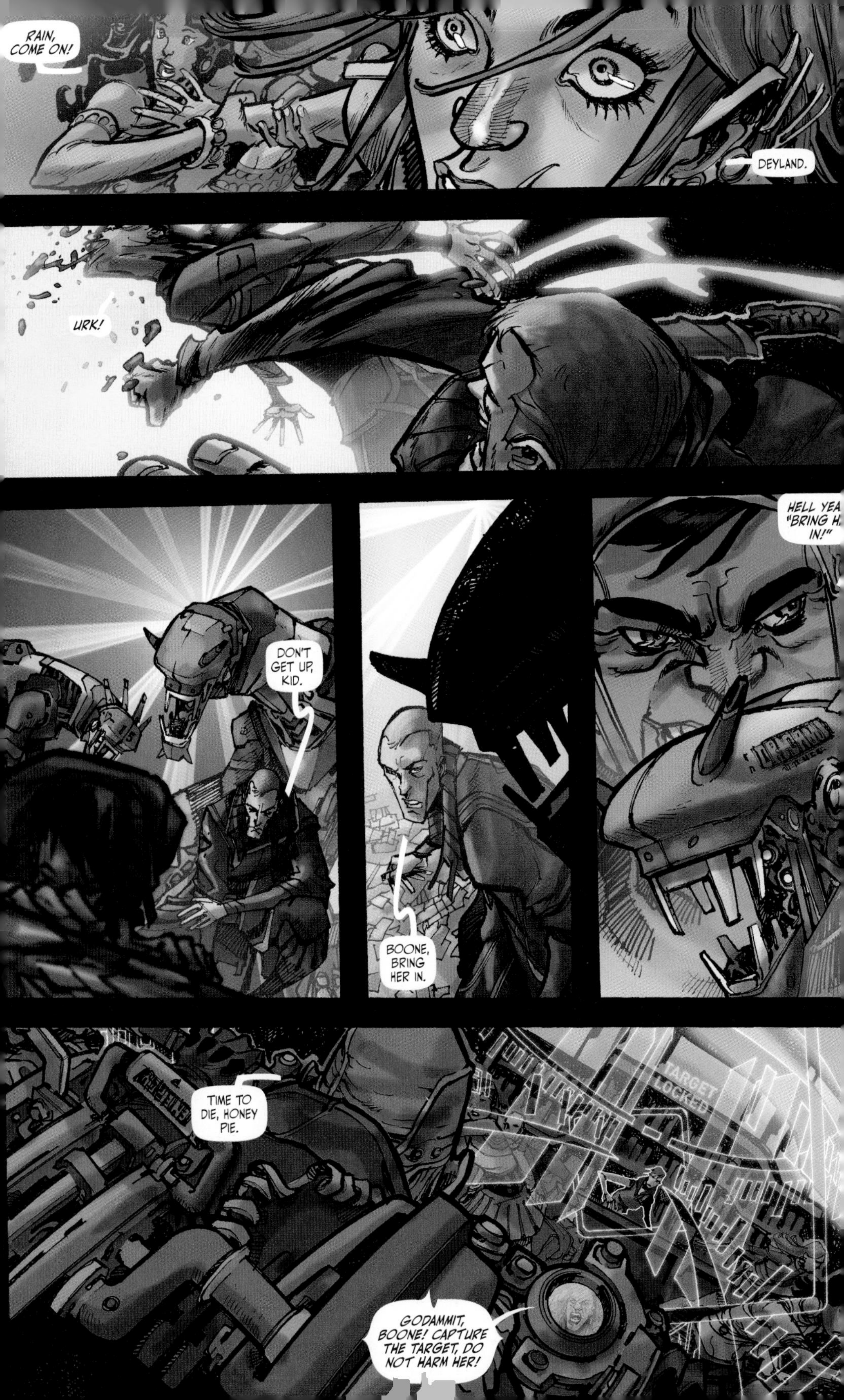
RAIN, COME ON!
DEYLAND.
URK!
DON'T GET UP, KID.
BOONE, BRING HER IN.
HELL YEA "BRING H IN!"
TIME TO DIE, HONEY PIE.
TARGET LOCKED
GODAMMIT, BOONE! CAPTURE THE TARGET, DO NOT HARM HER!

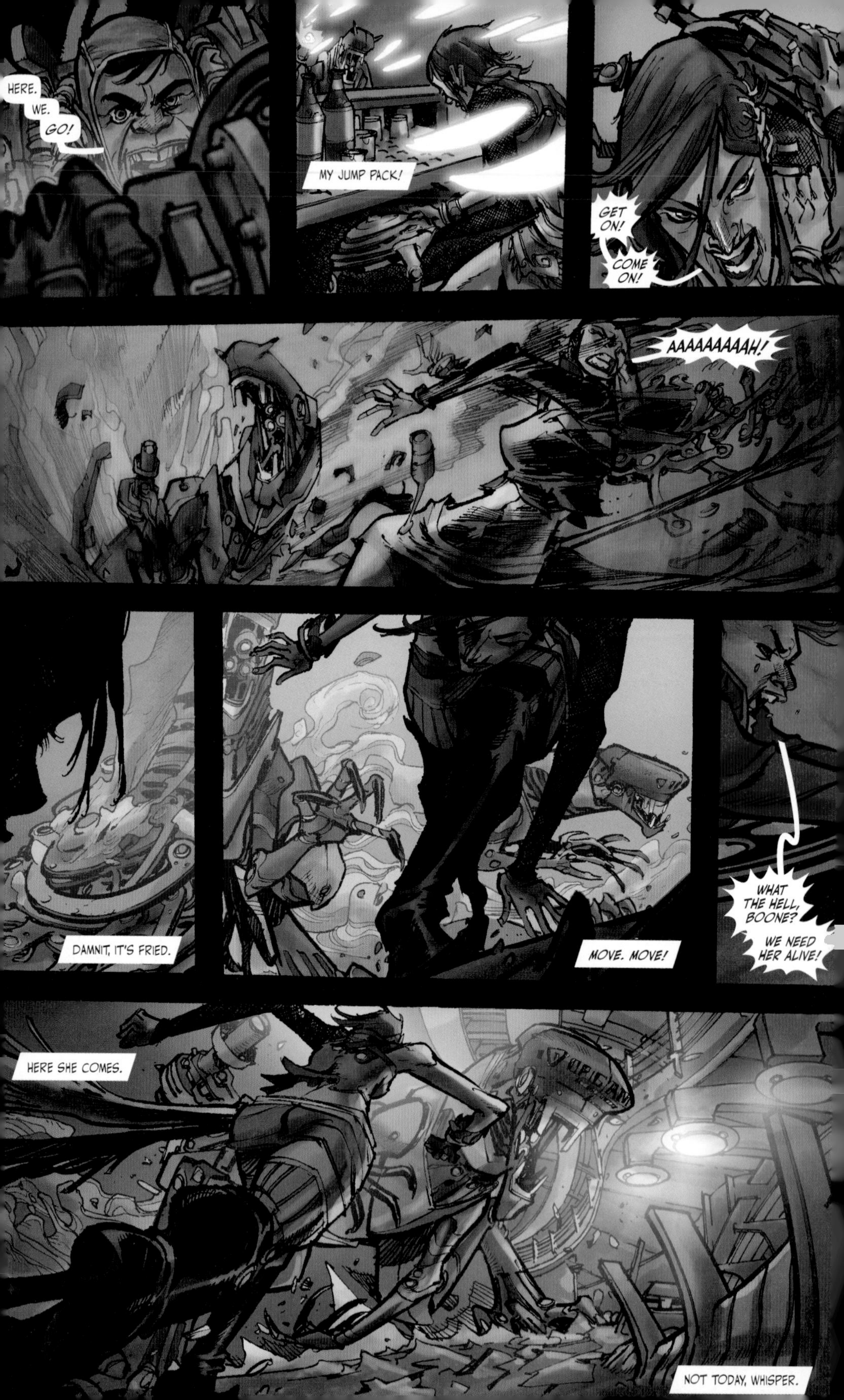

HERE.
WE.
GO!
MY JUMP PACK!
GET ON!
COME ON!
AAAAAAAAAH!
DAMNIT, IT'S FRIED.
MOVE. MOVE!
WHAT THE HELL, BOONE?
WE NEED HER ALIVE!
HERE SHE COMES.
NOT TODAY, WHISPER.

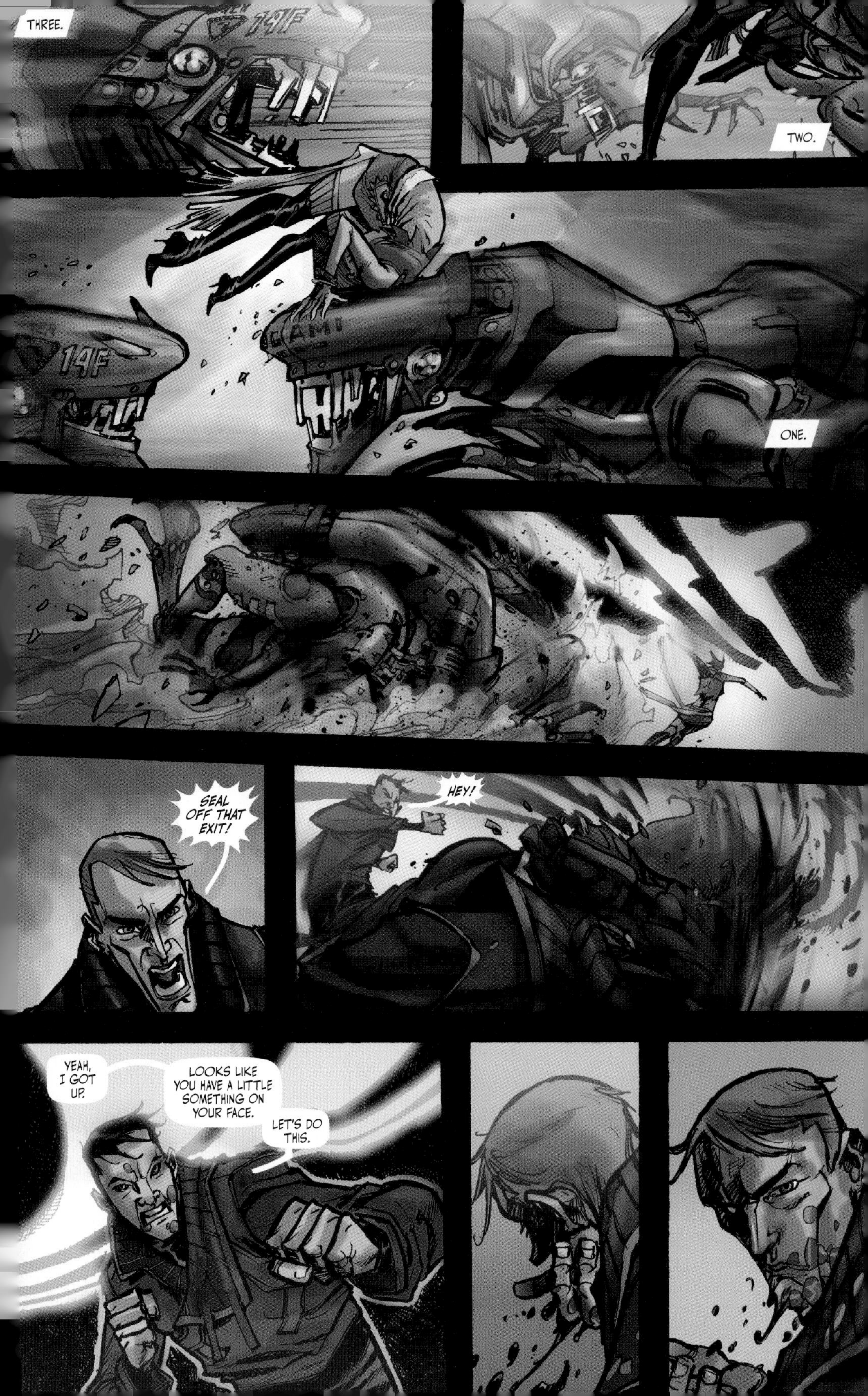
THREE.
TWO.
ONE.
SEAL OFF THAT EXIT!
HEY!
YEAH, I GOT UP.
LOOKS LIKE YOU HAVE A LITTLE SOMETHING ON YOUR FACE.
LET'S DO THIS.

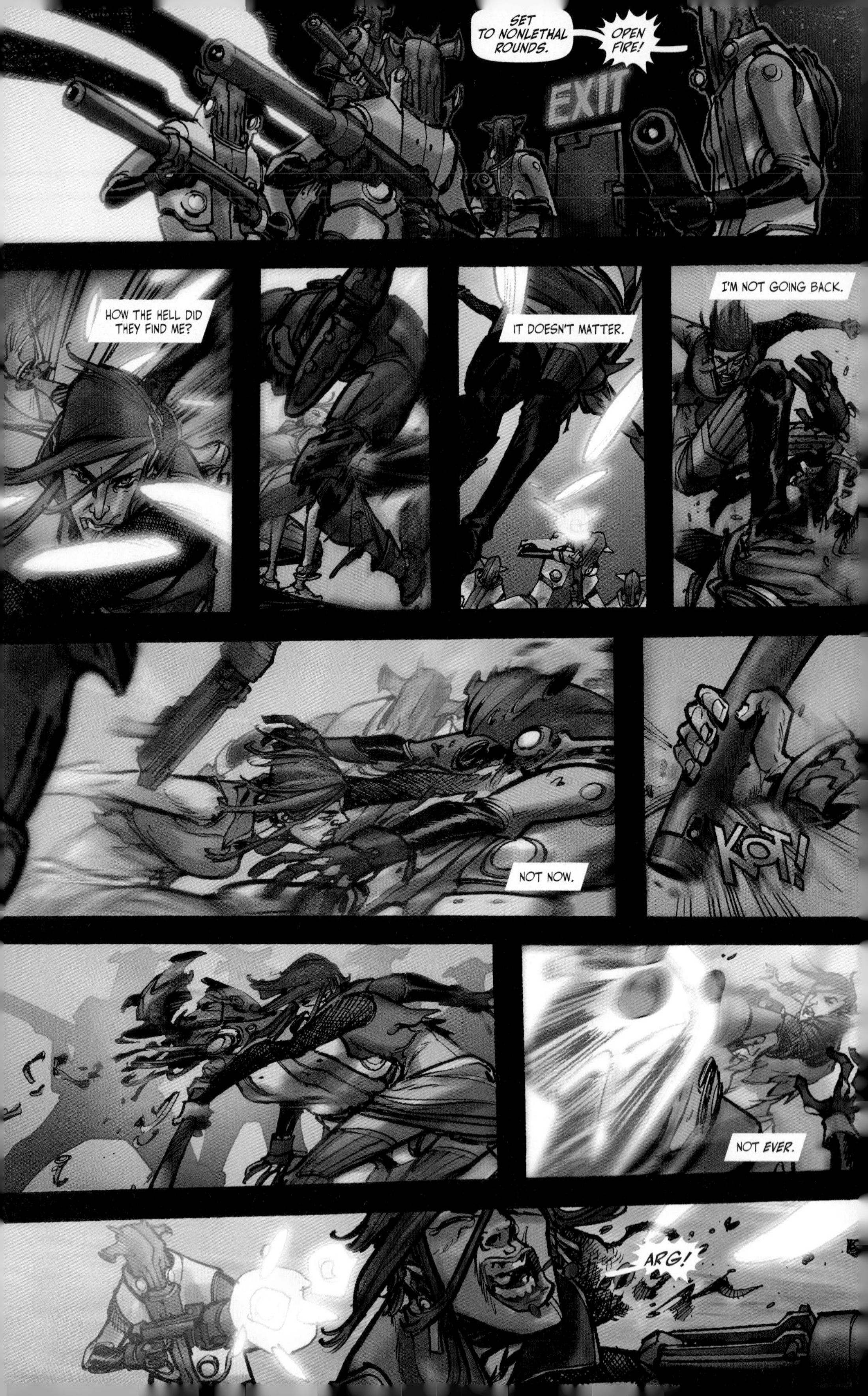
SET TO NONLETHAL ROUNDS.
OPEN FIRE!
EXIT
HOW THE HELL DID THEY FIND ME?
IT DOESN'T MATTER.
I'M NOT GOING BACK.
NOT NOW.
KOT!
NOT EVER.
ARG!

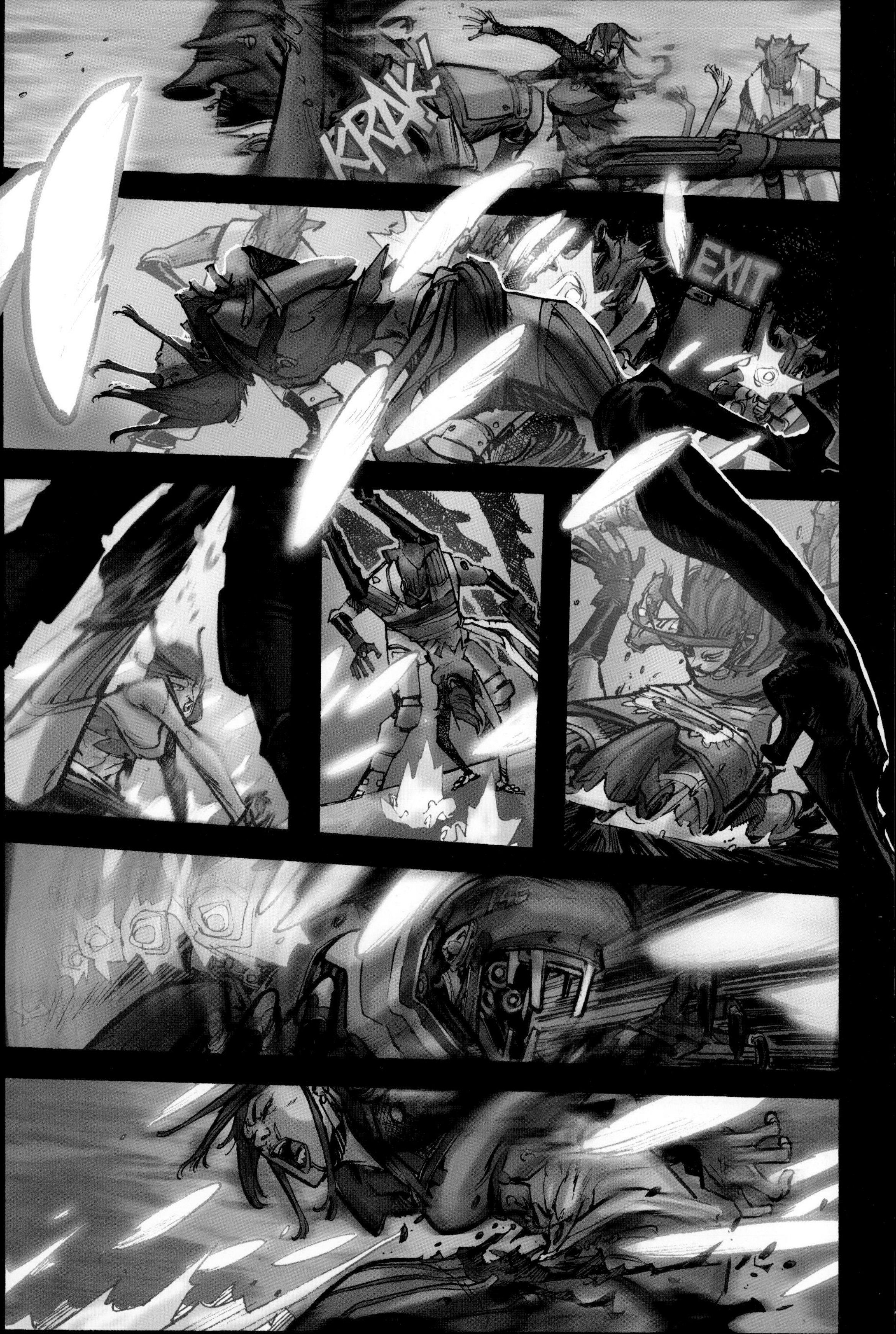
KRAK!
EXIT

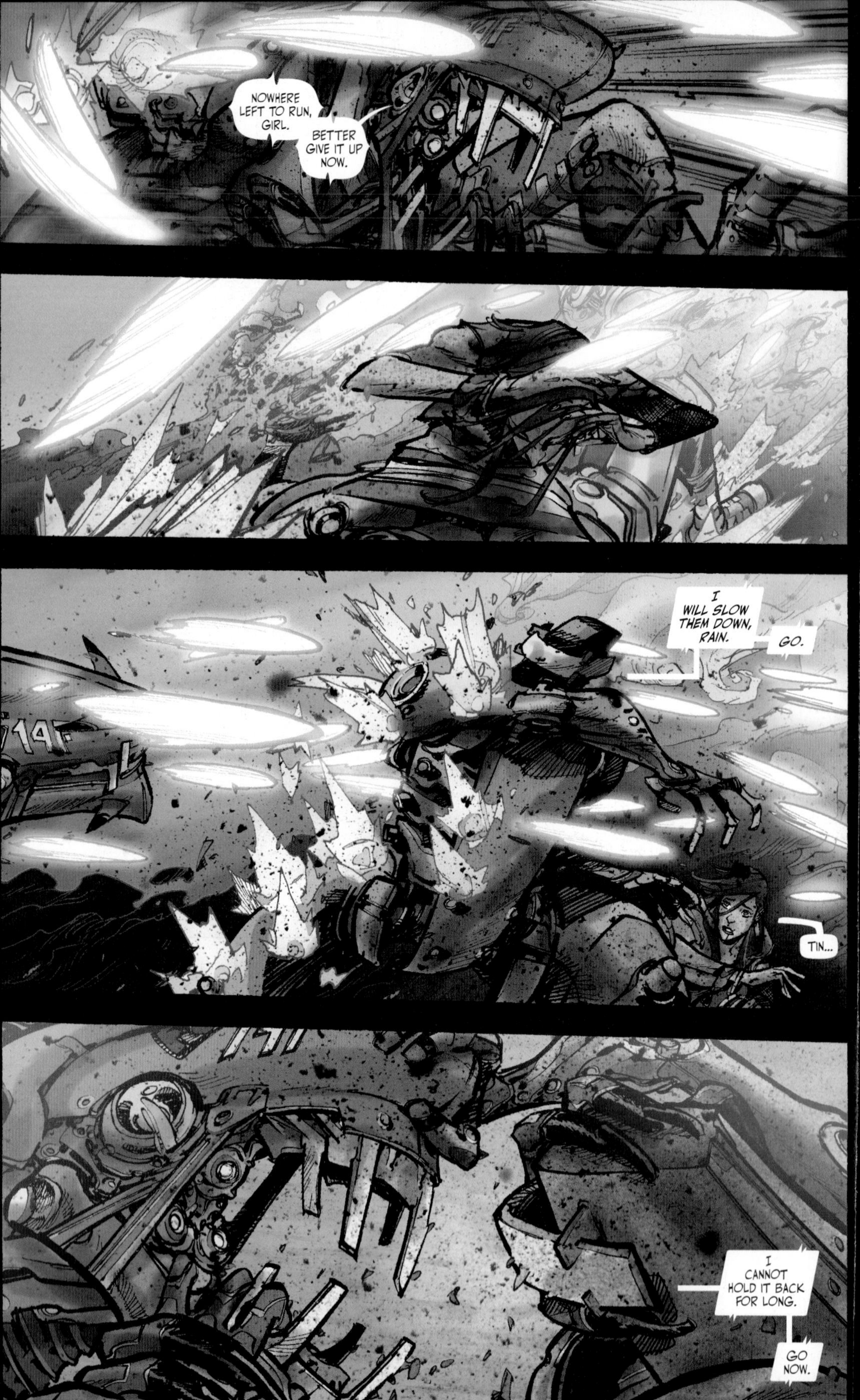

NOWHERE LEFT TO RUN, GIRL.
BETTER GIVE IT UP NOW.
I WILL SLOW THEM DOWN, RAIN.
GO.
TIN...
I CANNOT HOLD IT BACK FOR LONG.
GO NOW.

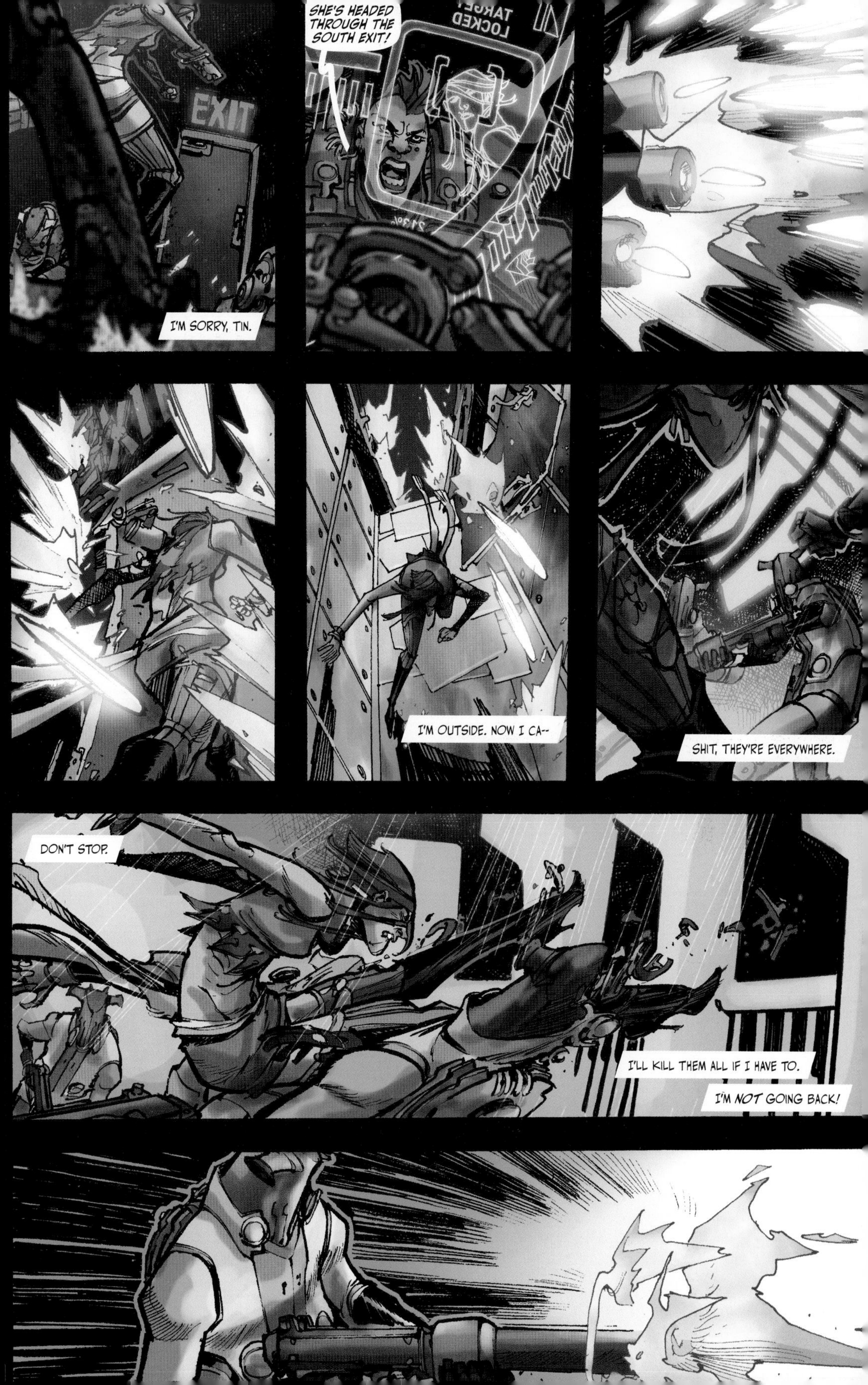
I'M SORRY, TIN.
SHE'S HEADED THROUGH THE SOUTH EXIT!
TARGET LOCKED
EXIT
I'M OUTSIDE. NOW I CA--
SHIT, THEY'RE EVERYWHERE.
DON'T STOP.
I'LL KILL THEM ALL IF I HAVE TO.
I'M NOT GOING BACK!

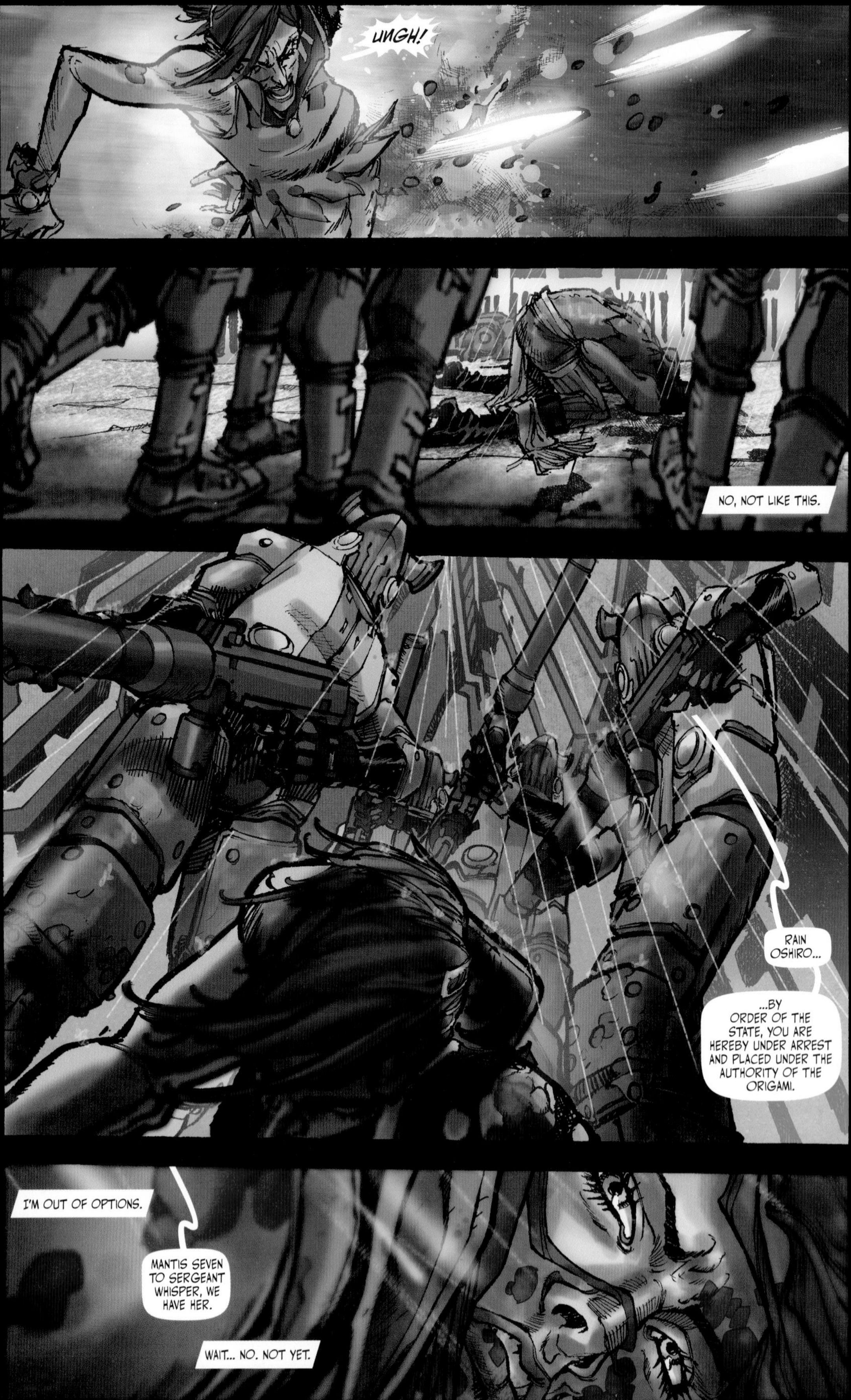

UNGH!
NO, NOT LIKE THIS.
RAIN OSHIRO...
...BY ORDER OF THE STATE, YOU ARE HEREBY UNDER ARREST AND PLACED UNDER THE AUTHORITY OF THE ORIGAMI.
I'M OUT OF OPTIONS.
MANTIS SEVEN TO SERGEANT WHISPER, WE HAVE HER.
WAIT... NO. NOT YET.

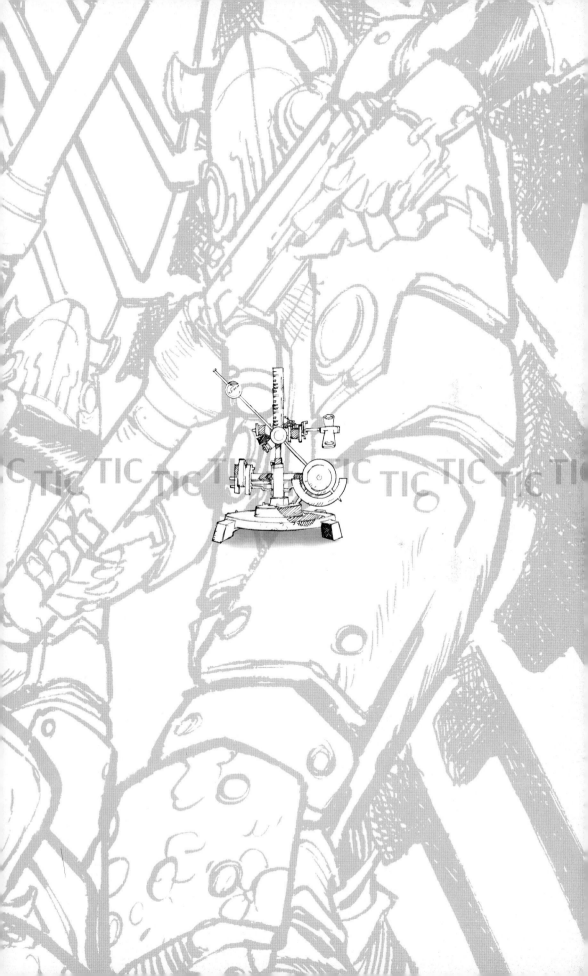

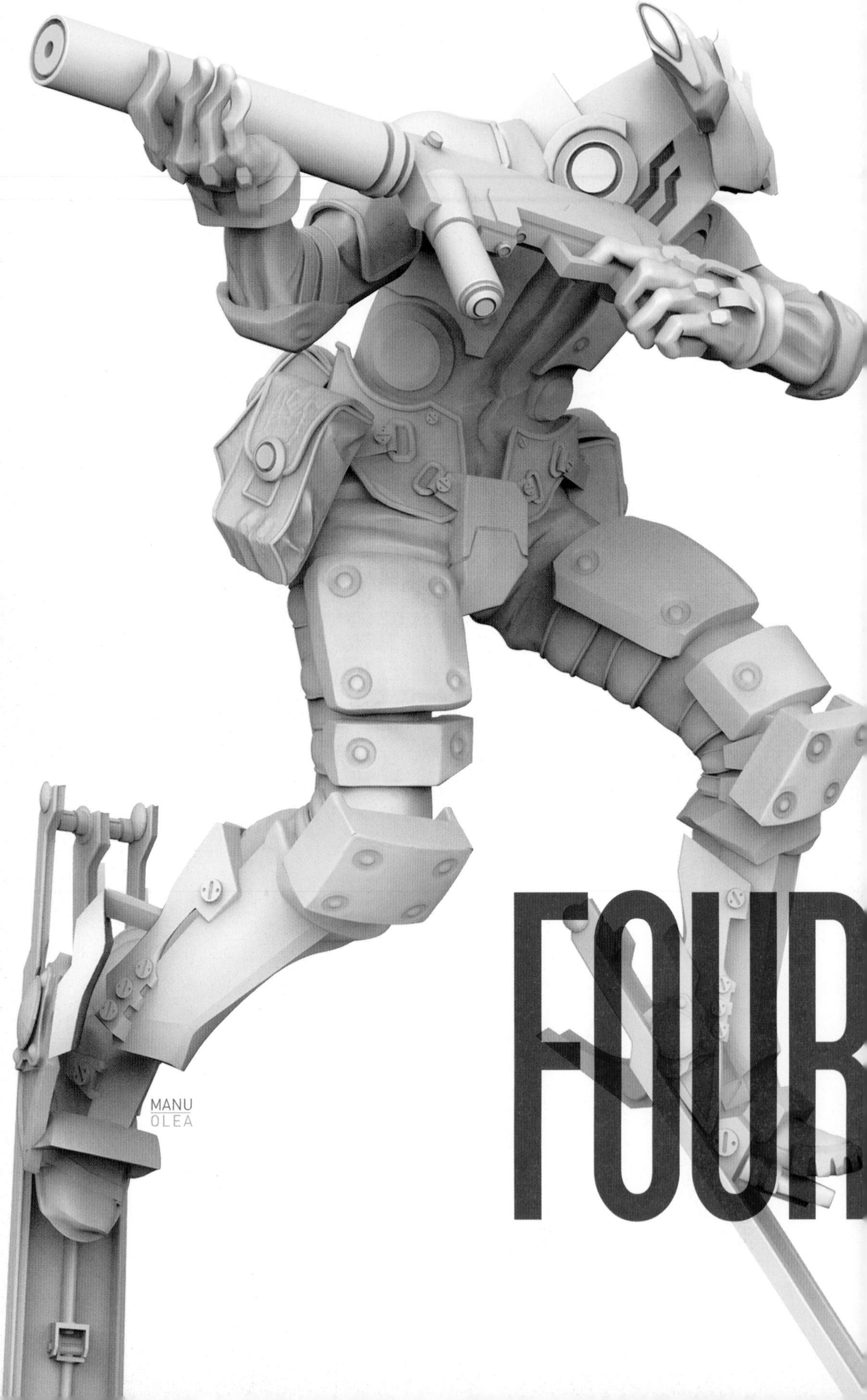
MANU
OLEA

FOUR

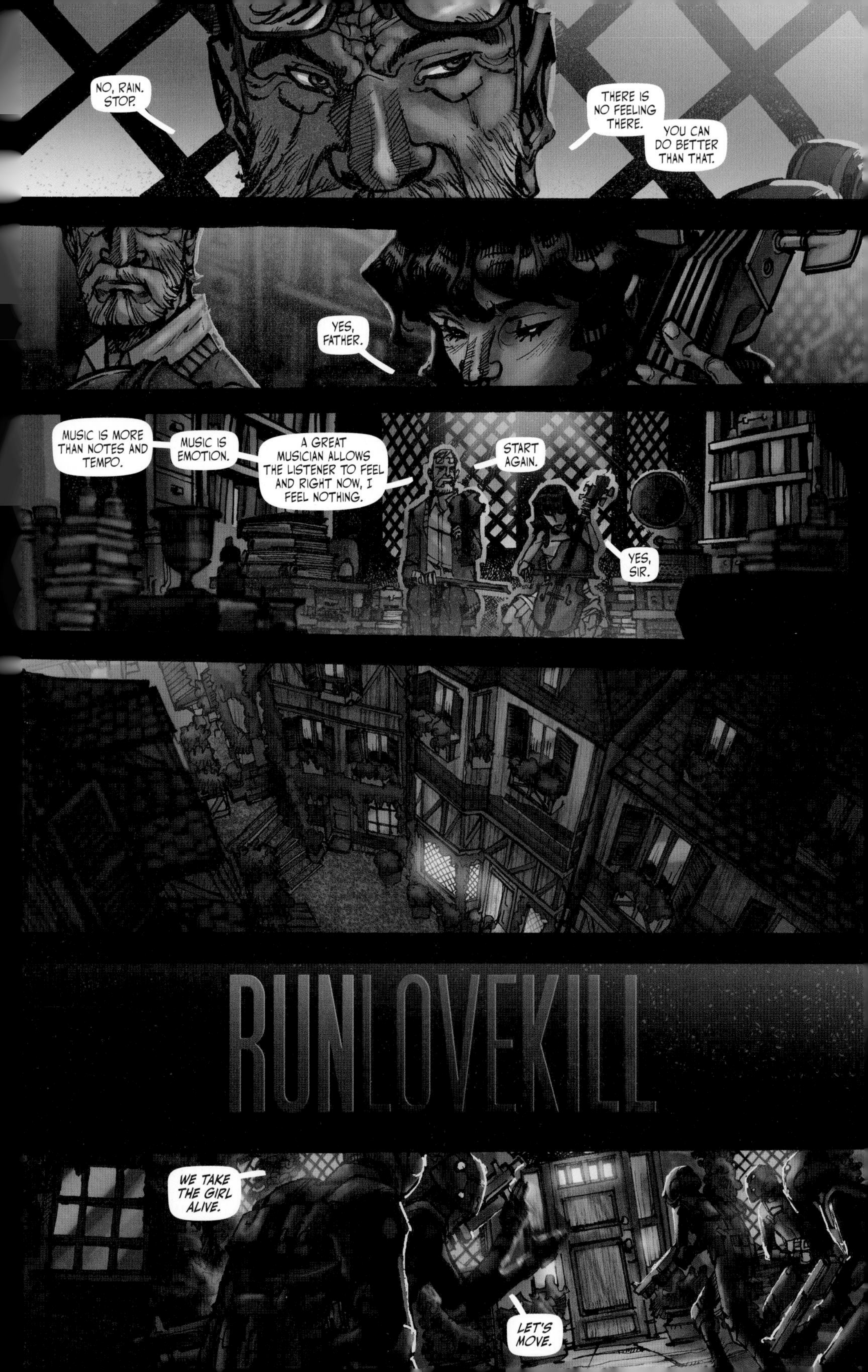
NO, RAIN. STOP.
THERE IS NO FEELING THERE.
YOU CAN DO BETTER THAN THAT.
YES, FATHER.
MUSIC IS MORE THAN NOTES AND TEMPO.
MUSIC IS EMOTION.
A GREAT MUSICIAN ALLOWS THE LISTENER TO FEEL AND RIGHT NOW, I FEEL NOTHING.
START AGAIN.
YES, SIR.
RUNLOVEKILL
WE TAKE THE GIRL ALIVE.
LET'S MOVE.

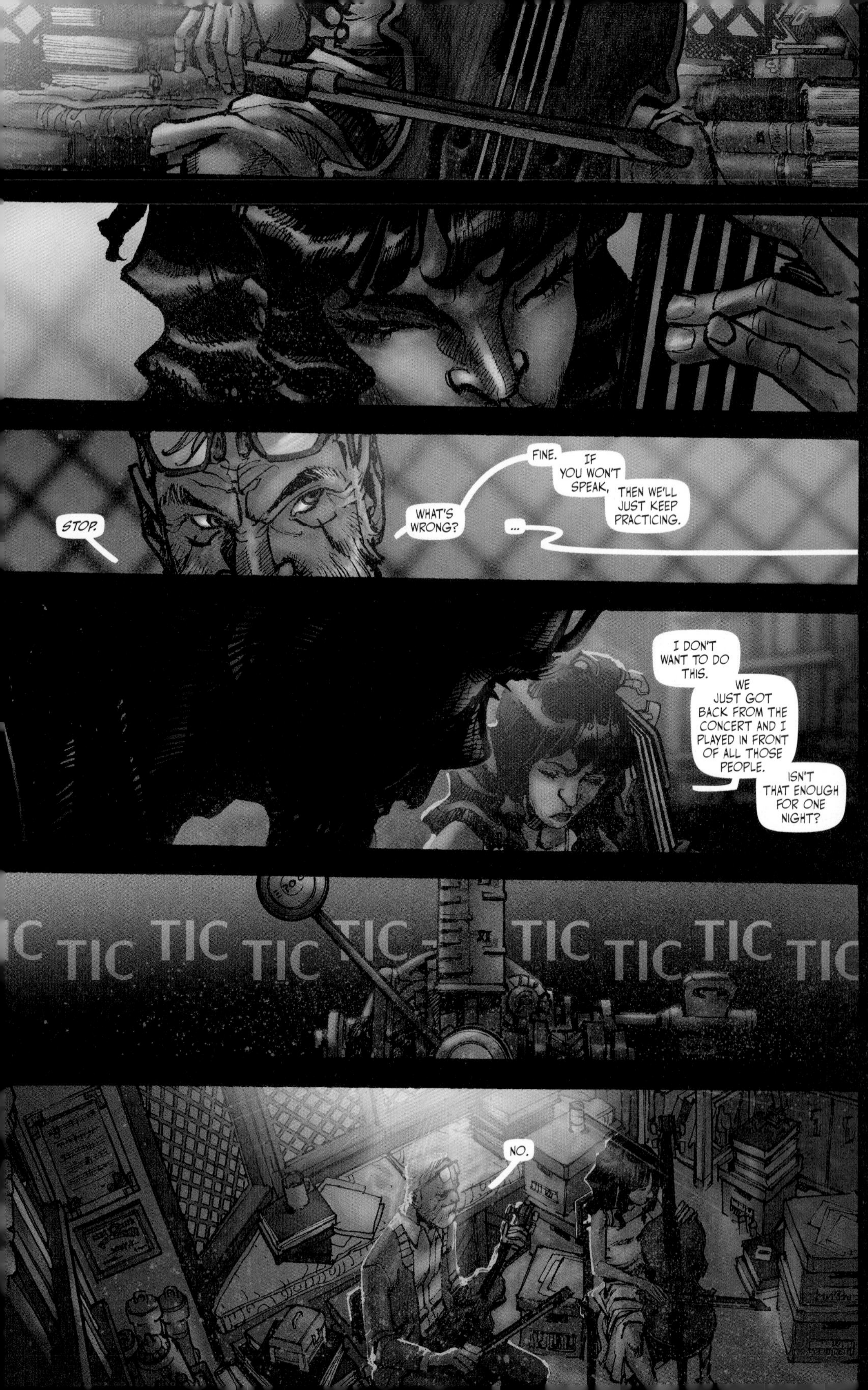
STOP.
WHAT'S WRONG?
FINE.
IF YOU WON'T SPEAK,
THEN WE'LL JUST KEEP PRACTICING.
...
I DON'T WANT TO DO THIS.
WE JUST GOT BACK FROM THE CONCERT AND I PLAYED IN FRONT OF ALL THOSE PEOPLE.
ISN'T THAT ENOUGH FOR ONE NIGHT?
TIC TIC TIC TIC TIC TIC TIC TIC TIC
NO.

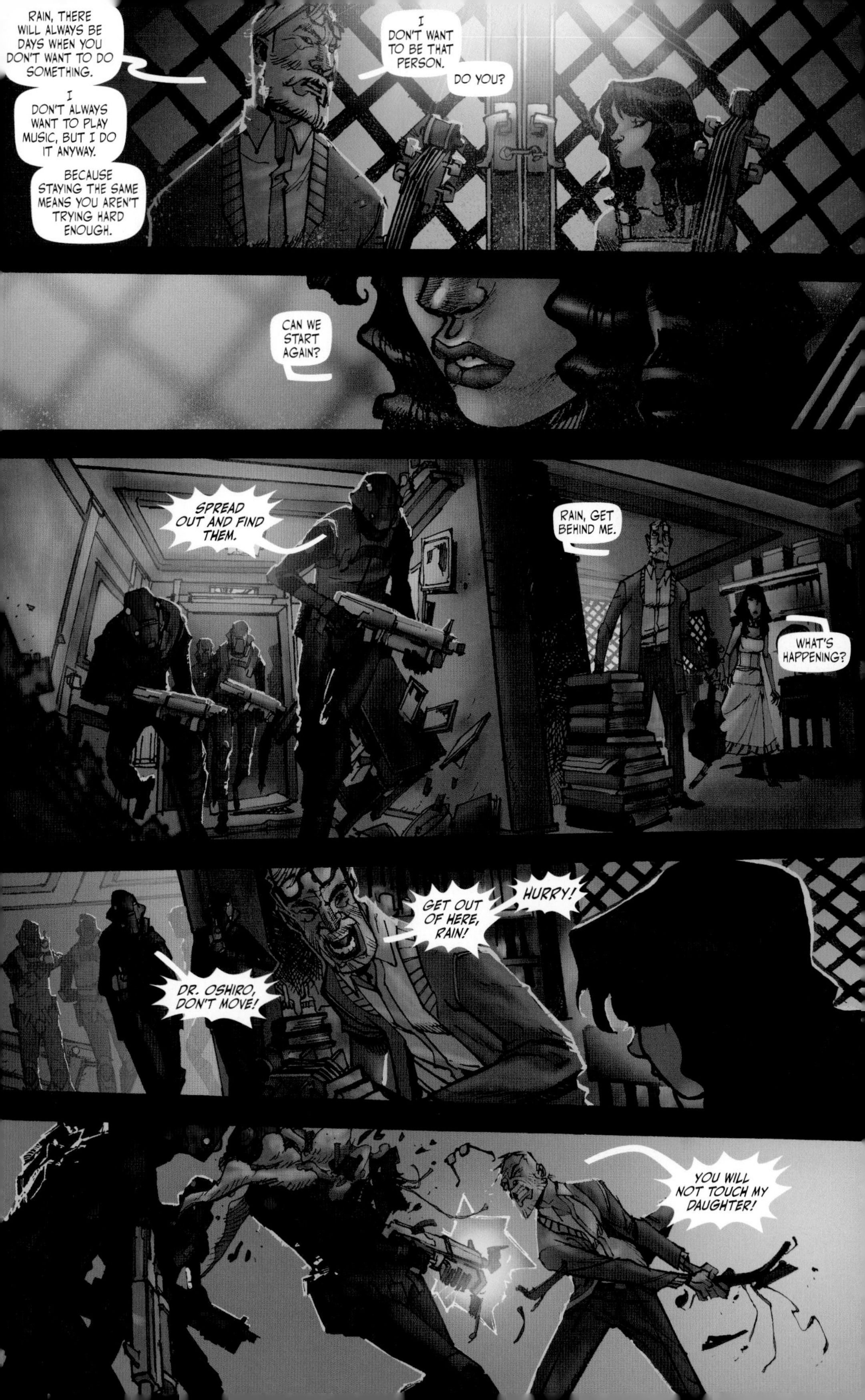
RAIN, THERE WILL ALWAYS BE DAYS WHEN YOU DON'T WANT TO DO SOMETHING.
I DON'T ALWAYS WANT TO PLAY MUSIC, BUT I DO IT ANYWAY.
BECAUSE STAYING THE SAME MEANS YOU AREN'T TRYING HARD ENOUGH.
I DON'T WANT TO BE THAT PERSON.
DO YOU?
CAN WE START AGAIN?
SPREAD OUT AND FIND THEM.
RAIN, GET BEHIND ME.
WHAT'S HAPPENING?
GET OUT OF HERE, RAIN!
HURRY!
DR. OSHIRO, DON'T MOVE!
YOU WILL NOT TOUCH MY DAUGHTER!

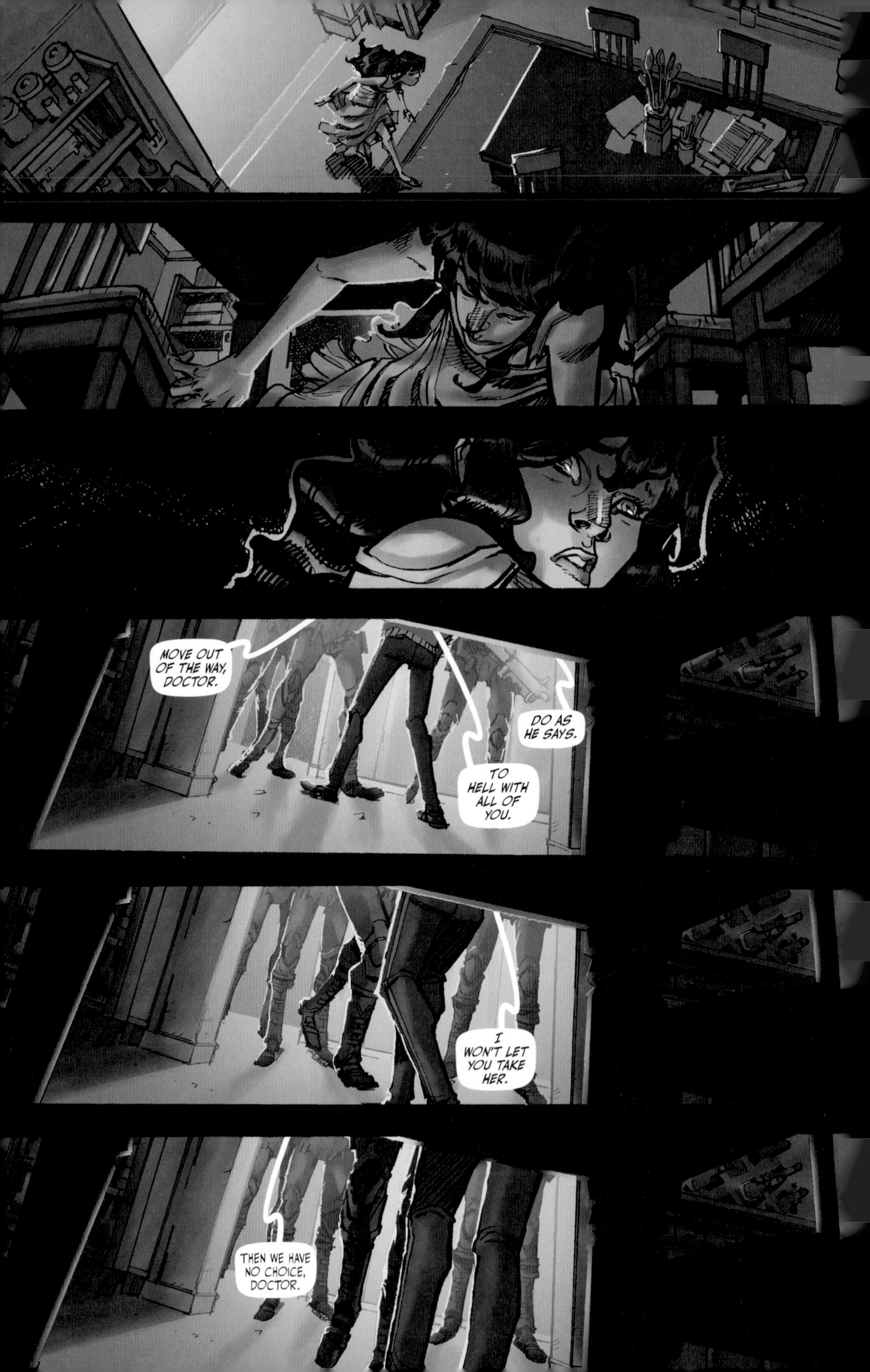
MOVE OUT OF THE WAY, DOCTOR.
DO AS HE SAYS.
TO HELL WITH ALL OF YOU.
I WON'T LET YOU TAKE HER.
THEN WE HAVE NO CHOICE, DOCTOR.

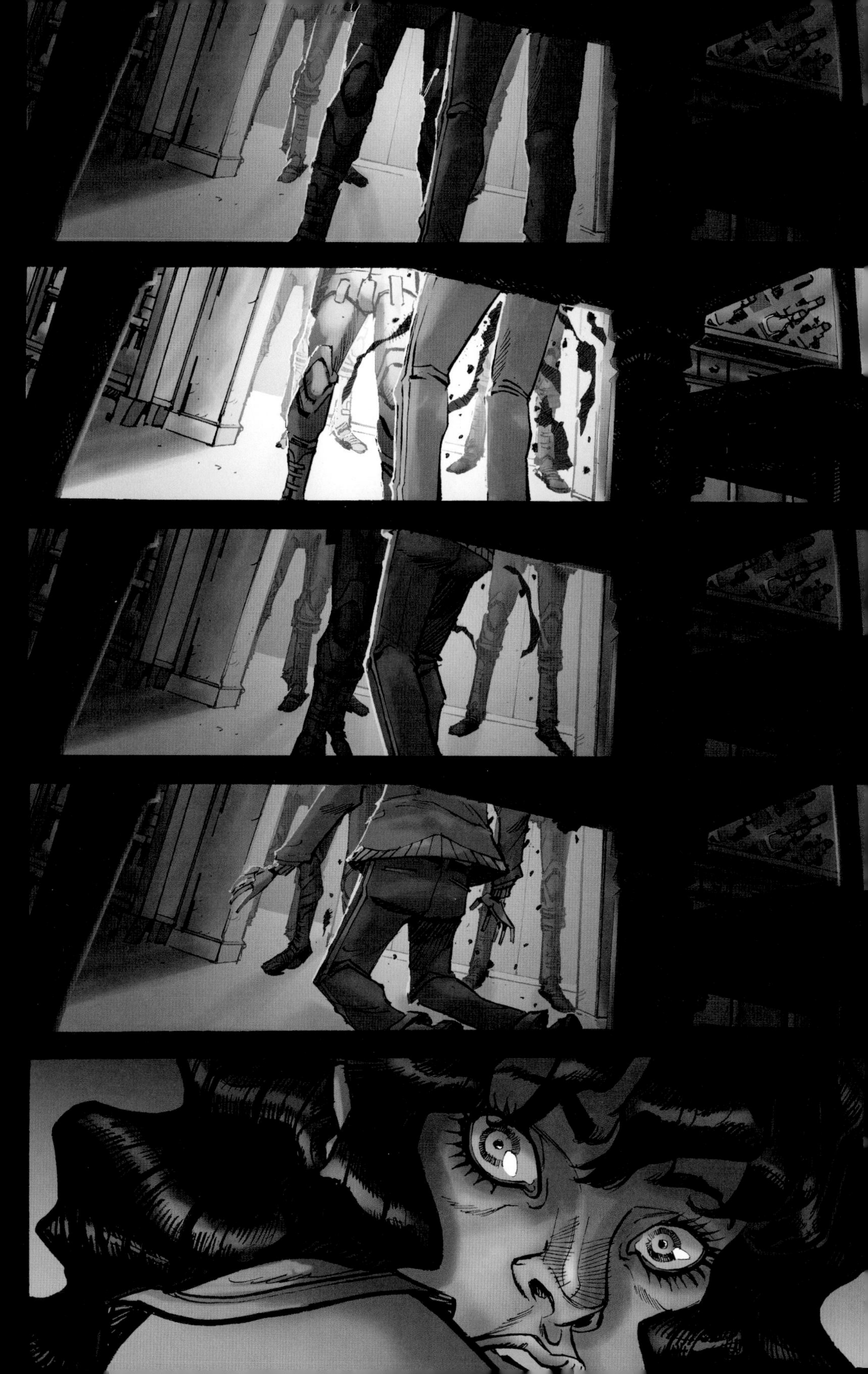

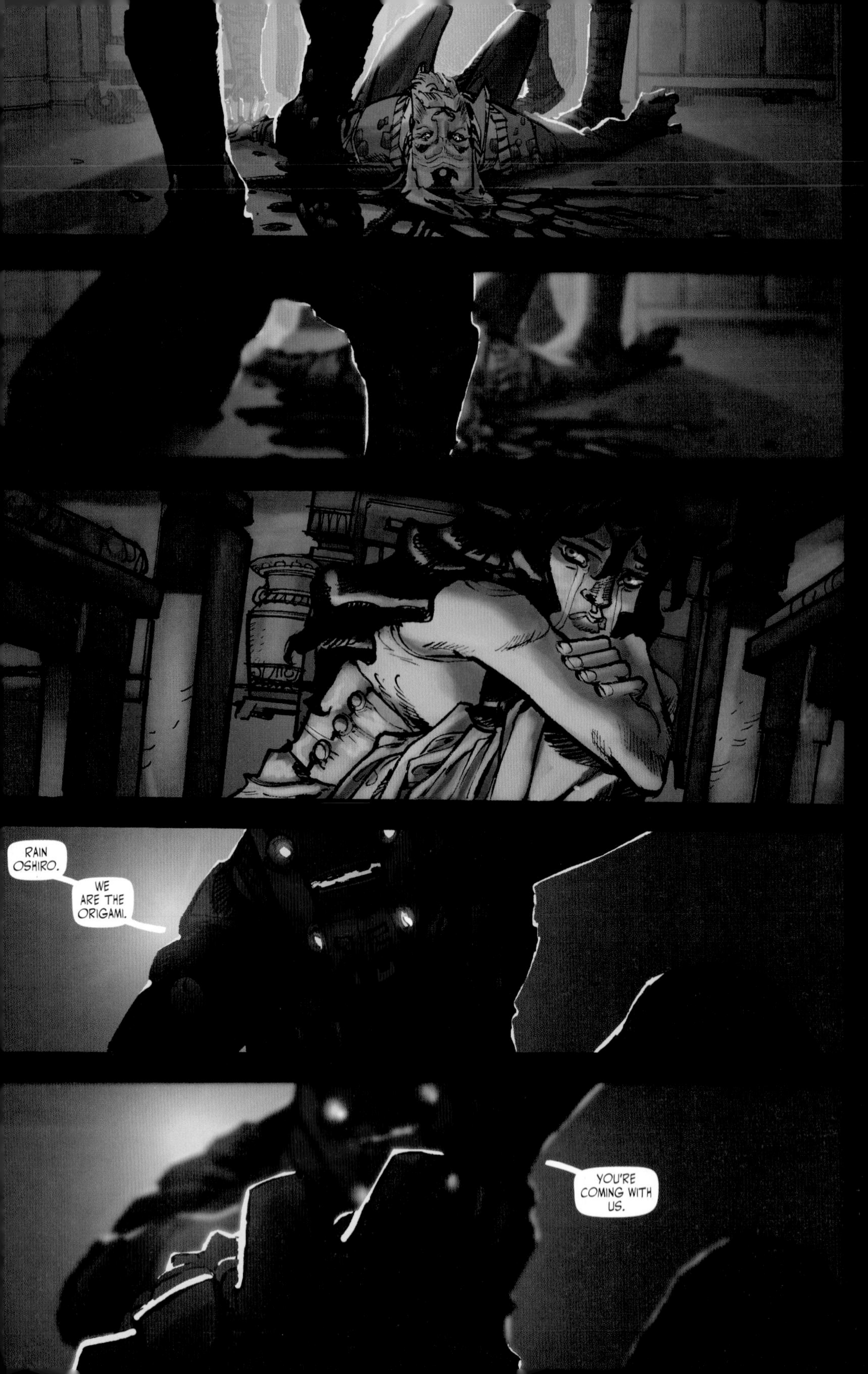
RAIN OSHIRO.
WE ARE THE ORIGAMI.
YOU'RE COMING WITH US.

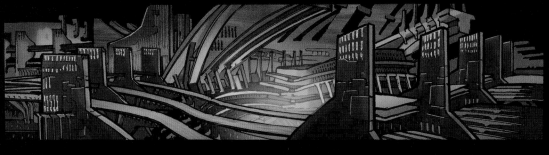

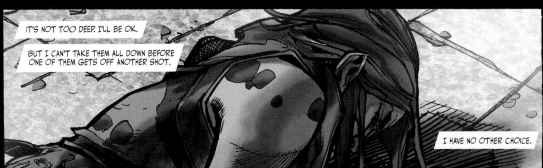

IT'S NOT TOO DEEP. I'LL BE OK.

BUT I CAN'T TAKE THEM ALL DOWN BEFORE ONE OF THEM GETS OFF ANOTHER SHOT.

I HAVE NO OTHER CHOICE.

COMMANDER, THE TARGET IS DOWN.

WE'RE RESTRAINING HER NOW.

NOW'S MY CHANCE.

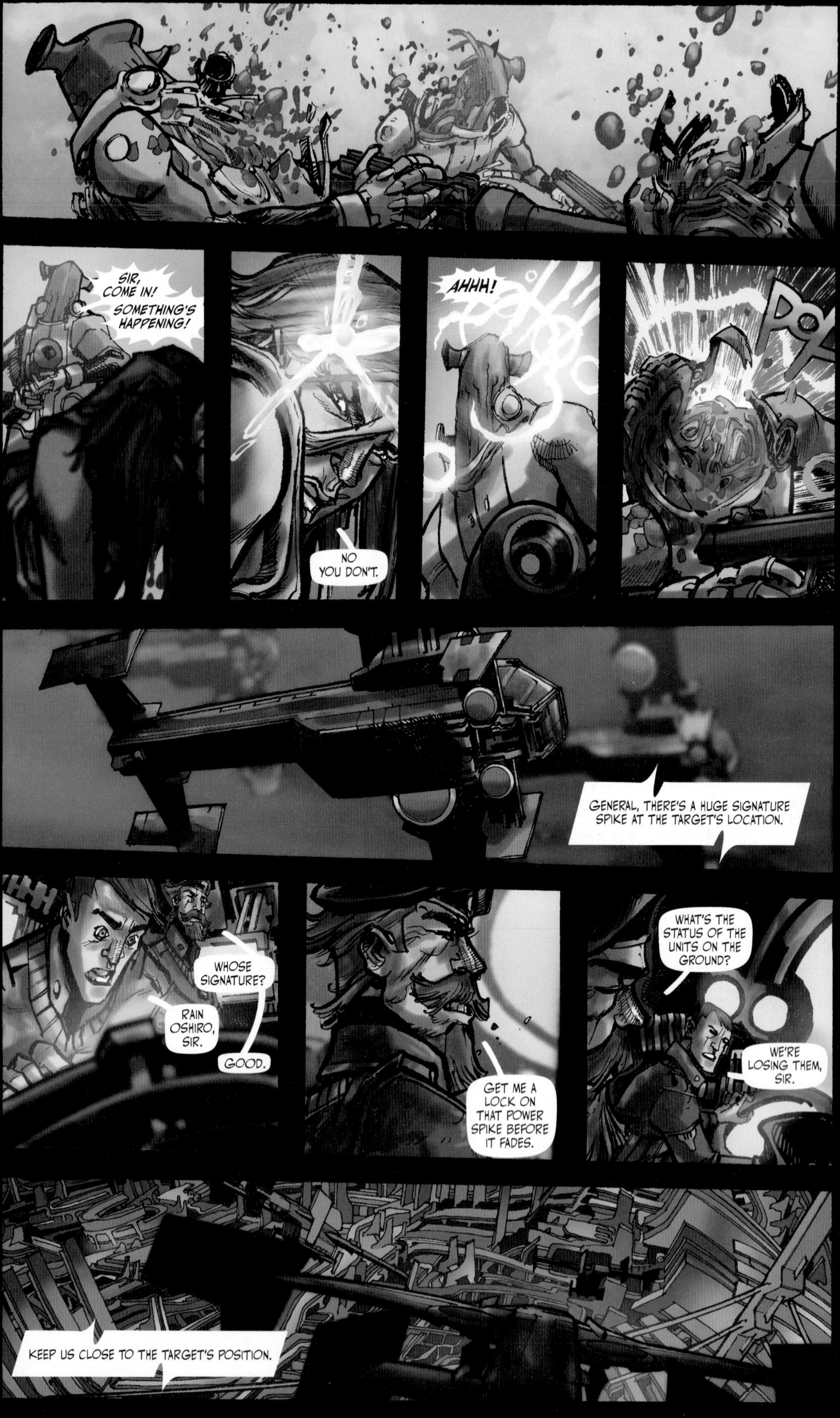
SIR, COME IN!
SOMETHING'S HAPPENING!
NO YOU DON'T.
AHHH!
GENERAL, THERE'S A HUGE SIGNATURE SPIKE AT THE TARGET'S LOCATION.
WHOSE SIGNATURE?
RAIN OSHIRO, SIR.
GOOD.
GET ME A LOCK ON THAT POWER SPIKE BEFORE IT FADES.
WHAT'S THE STATUS OF THE UNITS ON THE GROUND?
WE'RE LOSING THEM, SIR.
KEEP US CLOSE TO THE TARGET'S POSITION.

MAYBE THIS WILL EVEN THINGS UP.

JANUS, COME IN. THE TARGET IS MOVING.

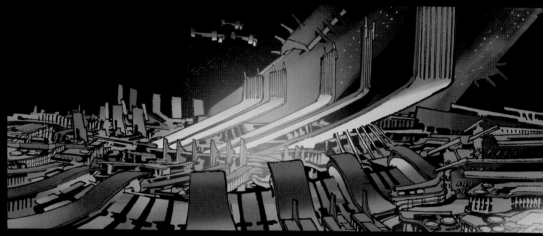

I HAVE TO GET SOME DISTANCE FROM HERE.

IT MIGHT NOT BE TOO LATE TO GET OUT OF THE CITY.

GOTTA TRY.

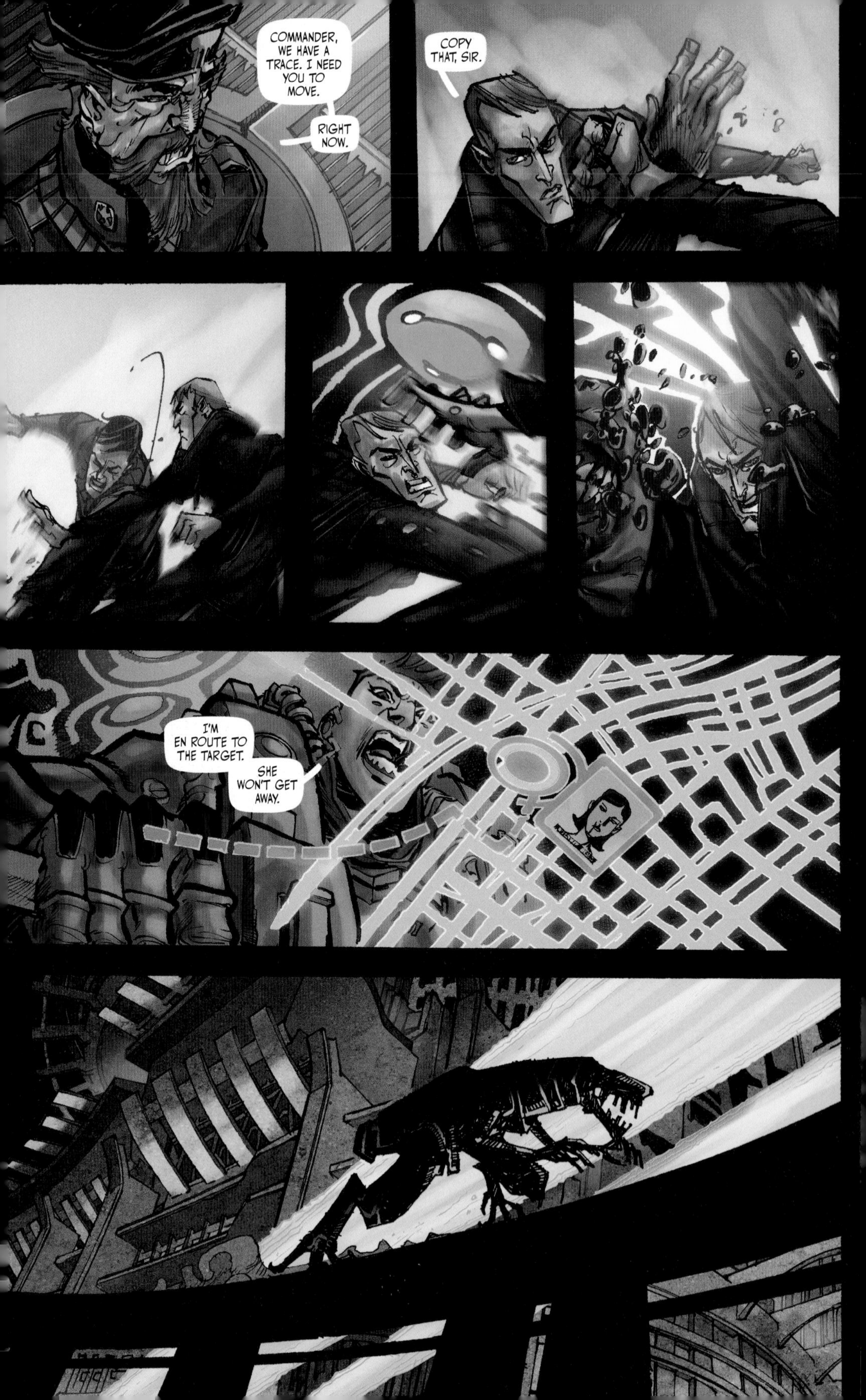
COMMANDER, WE HAVE A TRACE. I NEED YOU TO MOVE.
RIGHT NOW.
COPY THAT, SIR.
I'M EN ROUTE TO THE TARGET.
SHE WON'T GET AWAY.

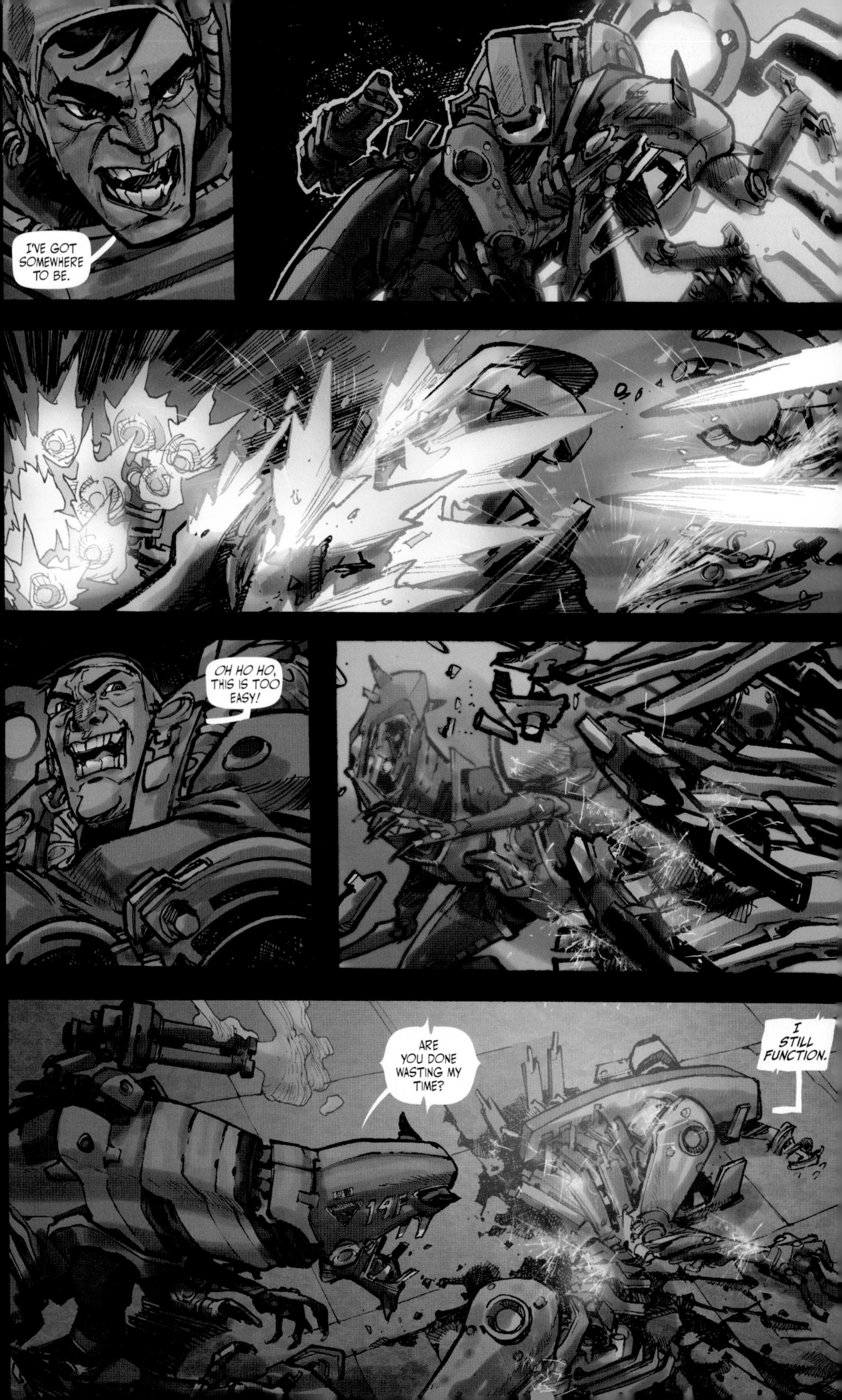
I'VE GOT SOMEWHERE TO BE.
OH HO HO, THIS IS TOO EASY!
ARE YOU DONE WASTING MY TIME?
I STILL FUNCTION.

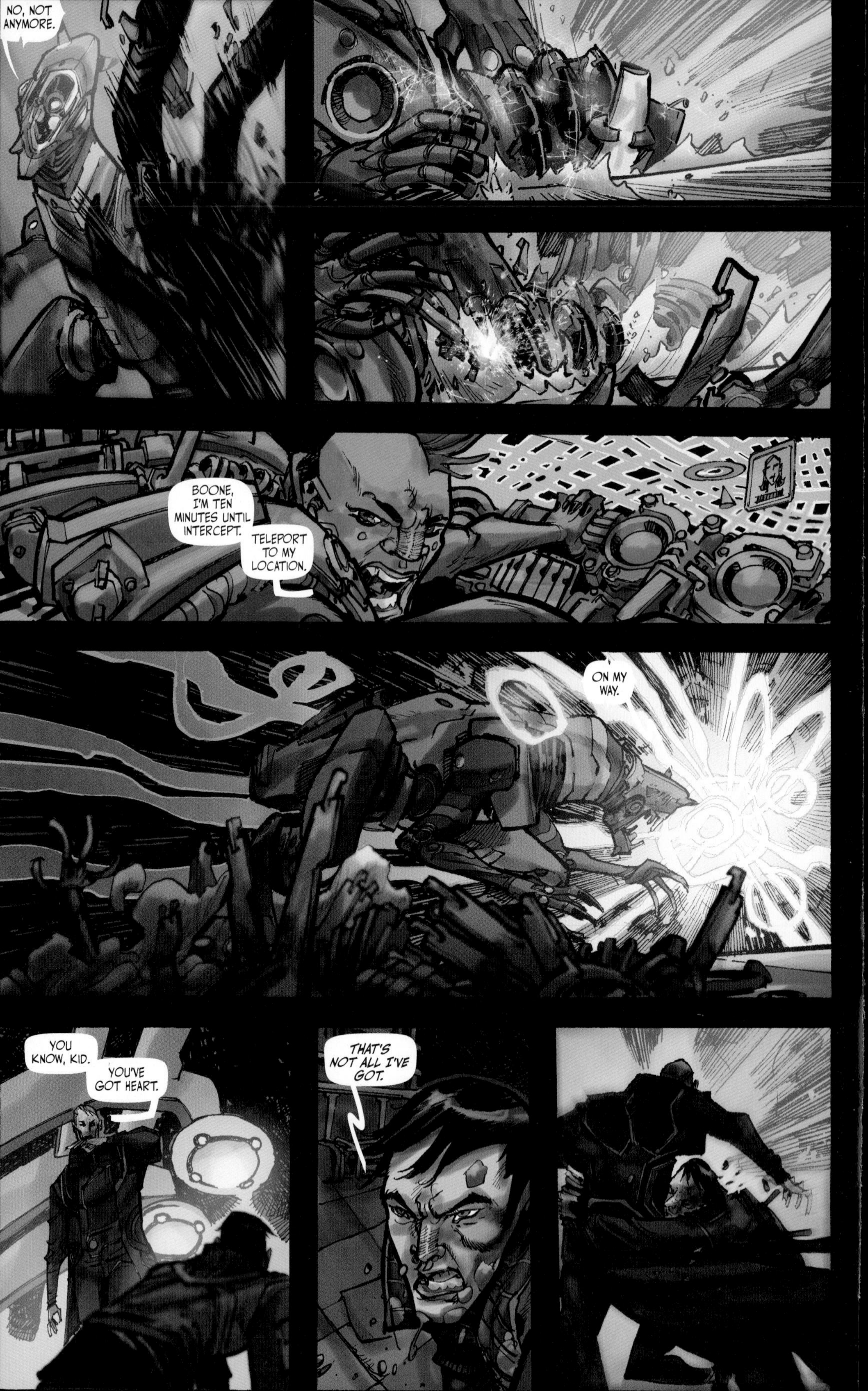
NO, NOT ANYMORE.
BOONE, I'M TEN MINUTES UNTIL INTERCEPT.
TELEPORT TO MY LOCATION.
ON MY WAY.
YOU KNOW, KID.
YOU'VE GOT HEART.
THAT'S NOT ALL I'VE GOT.

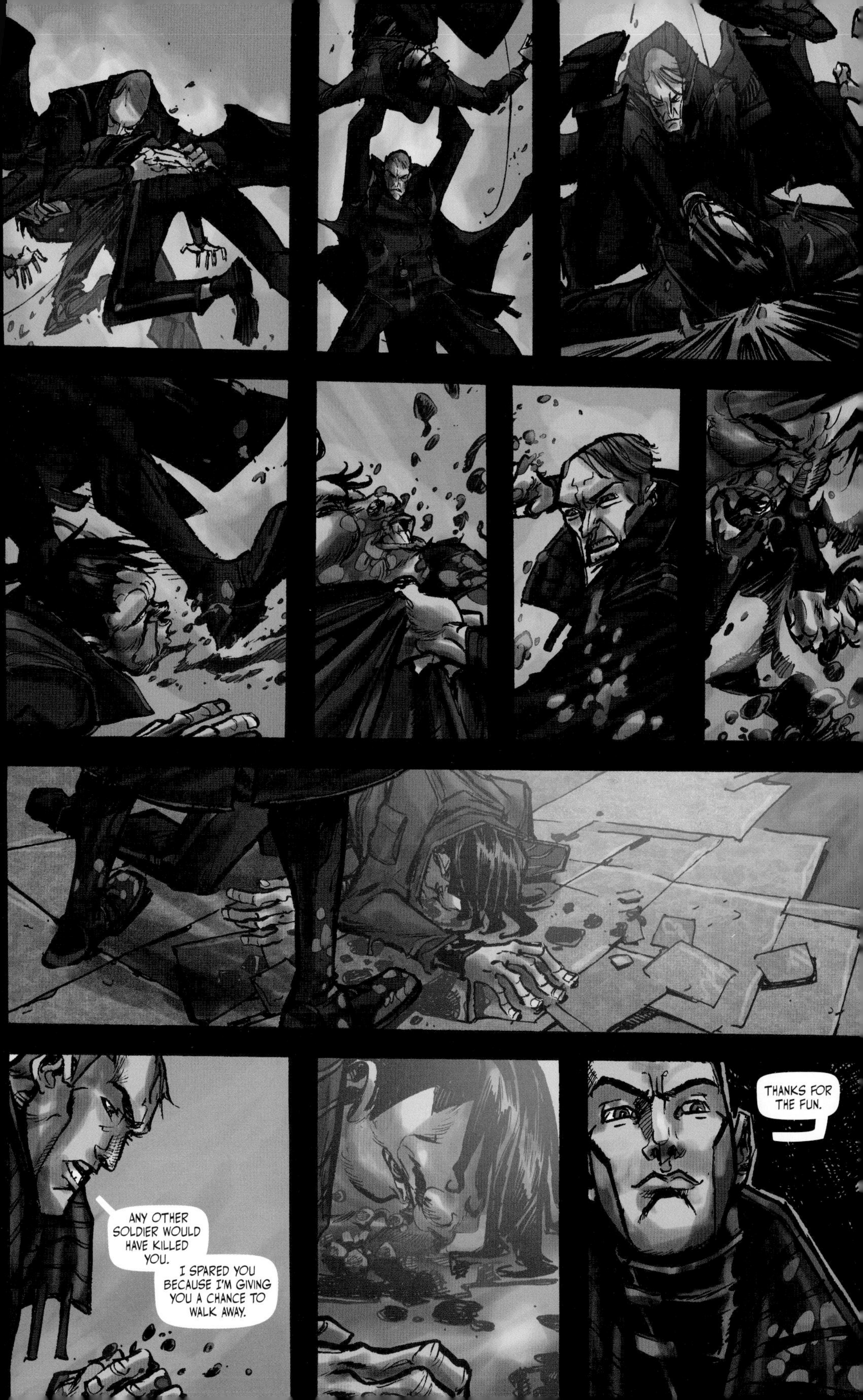
ANY OTHER SOLDIER WOULD HAVE KILLED YOU.
I SPARED YOU BECAUSE I'M GIVING YOU A CHANCE TO WALK AWAY.
THANKS FOR THE FUN.

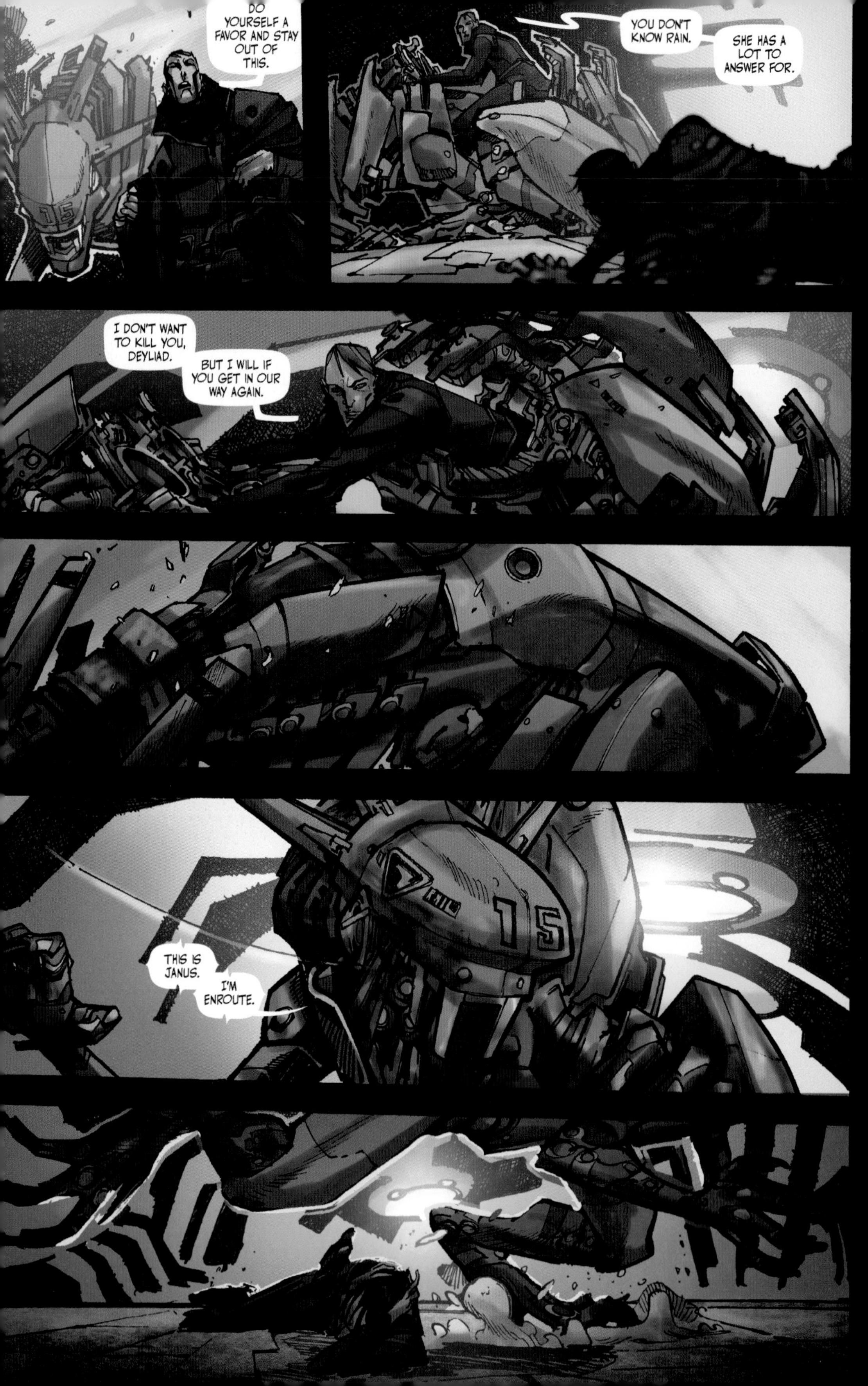
DO YOURSELF A FAVOR AND STAY OUT OF THIS.
YOU DON'T KNOW RAIN.
SHE HAS A LOT TO ANSWER FOR.
I DON'T WANT TO KILL YOU, DEYLIAD.
BUT I WILL IF YOU GET IN OUR WAY AGAIN.
THIS IS JANUS.
I'M ENROUTE.

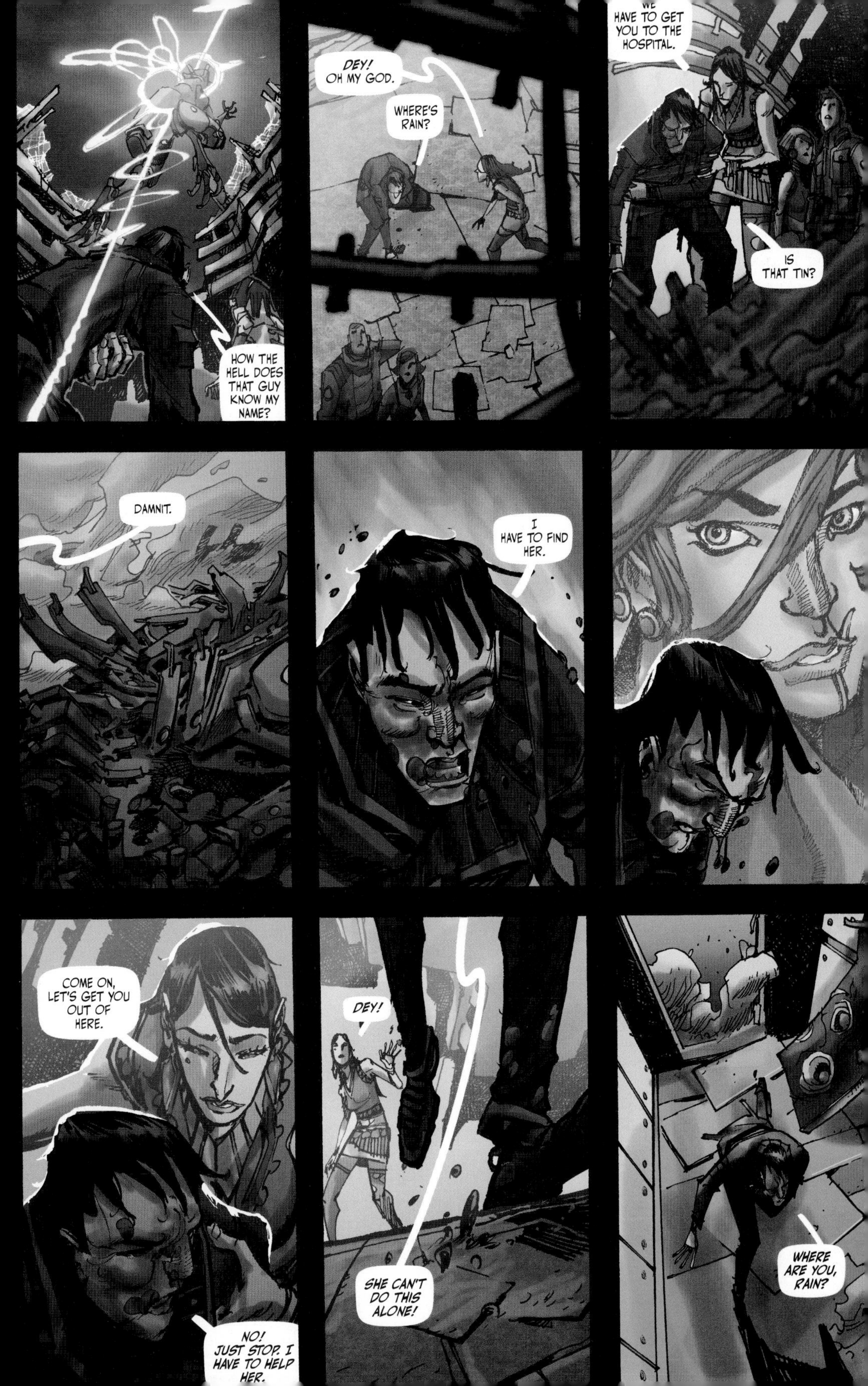
HOW THE HELL DOES THAT GUY KNOW MY NAME?
DEY! OH MY GOD.
WHERE'S RAIN?
WE HAVE TO GET YOU TO THE HOSPITAL.
IS THAT TIN?
DAMNIT.
I HAVE TO FIND HER.
COME ON, LET'S GET YOU OUT OF HERE.
NO! JUST STOP. I HAVE TO HELP HER.
DEY!
SHE CAN'T DO THIS ALONE!
WHERE ARE YOU, RAIN?

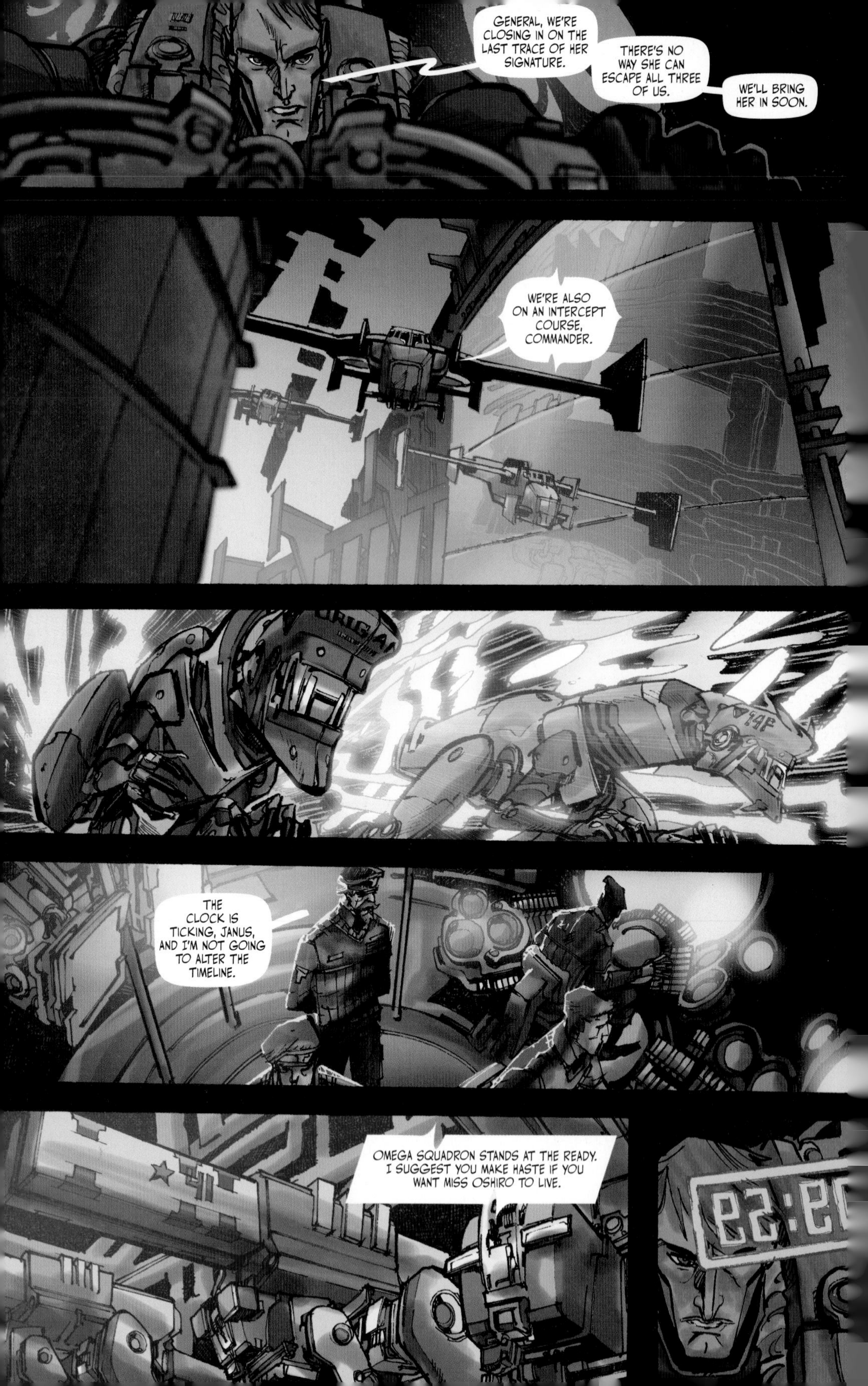
GENERAL, WE'RE CLOSING IN ON THE LAST TRACE OF HER SIGNATURE.
THERE'S NO WAY SHE CAN ESCAPE ALL THREE OF US.
WE'LL BRING HER IN SOON.
WE'RE ALSO ON AN INTERCEPT COURSE, COMMANDER.
THE CLOCK IS TICKING, JANUS, AND I'M NOT GOING TO ALTER THE TIMELINE.
OMEGA SQUADRON STANDS AT THE READY. I SUGGEST YOU MAKE HASTE IF YOU WANT MISS OSHIRO TO LIVE.

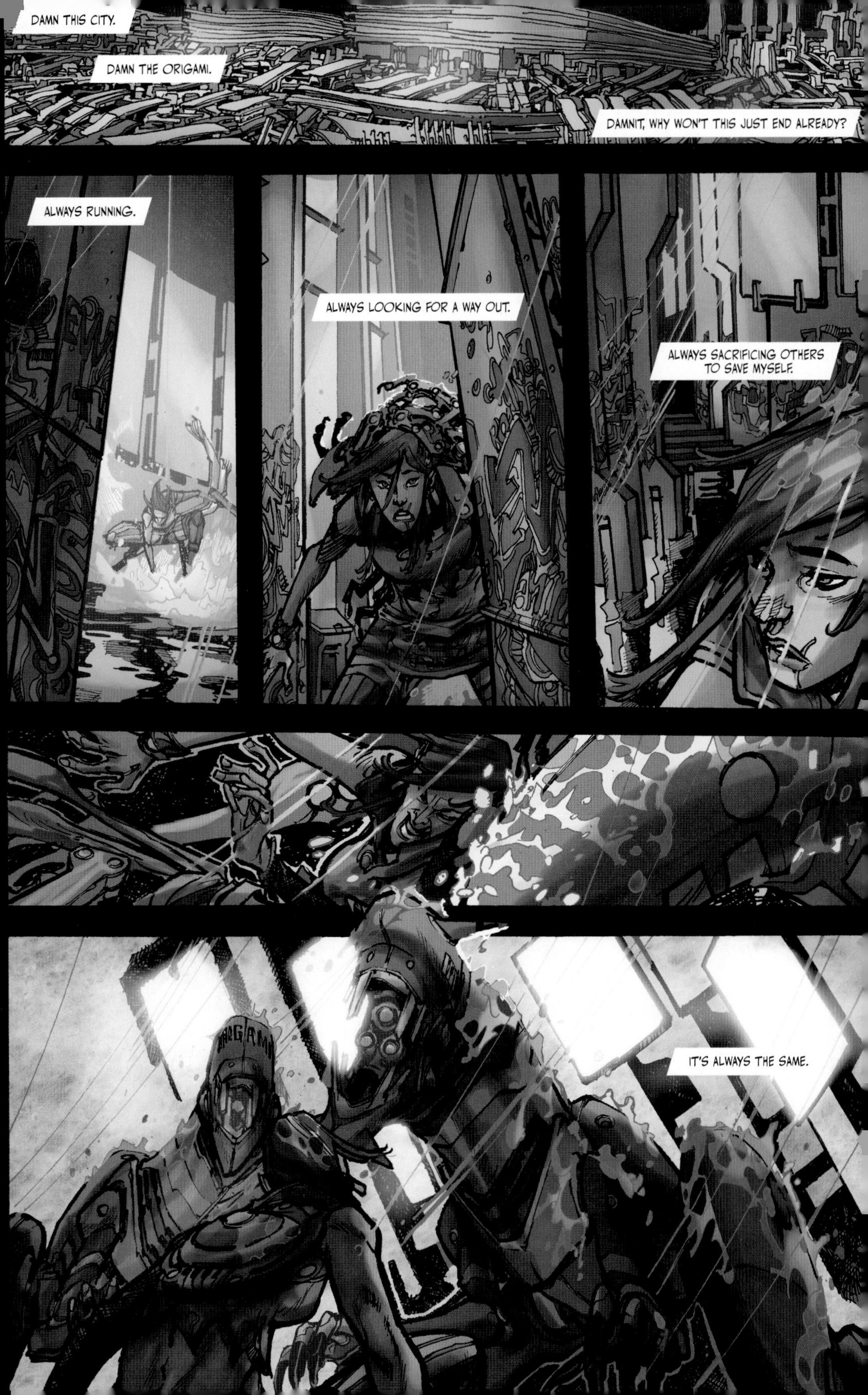
DAMN THIS CITY.
DAMN THE ORIGAMI.
DAMNIT, WHY WON'T THIS JUST END ALREADY?
ALWAYS RUNNING.
ALWAYS LOOKING FOR A WAY OUT.
ALWAYS SACRIFICING OTHERS TO SAVE MYSELF.
IT'S ALWAYS THE SAME.

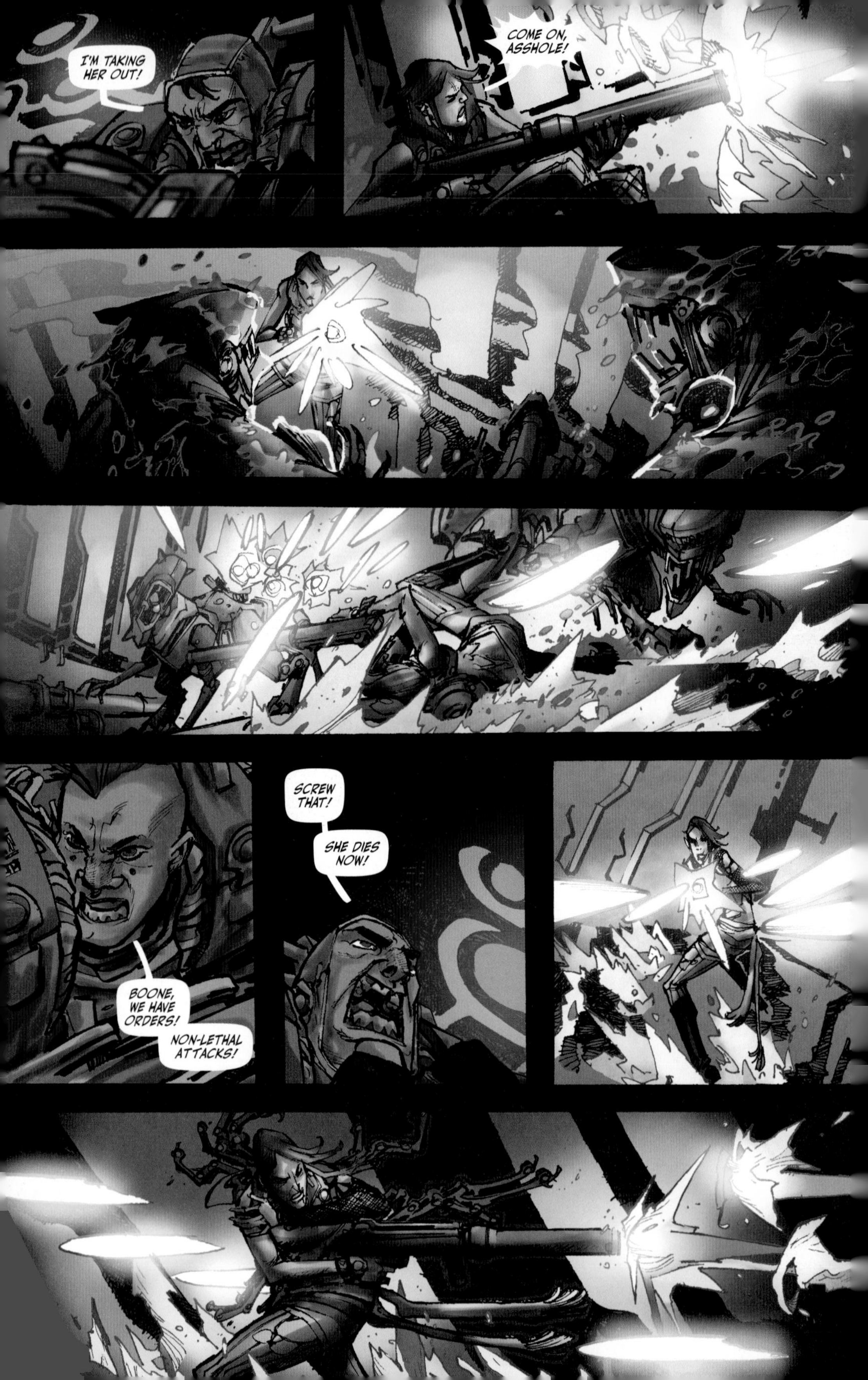
I'M TAKING HER OUT!
COME ON, ASSHOLE!
BOONE, WE HAVE ORDERS!
NON-LETHAL ATTACKS!
SCREW THAT!
SHE DIES NOW!

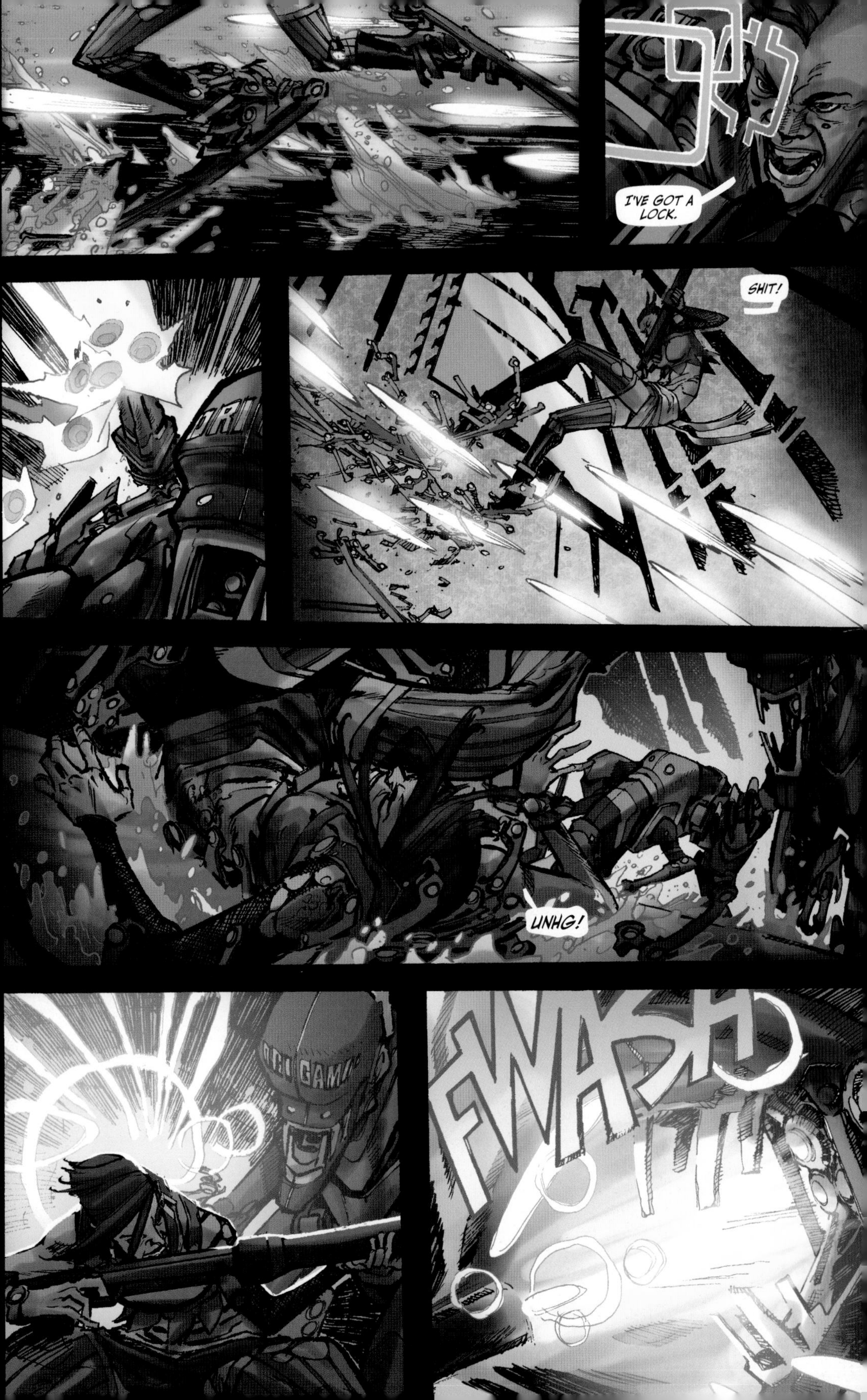
I'VE GOT A LOCK.
SHIT!
UNHG!
FWASH

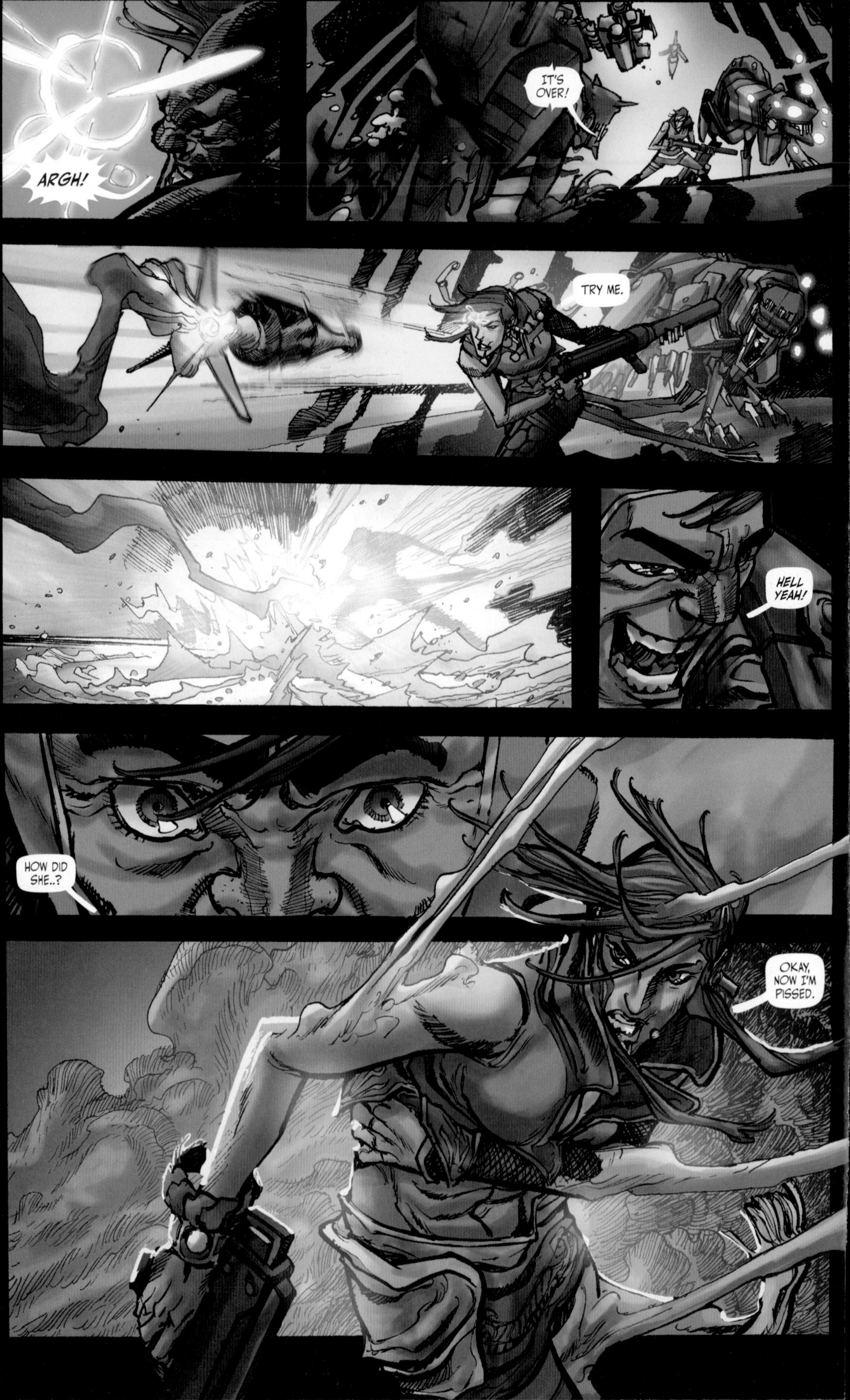
ARGH!
IT'S OVER!
TRY ME.
HELL YEAH!
HOW DID SHE..?
OKAY, NOW I'M PISSED.

DESIGNING
RUNLOVEKILL

RUNLOVEKILL's visual identity comes from the combined efforts of three artists, Eric Canete, Leonardo Olea and Manu Fernandez. The following pages give a glimpse at Eric's pre-production designs and thumbnails, Leo's color art and graphic design and Manu's 3D renderings. We hope you enjoy.

CONCEPTS

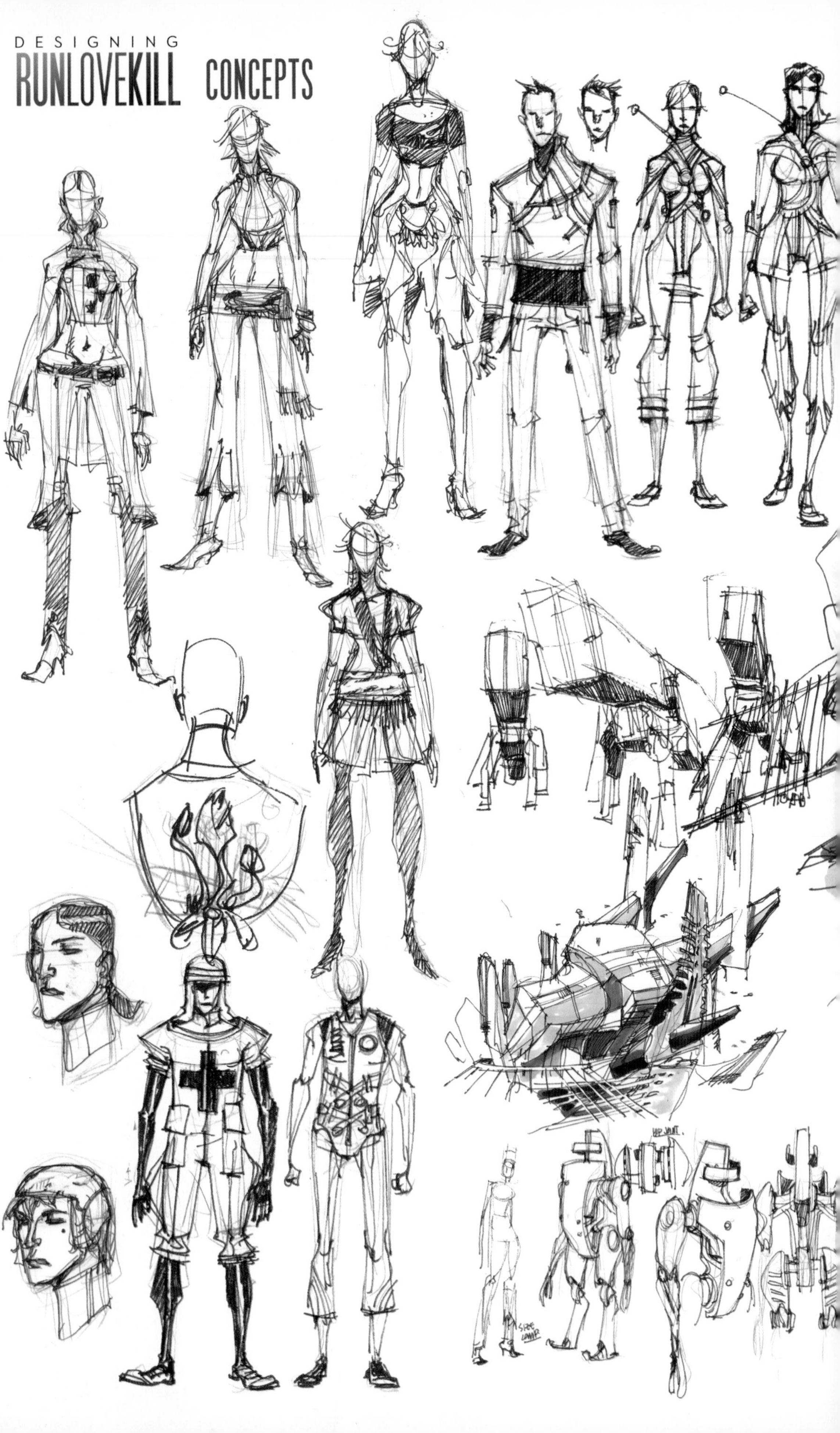
HIP JOINT.

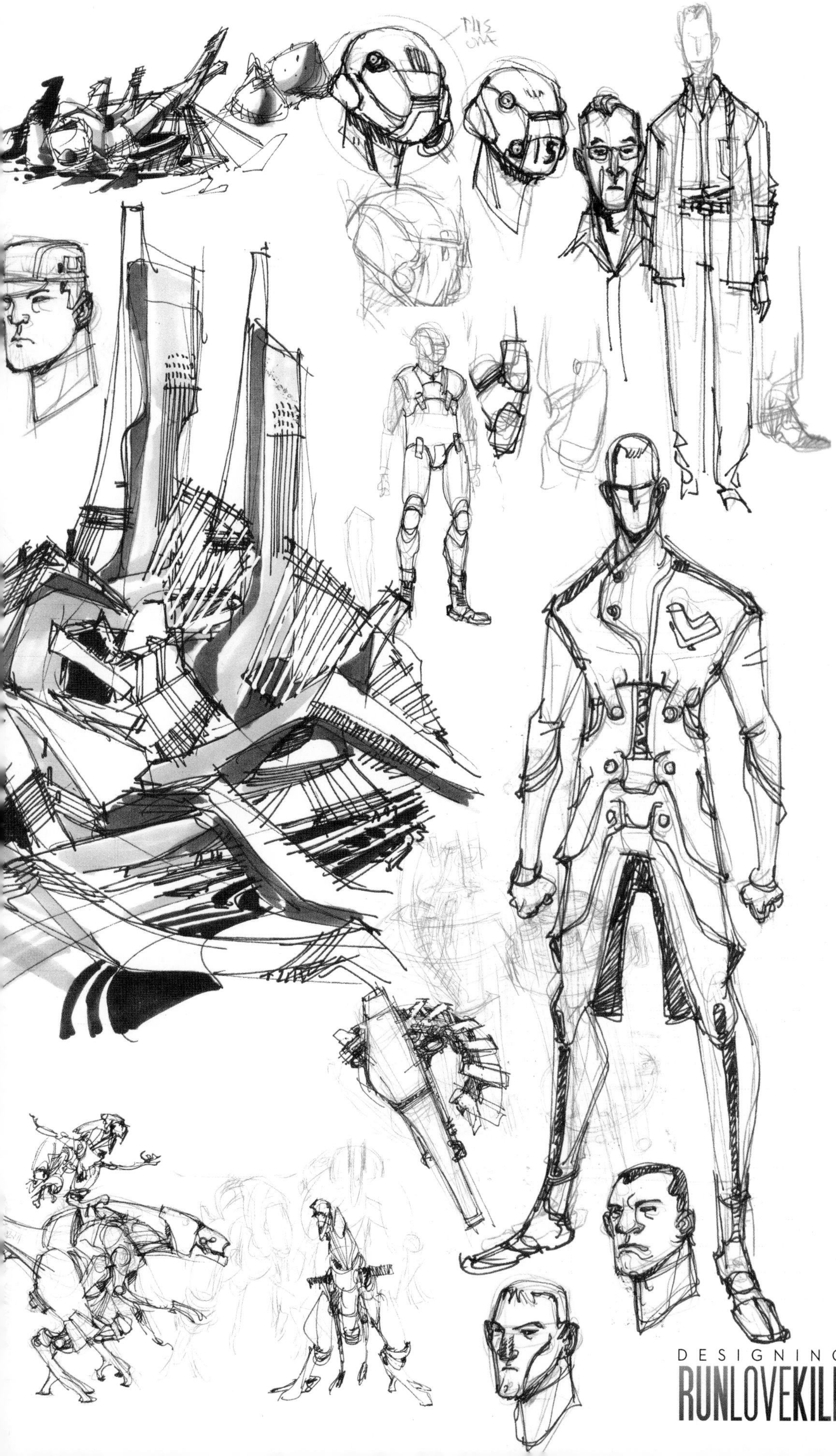
THIS ONE

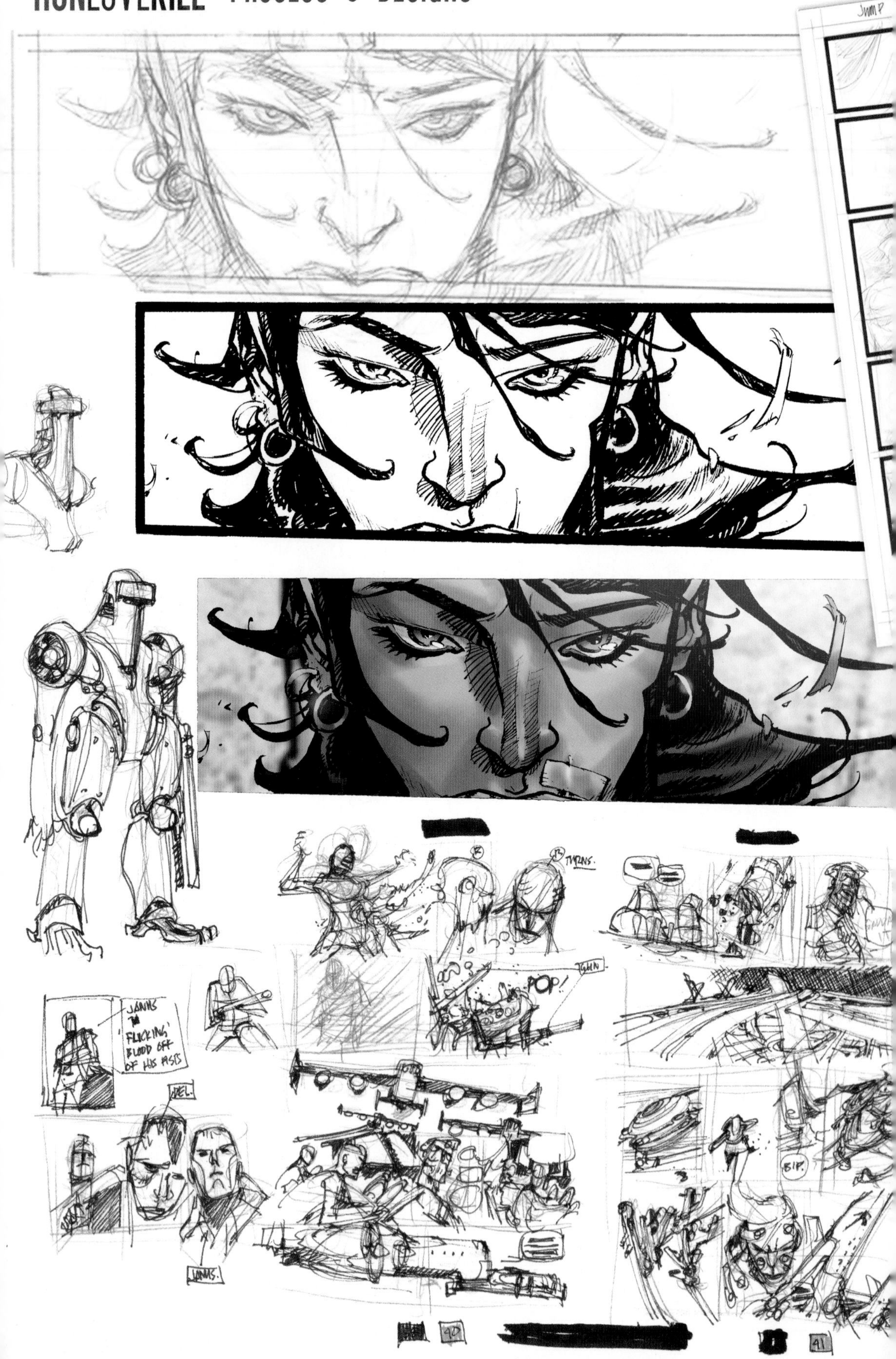
TURNS.
POP!
BIP.

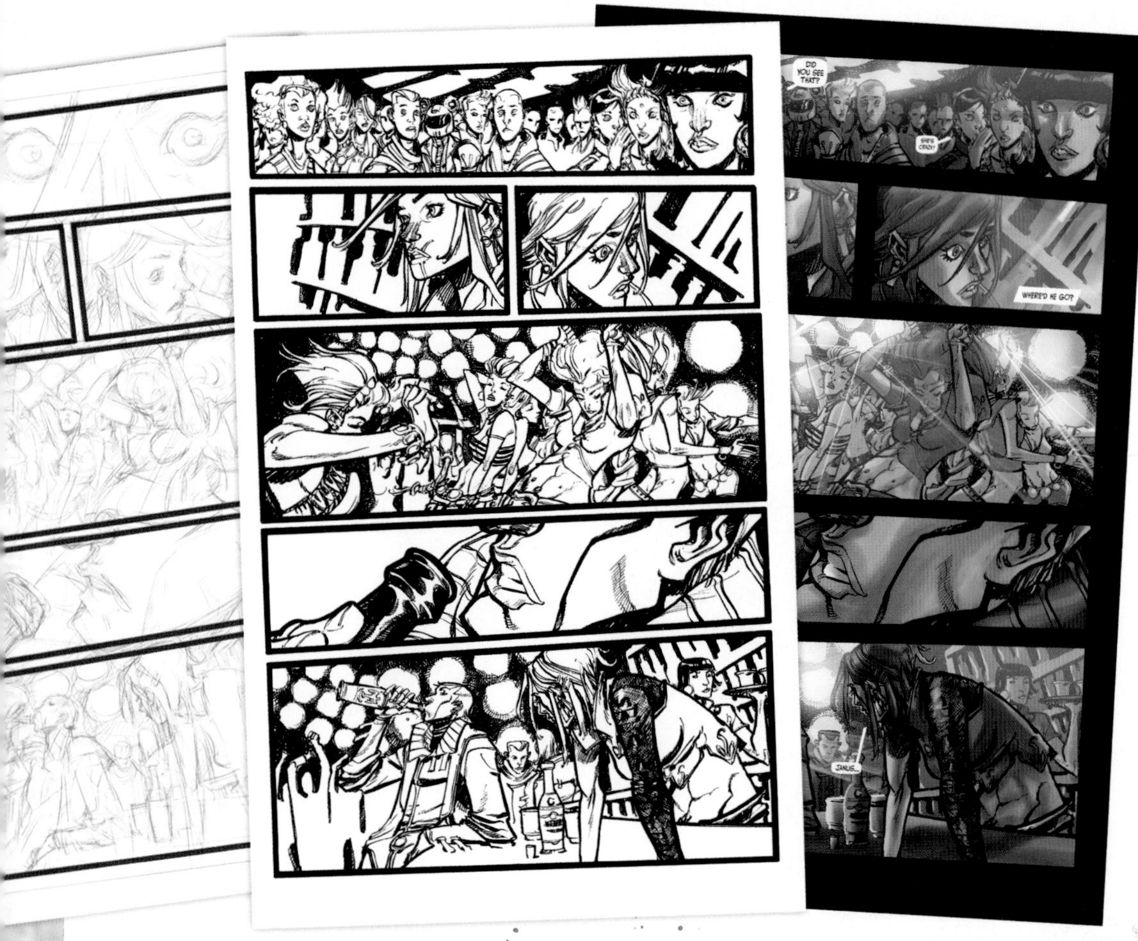

DID YOU SEE THAT?
SHE'S CRAZY!
WHERE'D HE GO?
JANUS...

RUNLOVEKILL

RUNLOVEKILL

JUMP

jump

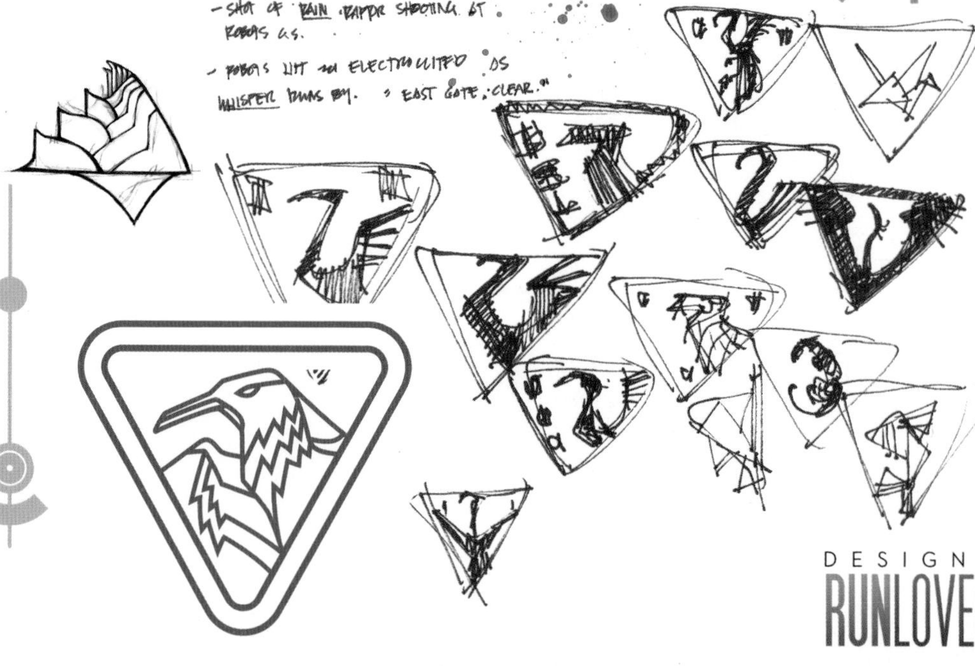

- SHOT OF RAIN. RAPTOR SHOOTING AT ROBOTS
- ROBOTS ELECTROCUTED AS WHISPER
EAST GATE: CLEAR."

DESIGNING
RUNLOVEKILL

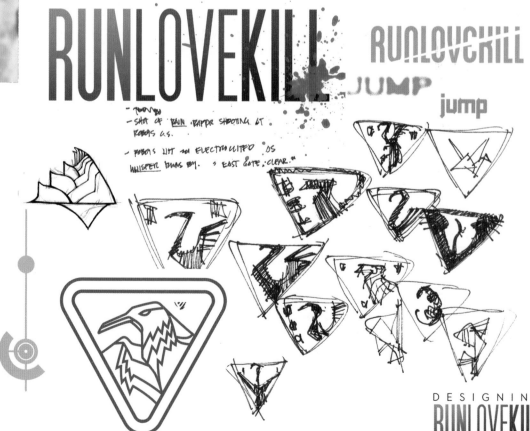

DESIGNING
RUNLOVEKILL
3D

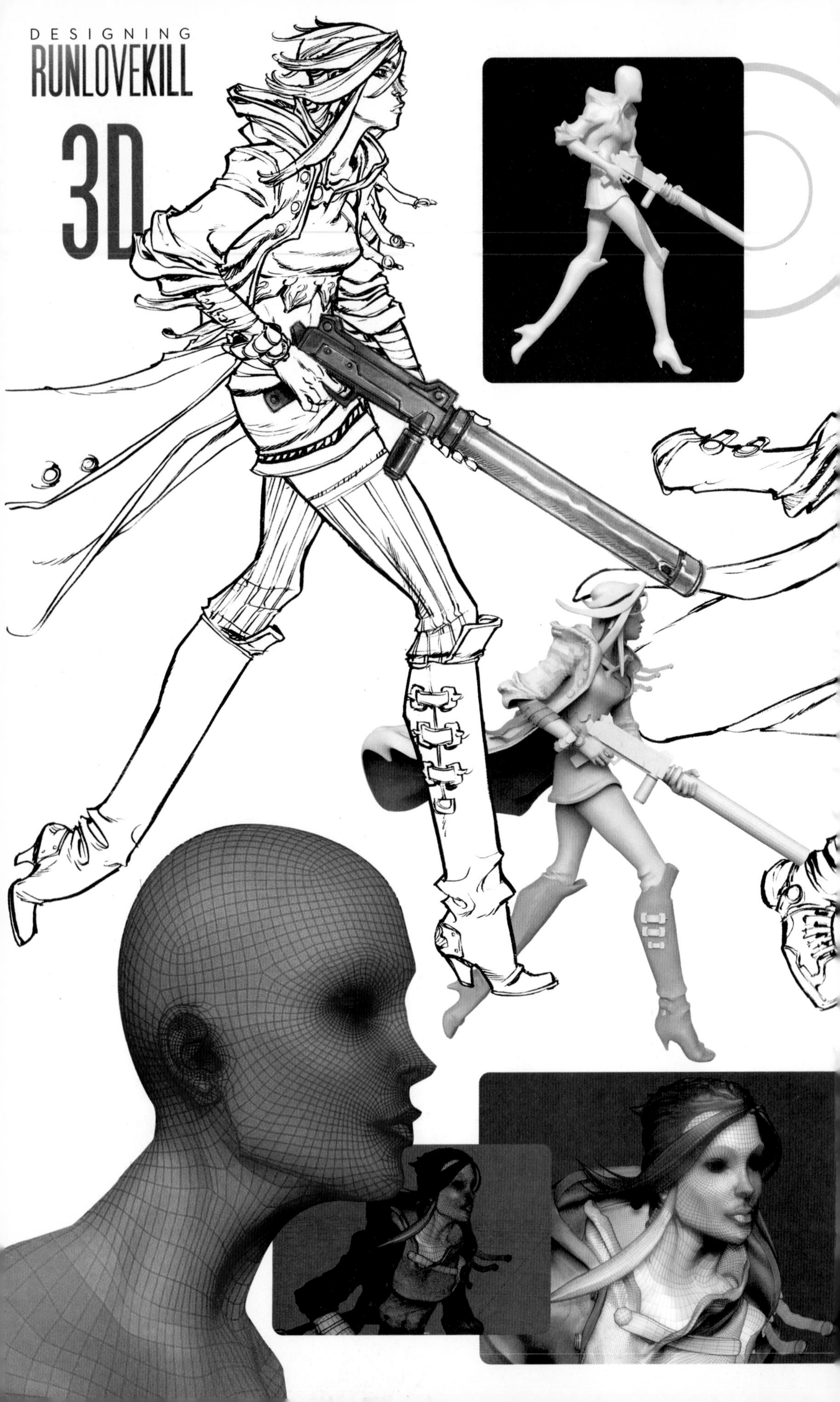

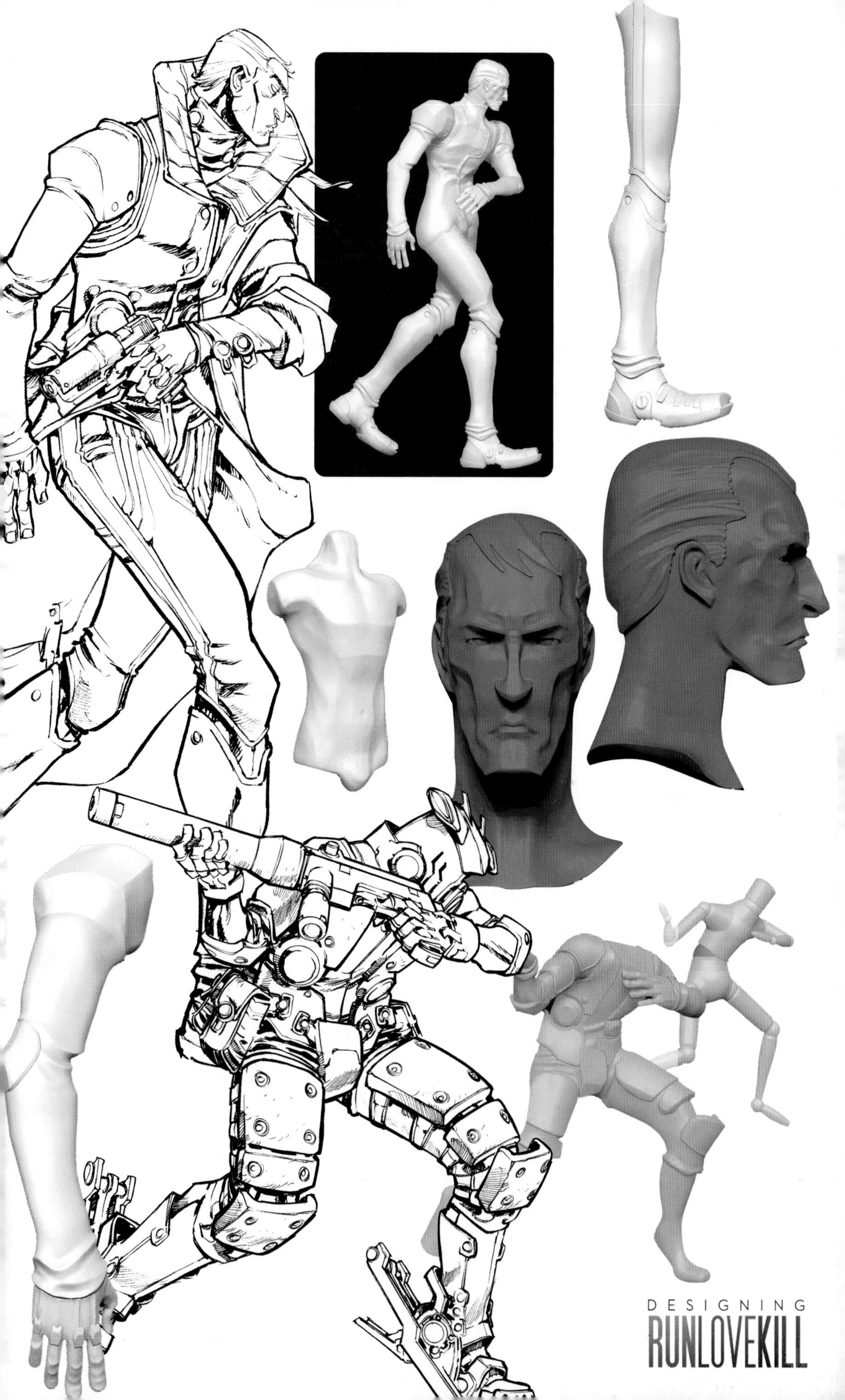

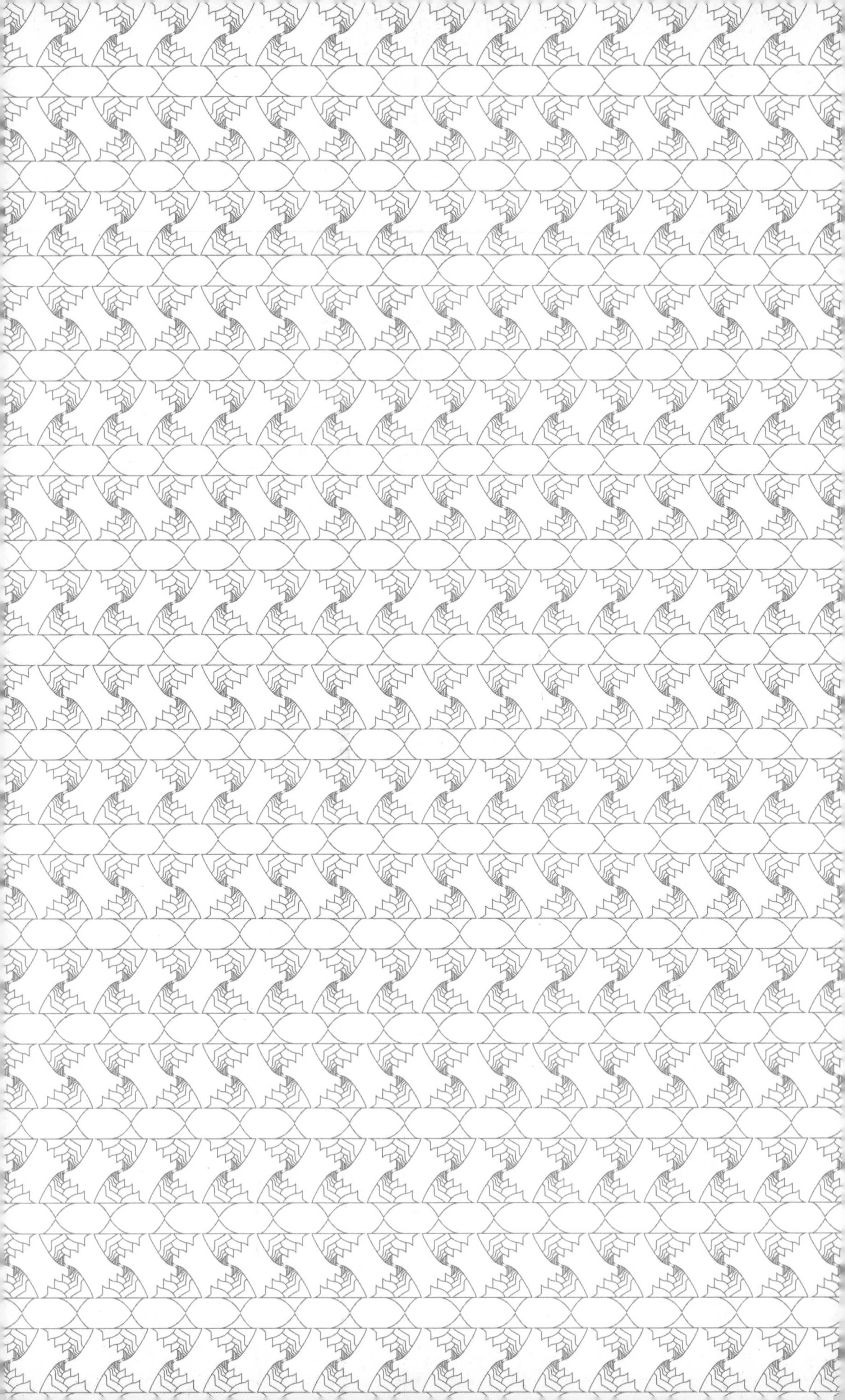